Tempted by You

I0598061

by TIFFANY CLARE

Tempted by You
By Tiffany Clare
Copyright © 2014 by Tiffany Clare

Cover design by Lou
Cover photograph Seam Nel
Formatting by Champagne Formats

ISBN-13:978-0-9937196-2-2

To my friends Ang & Di.
A shared love for music brought us together
anddefined us even at so young an age.

Chapter One

Do not ever conceal yourself from me.
–Ludwig van Beethoven

London, 1855

"YOU COULDN'T HAVE COME AT a better time." The duke took Rosalie's ermine-lined cloak and passed it to a waiting footman. "I leave for Maidstone first thing in the morning."

Rosalie grasped his arm in greeting. "I thank my blessings to have caught you at home at all."

Nathan, the Duke of Vane, kissed her cheek lightly. Threading his arm through hers, he took her deeper into his town house. "What crisis brings you here so late in the evening, Rosa?"

"I had no one else to turn to. Not for this matter."

Nathan's gait matched her smaller steps as they walked the length of the corridor.

"It's Daniel, isn't it?"

On hearing the censure and disappointment in his voice, she nibbled her lower lip. How often had she turned to the duke for help? Too often, but it was second nature for her to seek him whenever something was awry with her brother, which of late was happening with frightening regularity.

"He's never been absent from society for longer than a week. I'm worried he's found himself in deeper trouble than he has in the past."

They paused in the hall so Nathan could lift the door latch to admit them into the sitting room. "Your brother has a heart for adventure. Give him a few more days to turn up. He always has in the past."

Her brother was her weak spot and had been since the day her father had forced her to leave her childhood home. She'd done her best to watch over Daniel, trying to keep him out of trouble. But her brother had grown more reckless over the past year.

"You should have sent a note with your maid, Rosalie. I'm in no shape to assist anyone in my current mood. That's why I'm escaping Town for some fresh air."

What would she do if she couldn't rely on the duke? Who would she go to?

Nathan's hand squeezed her wrist before he released her. "Anna left me."

Rosalie's hand covered her mouth too late to muffle the sound of shock that escaped. "What do you mean, she left you? When did this happen?"

"A week ago. I thought she'd have come back to me by now. I haven't been myself for days." His declaration was so calm that she thought he was teasing her, but Nathan would never jest about Anna leaving him. His voice turned colder. "This is not a discussion I want to have, Rosa. I'll be of little help to you right now."

Oh, God, how could she not have known? Word must have spread about the duke's mistress of ten years leaving him. No wonder her worry for her brother seemed inconsequential.

But it was of no less importance.

She reached for his arm and pressed it comfortingly. "I'm so sorry, Nathan. I had no idea."

"Thank you, love. I'm working it out in my own way." There was an underlying determination to his voice that had her re-thinking the reason for Nathan's escape from Town.

"You're going to go after her aren't you?"

The duke chuckled. "I should have known I wouldn't be able to keep you in the dark for long."

"Do you know where she went?"

"I think she is at her sister's, which is the other reason I'm heading for Maidstone. I'll be closer to her." With a hand resting over her lower back, he led her to a settee. "Enough about my troubles. Let me reiterate my thoughts on Daniel. Your rogue brother will turn up sooner or later. He always has in the past—and when you least expected it."

How did she explain the gut feeling she had? Nathan was right in a sense, but this seemed different from the other times Daniel had disappeared because he'd taken on too much debt or thumbed his nose at the wrong man.

Rosa took a deep breath, closed her eyes to collect herself, and to stall the tears threatening to make her a veritable watering pot. She needed a level head and histrionics would help no one. "This feels different, Nathan. Can you assist me before you leave tomorrow? I can't go into the places you can, or ask the right questions of the right people."

Was it selfish of her to request his help when he had problems of his own to work through? As soon as the thought crossed her mind, she dismissed it. This was her brother—she would do any-thing to make sure he was alive and well—and Nathan had never been the type of man to turn his back on a friend in need.

"I can't do this alone," she pleaded.

The cushion next to her lowered as the duke sat beside her. He settled his hands over her fidgety fingers, his steady warmth calming her nerves. "I can ask around tomorrow. But if I'm going to make Maidstone by nightfall, I won't be able to ask at many places."

A huge sigh of relief washed over her. "That's all I need to hear."

"Stay for dinner, Rosa. I'll have a guest room made up for you. You're too far from home to head back tonight."

The invitation to stay the night caught her off guard, but it made sense if he only had a short time with her in the morning. "I had no intention of intruding, especially considering everything that has happened in your life. I don't want to inconvenience you if you're closing up the house."

"Don't apologize." He brushed his hand over her arm and grasped her hand again to squeeze it reassuringly. "I don't deserve your kindness when I'm abandoning you in your time of need. Stay the night. We can discuss over a cup of ratafia what you last remember your brother doing. We'll send out notes first thing in the morning to those we trust to see if they've heard of his whereabouts."

He made a good point that was hard to argue.

"Allow me your company. It'll make up for me acting like a boor," Nate insisted.

That got a smile out of her. "I can't refuse your generous offer."

"I should warn you that we have company."

That put a damper on her plans to stay. She would not interrupt a dinner affair. "Guests?"

"My brother is here and some friends arrived a few hours ago—to cheer me up, I'm afraid."

Thaddeus was Nathan's younger brother and a renowned composer. They'd never officially met, but she knew of him. "I hope they are providing some cheer."

"No, but I can't seem to get them to leave. I invited them to dine so long as they leave me shortly after so I can at least wallow alone for the remainder of the night." His comment was said in good humor.

"They don't know you plan on leaving, do they?"

"That would ruin my element of surprise. I can't risk word getting back to Anna, not when she's done a fair job of staying away from me this long."

"I don't mind waiting for your dinner to conclude before we discuss my situation further." She didn't care to dine with men she didn't know, close friends to Nathan or not. Her profession as a muse and courtesan made men think they could treat her as though she were easily bought property. And that couldn't be further from the truth.

"I insist you stay," Nathan said.

As he made his way to his feet, she clutched the sleeve of his jacket and stood with him, wanting to tell him how appreciative she truly was. "I can't thank you enough for this, Nathan. And I couldn't ask for a better friend. I will dine with you this evening and take you up on your offer to stay the night."

"I wish I could do more, but I have plans that cannot be changed. We'll figure this out." He kissed her cheek, the brush of his lips brotherly and kind. "The piano is yours if you wish to play until we dine. I'm going to try and rid myself of my other company, though I can't promise anything."

She ducked her head with a small smile. "How well you know me." He knew she was selective in who she would dine with.

"Always, darling." He pinched her chin with his thumb and forefinger. "I'll see you in short order."

He walked out of the room, clicking the door shut behind him.

The invitation to stay calmed her nerves a great deal. Her heart slowed to a less frantic pace as she took in a deep breath. It had been a smart decision to come here, though in reality she should have done so much sooner.

Nathan appeared to be many things to the casual observer, but she knew the man beneath that carefree persona he presented to society. He was loyal, considerate, and he would never let a friend down. Intuition had led her here for that reason alone and she was glad for it. Nathan would do what she could not do alone.

He would find her brother.

Rosa backed up a few steps, until her skirts hit the chair tucked under the piano. She turned and curled her hands over the rounded top of the chair and pulled it out so she could settle herself under the keys. While she waited for Nathan to come back to the music room, she could forget her troubles in her music.

THADDEUS DE BURGH FELT LIKE a voyeur. Technically, he wasn't a voyeur but an eavesdropper; he had actively listened to his brother talking in hushed tones with a lady Teddy did not recognize. While he could have walked away and left his brother to his newest guest, he'd been intrigued by his brother's change in character on seeing this woman; he was gentle and kind with her even though Nathan had been gruff and moody since Teddy's arrival. Teddy didn't know who she was, though he thought he'd seen her before, perhaps at a play or musicale.

While he might not know her, he had felt the weight of her grief and concern as she'd begged for Nathan's assistance to help her find her brother.

The door between the library and music parlor was slightly ajar. Gaslights flickered orange tendrils up the walls and along the floor, giving him a clear glimpse of the lady within the music room.

The lady's dress was of fine cornflower blue silk and scooped invitingly off her shoulders, tempting a man to trace the delicate lines of her collarbone and shoulder blades where they peeked out above the fabric at the back.

Rich, black curls piled atop her head, and a few enticing strands fell here and there down her neck, practically begging for his fingers to tuck them back beneath the bits of lace and matching blue silk ribbons woven through her locks. The line of her neck was graceful, her skin snow-white, not a freckle or beauty mark in sight. Even in profile, he could tell she was pretty, with her high cheekbones and her plump, kissable lower lip.

Who was this mysterious and fascinating creature? And what

could *he* do to help her once his brother left for Maidstone?

The temptation to talk to her—not only to distract himself from a composition that was going nowhere, but also to find a way to help her—was a bloody siren singing in his ear at a deafening volume. Without making a sound, he slid the pocket door completely into the wall as he entered the music room.

The woman's posture was perfect, her arms slender, elbows held aloft at the right angle as she started a series of simple scales and arpeggios with her right hand, followed in succession with the left hand as she warmed her fingers on the old family Broadwood.

He clasped the top edge of a chair and held firm as he listened to the music she all but sang with her hands as she moved away from scales and into a romantic sonata. He had never heard a more moving or passionate pianist. And she played for no one but herself. What would she sound like playing for an audience?

Her technique was flawless, her talent inarguable. Her mind seemed swept away by the music; that was clear in her body language, and in the way she moved gently in synchronization with the slow-paced larghetto. There were no sheets of music to aid her. She simply played where her heart led.

Again, he asked himself: Who was this woman? Why hadn't he ever heard her play before now? Why hadn't Nathan told Teddy of her natural brilliance?

He took another step closer when the chords changed to a familiar concerto. How tempted he was to sidle up next to her and place his hands on a higher octave and join in. Would she welcome him to play a piece for four hands?

She bent slightly forward, shoulders leaning close to the keys, and started a new piece. A smooth melodic cantabile, and a very picturesque tune. He could quite literally stand here all day and listen to her play. This was a piece she knew well. Sadness and joy danced around each note, as though she yearned for something long gone or out of reach. Was she thinking of her brother as she played the music? The melody diminished to a softer, quieter tone but remained as stunning as the rest of the piece had been.

He walked over to stand by her right side. The smell of lilacs teased him, the scent light and pleasant. She'd taken off her gloves to play, revealing long, delicate fingers, nails buffed short—ideal for playing the piano. Those slender fingers danced seamlessly across the keys as if she were born at the piano, as if she spent day and night pounding at the keys.

Every nerve ending in his body came alive with awareness, and his heart picked up in speed the more she played. The passion, the beauty of her music struck him speechless.

She didn't acknowledge him, so he assumed her to be so involved with the piece that she didn't realize he stood next to her. He couldn't help but reach for the keys in front of him. Taking the higher register, he mimicked her melody half a beat behind. The piece was simple, yet made complex with complementary harmonies playing over and with one another. And it was incredibly beautiful, as beautiful as Beethoven's *Eroica* the first time he'd heard it in concert.

She stopped suddenly with a sound of fright and fell off the side of the small round chair. She landed hard on the floor in a flounce of blue-and-white silk, the wash of color like a Mediterranean wave throwing itself onto a sand-covered shore.

"Let me help you up," he offered, reaching for her before she uttered a word.

"You've caused me to have the worst palpitation!" She took an audibly deep breath as she pushed herself up from the floor.

"My apologies—"

He couldn't finish his words when she looked up at him. She had the bluest eyes he'd ever seen. A clear, topaz blue that was easily four shades lighter than her dress. Yes, he'd seen her in passing from time to time in her brother's company, but they'd never been properly introduced. It seemed odd to him that he hadn't noticed her condition before.

The emptiness that met his gaze drained him of all the warmth that had infused him the moment he'd heard her playing.

In his mind he had pegged her as an undiscovered virtuoso, but that simply couldn't be the case. In fact, such a thing was damn near impossible for someone who obviously couldn't read sheet music, no matter how beautifully she played.

She could not see him, not even an outline of him. It was evident in her vacant, blind gaze. But the way she played...

She intrigued him like no other person ever had and he had a sudden desire to know everything about her. It struck him that her conundrum with her brother was the perfect reason to learn all there was to learn about this woman. This woman's music had inspired him to a whole new level. He wanted to write his composition with the same passion she exuded in her own music. Emulate it in such a way that those listening to his music would feel as he felt listening to hers.

Chapter Two

To send light into the darkness of men's hearts – such is the duty of the artist.
– Robert Schumann

ROSA GRASPED THE GENTLEMAN'S STRONG, warm hand. His grip was firm and steady as he pulled her easily back onto her feet. The tantalizing scent of amber and sandalwood filled her lungs, awakening her senses. Her skirts were twisted about her legs, and she released her hold on her rescuer to right her dress. His other hand slipped away from her arm the moment she was steady.

"I didn't hear anyone enter. I must apologize for the fright I surely gave you."

He chuckled, the timbre an uplifting baritone. The laugh was so similar to Nathan's that she was instantly put at ease in this unfamiliar man's company.

"It is I who must apologize for the awkwardness of this introduction. I beg your pardon and forgiveness for giving *you* such a scare, madam."

"I had forgotten where I was for a moment."

"I had thought as much. But that doesn't excuse me for listening at the door instead of letting you know of my presence."

She smoothed one hand over the polished top of the piano in search of her gloves. She was unsure how she should respond to him. She wanted to ask how long he'd listened to her playing, but the words stuck in her throat. Once again, the stranger's warm hands clasped around hers; this time he placed her satin gloves into her palms.

He stood so close to her that the warmth of his presence brushed teasingly over her skin where her upper arms were exposed.

"Thank you." Her knuckles immediately dropped to the piano keys, and she ran them gently over the blacks. Would it be obvious to him that it was a nervous gesture? She hadn't anticipated being in anyone's company other than Nathan's at least until dinner. While this introduction was unexpected, it was not the least bit undesirable. Anyone who could distract her from worrying about her brother was welcome to spend time with her.

"I honestly didn't mean to intrude. I'll leave you to your playing," the stranger said.

"Wait—" She stretched her arm out to him, but he was already beyond her reach. "Might I have your name?"

"Thaddeus de Burgh."

She felt like a ninny for not having put the pieces together before now; his laugh *was* similar to Nathan's.

"Yours, madam?"

"Rosalie Montgomery, my lord." She curtsied.

Was her surname familiar to him? She hoped he did not make the connection with Amaryllis Montgomery—her given name—once named the Royal and Imperial Virtuosa in Austria, the highest honor a musician of seventeen could achieve. She knew all about Thaddeus de Burgh and his passion for creating music.

Those who once knew her would hopefully never see how far she'd truly fallen. Especially this man, who was a composer—or had been. If memory served her correctly, he'd stopped making appearances a number of years ago.

"You play the piano well," he said.

The knot that had formed in her stomach eased. He did not recognize her name. Had he, he would have certainly said so.

"It's no more than a pastime. Needlework can be quite painful to practice, considering my *condition*."

"Not merely a pastime, Miss Montgomery." Laughter infused his voice. "I would be a content man if half the students I instructed showed the aptitude you just displayed and in less than a quarter hour at the keys."

"Thank you," she said, taking the compliment without any shyness. "It is an honor to be praised by you."

There was also no denying that it sent a sharp thrill of pleasure right down to the tips of her toes that he'd listened to her playing for that long. It had been awhile since she'd been complimented on her musical acuity—eight years to be precise.

"I feel at a disadvantage that you seem to know more about me than I you," he said. "After all, we've never been introduced."

"I've been your brother's friend for many years. He talks of you and your sister often enough that I'd be hard-pressed not to know of your accomplishments. Nathan is proud of what you've accomplished."

De Burgh made a derisive sound in his throat. "Nathan exaggerates."

"Perhaps the assessment is my own." She had heard him in a string ensemble once. He had played the violin with so much passion that it sounded like angels singing in her ears.

"Did Anna send you to check on Nathan?" he asked.

Why would he think Nathan's ex-mistress would send her? While she knew the woman and had been a friend of hers over the years, they were not confidantes. Anna would never ask Rosa to choose between two friends in a rift.

She shook her head. "I only just learned of Nathan and Anna's separation. I came to ask a favor of your brother."

"What did you ask for?"

Why did de Burgh want to know why she was here? Was it genuine concern or did he have another reason?

Rosa pressed her lips together. "It is of a personal nature."

"I'm not sure if you've noticed, but Nathan's not his usual carefree self." De Burgh's exhalation was full of frustration—not with her, but for his brother. "He's not necessarily in the right frame of mind to help out a friend."

She folded her hands together, well aware of that fact. She knew Nathan would only assist her until he left for Maidstone. And she also knew that that wasn't enough time to help her find her brother, but it was better than no help at all.

Did de Burgh ask so many questions because he wished to help her in his brother's stead? That seemed odd, especially considering they were strangers.

"Will you be staying the night?" he asked.

"Your brother insisted."

"He can be rather forceful when he's got his mind made up about something. I can lend you my carriage if you wish to return home tonight."

Ah, the crux of his interest was as clear as a cloudless day; a shame she hadn't come to the conclusion sooner. He must know that she wasn't precisely a lady.

Did de Burgh think to proposition her for his effort? She sighed heavily, disappointed by him and by her circumstance. "I do not seek male companionship."

"Perfect." There was a hint of amusement in his voice. "Because I do not seek a mistress."

She opened her mouth to respond, then closed it. What could she say to that? "What is it you want of me, my lord?"

"You require something from Nathan, and I do not believe he can help you at present. I on the other hand am more than willing to assist you if you allow me to use your musical insight

13

selfishly for my own."

Taken aback by the request, she thought carefully on her response, since that was the last thing she'd expected him to ask. "And you think I'd be useful to someone with your reputation in music?"

He made a derisive sound. "Hardly a reputation worthy of boasting about. However, I am working on a new concerto. I haven't made an appearance of a professional nature for some time, so this piece is near and dear to me. It must be beyond perfect when it's debuted. Listening to you tonight, I realized that I needed the assistance of someone as passionate about music as I am."

Though she knew de Burgh wasn't active in his compositions, she should have known better than to assume he had given music up. The drive to create did not simply stop; it pressed forward like the force of a babe being brought into the world. To create, even for her, was an undeniable need.

"What can you possibly learn from me?"

"I'm not easily moved by a simple piano piece, but you have managed to surprise me, Miss Montgomery. I could use your insight. Another ear would be more than welcome with my latest compositions."

She chewed on her lower lip, mulling the idea. Why was she even entertaining such madness? It was ludicrous to entangle herself with this man, but music was her knee-bending weakness ... and also her greatest strength.

"You want a muse."

"In a sense."

Why not take his offer? He was a gentleman and would be able to enter the clubs her brother frequented. Provided de Burgh still agreed to the arrangement once she explained what she required.

"But you haven't any inkling of what I need," she pointed out.

"Then you will have to enlighten me."

How much of her brother's indiscretions and knack for

ill-wagered gambling should she reveal? It was better to be vague—for the time being. Maybe her skill in music alone would win him over. She nearly snorted at the idea. How ludicrous; if such a thing were possible she would never have had to play the role of courtesan.

"My brother has not been seen for a week. I wish to locate him."

"A simple enough task." There was no hesitation from de Burgh. "Will you agree to spend an evening around Town with me tomorrow? We can discuss our mutually beneficial arrangement in further detail."

Why was he so quick to offer his help? Did it matter? She couldn't refuse his offer. She had a feeling, knowing Nathan as she did, that she could trust de Burgh implicitly. Besides, his name would provide entrance into more places—nearly as many as Nathan's she was sure—than hers.

"I would need you to attend the gentlemen's clubs and quietly ask after my brother, starting in the morning. I'm quite anxious to locate him."

"I am completely at your service, madam."

Put simply, it would be madness not to accept his proposal.

"Then I accept your offer, de Burgh."

She stuck out her hand; she had every intention to seal their deal with a handshake, since she could not see his expression. His grip was strong and steady. When their grasps loosened, he curled his fingers around hers and raised the back of her hand to his mouth. The tips of his fingers were callused, most likely from the strings of his violin. His breath was warm on the back of her hand as he lingered for a while before pulling away.

"Do you dine with us this evening?" His voice deepened, as though it were an intimate question.

Did he wish to tempt her into a liaison, too? Did it make her a terrible person that she wanted to encourage a flirtation? And why shouldn't she? They shared similar interests and were about to embark on a mutual pursuit that would be more fulfilling than the lonliness she felt of late. She hadn't been a part of the music world and in the company of the people who made up that world for so many years. The yearning that bloomed in her chest chased away the constant loneliness that stabbed at her heart whenever she thought of her old life.

"What is it you seek, my lord?"

"Your company."

She took a step toward him. He was like having a taste of the rich and forbidden once again.

Her desire to spend time with de Burgh felt like a betrayal of her brother. There were family secrets that had to remain forever buried and protected, but could she keep them buried when de Burgh was a temptation she didn't think she could deny herself for long?

"Is that all you require of me?" she asked.

"I wouldn't dare trick you. I give you the truth." He cleared his throat. "Might I ask you a personal question?"

"By all means, but I may choose not to answer."

"What a refreshing woman you are, Miss Montgomery. I rather enjoy it when a beautiful woman tells me exactly what she thinks."

For the first time in days, she felt a genuine smile lift the corners of her mouth. "I'm glad you approve of my directness. Your question?"

"Where did you learn to play the piano?"

She hadn't been expecting that. She'd not reveal to de Burgh that she'd been playing the piano since she was three, or that she had traveled Europe extensively with her father, looking for the best instructors for her lessons. Or the fact that she'd played for royalty and with some of the greatest musicians of her youth.

Playing the piano had never been a passing amusement. It was as vital as water and as crucial as breathing to her. Without it, she couldn't truly live.

It was better to tell him as little about herself as she could. Half-truths and nothing more would have to suffice.

"Not so uncommon a question. I was not always as you see me." She motioned one hand toward her eyes. "My father taught me to play when I was a young girl. A carriage accident took my sight when I was seventeen."

They shared a moment of silence. Not the kind of quiet that grows awkward between two people who haven't anything to say to each other. There was something more complicated and elemental happening here. She wasn't sure how she felt about the odd familiarity after just meeting. It must stem from hearing about him through Nathan for so many years—she almost felt as if she knew Thaddeus de Burgh.

What would he say or ask next? She inched closer in anticipation. The only way to justify her reaction to this man was to remind herself that the past week had been fraught with so much emotion, worry, and fear for her brother and what trouble his latest scheme had gotten him into, and de Burgh served as a respite from her frustrations. He made her feel alive, almost as though she could see a spark of light in the pitch-darkness that was her life.

It was newfound hope—nothing more. She knew it would pass the moment she woke up, making this no more than a dream.

"I'm not presentable for dinner," he said abruptly, breaking the spell that had ensnared them. "But I promise to find you before we sup."

"Till then," she said, realizing her main interest in joining Nathan for dinner was because she wanted to learn more about Thaddeus de Burgh.

There was something about this man's character, the subtlety of his approach, and the steady cadence of his voice that offered safety and comfort. She felt she could let her guard down with him. Could she trust him like she trusted Nathan? There was no doubt in her mind that she could.

How had her original purpose in coming here deviated so far? Was she interested in de Burgh because he did not crassly proposition her as most men did? Or was it because he understood and appreciated music? Perhaps it was nothing more than the adoration she heard in his voice as he praised her piano skills.

No, it was because he offered her the one thing she needed most right now: his assistance in finding her brother. She knew Nathan would help in any way he could, but he was focused on his latest problem with Anna. De Burgh was in a much better frame of mind to help her.

With a soft tap under her chin, de Burgh tilted her head up. His touch was gentle and not at all brotherly like Nathan's was. What did he think to read in her face, or see in her eyes—eyes that could no longer make out the beauty that surrounded her?

"Dinner will be most pleasurable with you present, Miss Montgomery."

She made no response, just held perfectly still. What she wanted to do more than anything was touch the planes of his face, to see him with her hands. That would be too intimate a gesture, so she fisted her hands at her sides instead. He released her and stepped away. The air between them immediately cooled and she felt momentarily bereft.

The tread of his feet was the only indication that he'd left her standing there alone.

She sat on the chair and placed her right hand over the higher register, dancing out a Mozart gigue to match the skip of her heartbeat.

Could she enjoy an affair with de Burgh? Maybe even companionship for the short time they would work together? She was entitled to a small bit of happiness while she searched for her brother. Wasn't she? The fates were cruel to dangle temptation before her unseeing eyes.

Chapter Three

When I wished to sing of love, it turned to sorrow. And when I wished to sing of sorrow, it was transformed for me into love
— Franz Schubert

DRESSED FOR DINNER, TEDDY PAUSED in front of the piano in his room. He focused on the scribbled notes of his latest composition spread across the top. It was a mess, and without his usual inspiration; in fact, he hated it all and wanted to start it over again, but was running out of time. That thought conjured Miss Montgomery to mind. There was no denying that he did require her discerning ear, and her blindness didn't matter; he knew an exceptional pianist and musician when he heard one.

Apart from that, he felt that there could be something more between them.

He wasn't precisely sure why he had invited her to join him around Town tomorrow night, but the opera would be the perfect place for their first meeting of minds. It was a way for him to test her knowledge and understanding in music further. But a larger part of him wanted nothing more than to spend time in her company.

He had no intentions of traveling back to Maidstone with his brother. Not until Nathan wanted to talk to him, if such a time ever presented itself—Nathan was a private man, and Teddy fully respected that. Teddy, on the other hand, had his own life to attend to and a promise to Miss Montgomery that he would fulfill. A little intrigue with the mysterious pianist was more than enough to keep him in London.

He brushed his fingers across the stave paper. There were blocks of empty lines where notes should be dotting out melodic interludes or harmonic progressions between the instruments. Nothing seemed to be coming together for this composition.

The chords of Miss Montgomery's piece teased at his mind.

He wondered if he had been overthinking the process all this time, until the joy he normally found in writing music had diminished until it felt more like an unwanted chore. Perhaps the issues stemmed from being out of practice in composing?

For the past few years, he'd done nothing more than transpose popular works by Mozart, Haydn, Beethoven, and Bach, for the music publications in London. It was tedious, unfulfilling, thankless work. And if he never had to transcribe someone else's works again, he would be content.

Yet the pressure to produce something for the masses suddenly felt overwhelming.

He wondered what his concerto would sound like if Miss Montgomery were to play the piano solo. Then he wondered what kind of embellishments she would include and how she would interpret the piece to make it hers alone.

He was getting ahead of himself.

Luckily for him, a friend had offered him the opportunity of a lifetime. Teddy was to open the Season with the performance of the new concerto he'd feverishly worked on for the past six months. He would round out his month in residence at Hanover Square Rooms conducting Haydn's Symphony No.85.

This was his chance to prove himself as a composer. If he bungled this opportunity to play in a respectable place, he might very well be relegated to playing the music halls and pennies—places where the poor found a reprieve for a few shillings.

He had nothing left to lose except for his pride, though he'd been pitching pride into the fire for quite some time now, with one failed piece after another. Years ago, his ensemble pieces had been well received, but he wanted something grander, something that made him as respected a composer as any of the modern Greats.

He shut the lid on the piano keys, blew out the candle, and headed out the door.

Miss Montgomery had made something come to life inside him. The moment her fingers had sung out a tune, he'd felt inspired and had wanted to accomplish so much more. Her playing had been inspirational to say the least.

He shouldn't have left her in the music parlor to begin with, but had to because he had been close to reneging on his promise of wanting only her musical assistance; he'd nearly kissed more than her hand. Even though she'd made it quite clear she was not looking for companionship, there was a receptiveness offering more than her company when he'd kissed her hand—he'd been sure of it. Instead of making himself seem like an ass, he'd forced himself to walk away.

As though his thoughts conjured her up, he caught sight of her heading toward the dining room. The clever flip at the tail end of her frilly underskirts added an indecent, alluring quality to the way she strolled, her heavy skirts crinkling in rhythm with her easy stride. Trailing her fingers along the chair rail, she used it as a guide.

Dear Lord, what the mere sight of her did to him!

There was something about her that made him want indescribable things—of himself and his music.

Benedict Johnson, the cad, intercepted her before she could make it to the dining hall and whisked her into a small sitting room. Thaddeus wanted her all to himself.

He'd give her a minute to rid herself of Johnson. Otherwise, he would get rid of the man himself. As he approached, he realized their voices were lowered. Not wanting to intrude on a private conversation, he stood just outside the door waiting for an opportunity to interject; wondering how in hell Johnson knew her when Teddy hadn't even formally been introduced to her before today. Regardless of her past acquaintance with Johnson, Teddy planned to escort the lovely lady to dinner.

"I heard your brother's latest game is taking loans from the seediest of shylocks about Town and disappearing into the night with all their money. There's a price on his head, but I'm willing to help you in exchange for your company."

"I would never accept you, Johnson. I don't know how many times I have to tell you that. And don't ever think to put a price on me; I can help my brother just fine without your interference."

Her voice had the cadence of a lone viola—wistful, distant, the intonation even and clear, firm and without negotiation. Knowing now that Johnson's company vexed her, he turned toward them.

"You make a man feel as though he has to prove himself." Johnson's knuckle caressed her left cheek.

She flinched away, locked her hand around his wrist, and pushed him away. "There is nothing you can say or do to prove yourself worthy of my time, Johnson."

Slamming the door against the wall, Teddy strode into the room. He had no qualms about beating the blighter into the ground for distressing Miss Montgomery. This was his home, and while she was here she was under his protection.

Both heads turned at his sudden entrance.

"I shouldn't be surprised to find you accosting a guest, Johnson," Teddy snarled in warning.

Johnson sidled past Miss Montgomery, a sly, self-satisfied smirk on his face. "De Burgh."

"It would do you well to remember that this isn't your house."

He pointed an accusing finger at the man. "And you'll treat the lady with the respect she is due."

"Lady?" Johnson guffawed. "Really, de Burgh, think about what you're saying."

Miss Montgomery turned in his direction. A frown creased her delicate brow and her lips pursed in distaste.

"Get out of my sight, Johnson. And don't come back or more than words will pass between us."

Johnson held up his hands in surrender and backed toward the exit. "May the *lady* keep *you* warm, then."

Teddy clenched his hands at his side and took a deep breath after Johnson left. He still wanted to plant his fist between the man's beady eyes. The only thing that stopped him was the way Miss Montgomery stood by the chaise, her right hand curled tight around her blue topaz pendant, her fingers trembling slightly. Her expression was stark and distressed. He should have interrupted the moment Johnson had stolen her away. He would not make that mistake a second time.

"I cannot thank you enough," she said with a relieved exhalation.

"It is my fault you had to endure his company. I should have intercepted him before he had a chance to pull you in here. I've never liked that man; I have no idea what Nathan sees in him."

He stepped toward her, not sure exactly what he planned now that he had her alone and all to himself. Taking her in his arms to offer solace crossed his mind, but he didn't think she'd be receptive to his touch just now.

ROSA TOOK IN ANOTHER DEEP breath. Goodness. She tried not to think of what could have happened had de Burgh not come across her path. Johnson wasn't normally so confrontational, and she'd smelled the evidence that he'd been drinking; the stench had been on his breath, in his clothes, and everywhere around her when he'd grabbed her wrist. It was no wonder Nathan wanted to get rid of his guests before they dined; he knew how much she disliked Johnson.

A shiver of revulsion roiled in her stomach. It was best to put that man out of her mind and not think of him a moment longer. Except the part where he'd mentioned her brother. Who was her brother borrowing money from?

"I wanted to escort you to dinner, Miss Montgomery."

She relaxed her guard, instantly feeling at ease in de Burgh's company. "Thank you. And my friends call me Rosa," she offered. "I insist you do the same, since we will be friends."

"Is that what we shall call our arrangement? Friendship?"

There was that intimate—seductive, even—quality in his voice again. It was a velvety promise of sinful delight if she so much as took a nibble. Why did she have a feeling she was going to take a bite? Because every moment she spent with him made her feel safe and so very alive.

"It shall be many things, friendship included. I've no inclination toward brutes, and you've just saved me from one of the worst."

"How do you know you can trust me?"

Because she just did. Instinct and experience with men told her that she could trust this man. But she couldn't admit that after meeting him for the first time tonight.

"You would not have played my very own Galahad and knight errant if there were an ounce of cruelty in your character."

"Well spoken, my lady." Teddy took her hand and pressed a kiss to her glove-clad knuckles. Her breath caught in her lungs at his gallant gesture. She hated the thin material that stopped them from touching flesh-to-flesh as they had earlier.

She waited for him to release her, but he held fast. Tucking her close to his side, he threaded her arm through his and led them both toward the dining room.

"I've no intention of being discourteous, but I heard you turn down Johnson's offer."

"I meant what I said earlier." Her voice came out more firmly than she intended, but there was no negotiating for her company.

She chose whom she wanted to spend time with. End of story.

"I don't doubt that for a moment."

Was that disappointment she heard in his voice?

His thumb rubbed over the inside of her wrist, the action possessively intimate. "Despite what Johnson said, I do believe I'll be able to find your brother."

"I should make it clear that there is no amount of money I won't pay to help my brother out of any trouble he's found himself in."

"I do love a self-sufficient woman, Miss Montgomery." Amusement was evident in his response this time. "Let it be clear that I would never make such a vulgar suggestion as Johnson."

"Perfect. I cannot express how grateful I am for your kindness. And I insist you call me Rosa."

"Rosa." He rolled his "r" a little when he said her name. "Please call me Teddy. It is a name reserved for my closest friends. To everyone else I am simply de Burgh."

"Teddy, then." A smile curved her lips as she repeated his name.

"It's odd that we have never met before, but I feel as though I know you."

He couldn't mean he remembered her from when she was a young woman—at least she hoped not. "We have traveled in some of the same circles, so it's no wonder you feel that way."

"I must take your word for it. We'll have to share a list of our acquaintances to see how many near misses we've had in being introduced."

That was the last thing she wanted to do; it would not be difficult to follow the trail from the young *virtuosa* she'd been to the kept woman she'd become merely to survive.

"A woman should always remain a little mysterious."

"My curiosity has been irrevocably piqued where you're concerned, Rosa."

Regardless of their odd beginning tonight, everything was made a little better by simply being in his company. It also helped that he'd saved her from Johnson.

Admittedly, she was too jaded to fantasize about a knight in shining armor coming to her rescue. Fairy tales were for dreamers and her dreams had been crushed long ago. That truth didn't stop her from feeling as though she were a young woman with the whole world ready to be set down at her feet when de Burgh flattered her.

But she must try and remember that the world was no longer at her feet. A small piece of her had died the night of the accident.

"I hope you'll consent to letting me take you to the opera tomorrow evening."

"In what capacity, Teddy? Anyone who sees us publicly will assume one thing."

That she was his mistress.

And Rosa was no man's mistress. She must always have complete control of every situation she put herself in and something about being in this particular man's company made her feel as though she was surrendering that control to him.

"That you're there as my friend, as my lover, that I am your protector. They are mere words and only some of the names other attendees will give our union. We cannot hide from the world forever if we are to embark on a journey together." It didn't matter what they were to each other; the gossips would all have their own opinions. "Join me for a night at the opera. I'm actually attending to hear an oboist that I might hire for my upcoming performance."

"How can I partake in something so ... joyous when my brother is likely in trouble?"

"I will find him for you, Rosa. If your brother has found a spot of trouble, we will have to find a way to work around it. But until he's found, I presume we'll be constant companions. You can't stop living in the meantime."

Which theoretically was true. But how would he find her brother when he knew little about the places Daniel frequented? In fact, de Burgh knew nothing about her brother and that made the task so much more difficult.

"Will you visit your clubs tomorrow?"

"Those in which I hold memberships, yes. You'll have to help me draw up a list of clubs and places he visits, and the people he prefers to spend time with. While I help you with this, you cannot forget that you still need to live your life."

She let out the breath she'd been holding in anticipation of that exact answer. There was no doubt in her mind that she could trust Teddy implicitly with this task. He would not let her down. He was as good a man as his brother, if not better, for he didn't truly know her.

"I can agree to that, but tell me why we are listening to an oboist?"

"I want your thoughts, and your company."

"And which opera will we attend?"

"A surprise," he said. "I'll have the carriage pick you up mid-afternoon."

She pushed playfully at his arm since he stood so close; an electric hum ran through her body with his nearness. *When had she last felt this thrill for life? This kind of anticipation?*

"You cannot mean to keep me in the dark," she teased.

"Never, Rosa. You are too much a darling to be kept in the shadows."

Her cheeks warmed and her heart pounded anxiously in her chest. He had a sweet way with his words that made her melt a little on the inside.

"And afterward ... Will we part ways?" She was shocked that she even asked, but she might as well know his true intentions now.

They stopped for a moment and Teddy turned her to face him. He threaded his fingers through hers. She held firm and steady as his rougher hands explored hers more familiarly. Though confident was the last thing she felt with his tender touch. "I have a feeling we'll be far from done with each other."

Her eyes slid closed for the briefest moment with his caress.

"We'll have to see what tomorrow brings us, my lord."

"I'm afraid I have to insist you refrain from calling me 'my lord.'"

"That is easy enough to promise."

"We can apprise Nathan of our plans so he has one less worry before he leaves for Maidstone," he said.

"Might I ask a favor?" Her voice was barely above a whisper.

"I think I'd pull the moon from the sky for you, fair Rosa."

He said it so steadily and with so much conviction that she was momentarily taken aback. That he offered such a grand gesture when she knew she had not earned his kindness warmed her heart.

Her arm stretched out, fingers brushing against his torso, seeking knowledge of his person. He was solid beneath her careful exploration. She took a small step closer, swallowing against the lump of nervousness in her throat.

"Might I see you with my hands?" She could hardly believe she'd asked; it wasn't something she ever requested upon first meeting someone. In fact, she could count on one hand how many people she had asked since becoming blind. But it was too late to take the request back. Not that she wanted to.

"Yes," he responded without hesitation. Taking her hand, he slid it higher so it covered his heart. The steady beat beneath her palm was like a metronome that matched the tempo of her pulse.

"You're positive you don't mind? I know my condition can be unsettling." This was his last chance to refuse her.

"Not in the least." His voice was low, his body taut as a well-strung bow where she pressed her palm against his chest.

She slid her hand away from him to pull her gloves off. His warm fingers met hers as he relieved her of the satin burden. She raised her hands to his face, one to each of his cheeks. His skin was freshly shaved, smooth. Not a crease to be had around his mouth or his eyes.

"How old are you?" She didn't mean to ask; she supposed she could have found out in a less conspicuous way.

"Twenty-five."

A few years younger than her own age of twenty-eight.

She passed her fingers over his lips as he talked: not too full, not thin at all. She felt the tip of his tongue faintly against her fingers, then the heat of his breath fanned out over her. Had she imagined the carnal touch?

She closed her eyes, focusing only on him and not the sounds of dinner being set up in the room beyond. Teddy's jaw was nicely formed, his nose large and quite defined, a bump gracing the top ridge.

When her touch lingered, he said, "I broke it when I fell off my horse a few years back; rolled right down into a ravine. A tree stump stopped me at the water's edge."

"It is an attractive feature to many swooning ladies," she teased.

"Ah, but I've no interest in the swooning type."

She made no response, only smiled as she moved onward from his nose. The ridges of his brows were lined with short, well-groomed hairs, turned down at the edge. Bedroom eyes. What a thought to have when she should be dissuading any base reactions she had toward this man.

She didn't stop there. She rose to the tips of her slippered feet, because he had a good six inches on her, her fingers slid though his hair, which was thick, and longish, the texture rougher and heavier than her own.

"What color is it?"

His hand pressed lightly to her hip, holding her in place. "Dark brown. Almost black. Do you remember the shade of your own hair, before ..."

"Yes, like tar."

"Much prettier than tar. It's more like burnished ebony."

She dropped her hands away, opened her eyes and stepped away from their impromptu embrace. She couldn't do this. Not here, not now. A flirtation was one thing—an outright seduction something altogether different. Something she wasn't sure she could allow.

She put her hand out to the wall beside her, feeling a little off balance from his nearness.

It was then that she realized she'd made a devil's bargain. She *wanted* to spend time with Teddy. When was the last time a man had made her truly smile? She honestly couldn't recall a time since Michael. The bittersweet memory had her tilting her chin down, afraid something in her expression would reveal the momentary pain she felt when thinking about her dead fiancé.

If she let any man into her life like she had Michael, it would devastate her if she lost that deep a connection a second time.

No, it would do so much more than that. It would completely destroy her.

Had she agreed to this madness because Teddy made her remember everything she loved and craved most from her old life, the days and nights filled with music, laughter, and friends who understood and shared her aspirations? Did he wish to remain friends, or did he have something of a forbidden nature in mind? More importantly why did she hope for all those things from him?

"Come," he said, handing back her gloves and taking her hand. "Nathan will be looking for us if we tarry much longer."

Time would give her the answers she sought. And hopefully she wouldn't lose herself in the process.

Chapter Four

*It is strange how one feels drawn forward
without knowing at first where one is going.*
— Gustav Mahler

TEDDY SLID A CHAIR OUT for Rosa and guided her to her seat. She sat next to Nathan at the head of the table, so Teddy took the seat on her left, not liking the idea of sitting too far from her.

"It'll only be the three of us dining tonight after all," Nathan said. "I asked Fredricks to go with Johnson to the club," Fredricks being the other friend who had come to see Nathan to cheer him up.

"It gives us more privacy," Teddy pointed out. They would need to discuss Rosa's predicament, and the fact that Teddy had volunteered to help her in Nathan's stead.

"I hope your company didn't leave on account of me. Fredericks could have stayed." Rosa lowered her head and her hands twisted around the napkin in her lap. Teddy was surprised she seemed genuinely troubled that that might be the case. After the way she'd been treated by Johnson, he thought she'd be receptive to the idea of a more intimate dinner arrangement.

"And why shouldn't they leave on your account, darling?" Nathan reached for Rosa's hand, stilling her fidgeting.

Teddy's own fists clenched in his lap. Why the sight of his brother offering a kind caress to this particular woman should bother him was something he'd dissect later. He was developing a dangerous attachment to Rosa. A woman, he reminded himself, he knew very little about other than the minor details of her profession, her need for assistance in finding her brother, and her love of music.

"Don't think for one minute they wanted to spend the evening here," Nathan said. "They're happy to have been sent on to the club to cause mischief more to their liking. I know Fredericks was here out of pity, and I hate pity. Johnson was here merely to see me in my miserable state."

"I just wish I hadn't put you in that position," Rosa said apologetically. "Had I sent a card ahead of my arrival, we could have made proper arrangements to meet."

"It is never necessary. And need I remind you that Johnson knew better than to approach you. Had my head been clearer I would have removed him long before he had a chance to accost you." If Teddy wasn't mistaken, there was some underlying past that Nathan was referring to. "I'm thankful Teddy was able to remove him before something more could have come of your run-in."

"I doubt he'll cause me any harm, but thank you," she said, face still lowered in guilt.

"You are far better company than those two louts," Nathan added.

"And you didn't tell me your brother could be so charming." Rosa's tone lightened.

Nathan gave a throaty laugh, full of amusement. "I had no idea myself. I've barely seen him outside of his work and when he's all work, he's no play."

Teddy narrowed his eyes at his brother. While that might be true, there was something about Rosa that changed him and overcame his usual reluctance to entertain. She'd suggested that she was a muse—he supposed she was, in some senses of the word, considering his reaction and desire to spend time with her. Her mere presence enlivened and inspired him.

"I have agreed to assist her in finding her brother," he said to move the focus of the conversation away from him.

Rosa's spoon stopped halfway to her mouth and Nathan gave Teddy a quizzical look. So his announcement had been abrupt.

"I see," was all Nathan seemed able to say before taking a long drink of his wine.

Rosa dabbed at her mouth with her napkin before sitting up straighter in her chair, turning slightly to face Nathan. "When Teddy offered to assist, I could hardly say no. I know you have to go after Anna, and it would tear me apart inside if I were the person stopping you."

"It's a fine idea. I can't thank you both enough."

Nathan set his wineglass down and leaned against his chair, arms outstretched on the table.

"Just win her back," Rosa said as she slid her hand across the table in search of Nathan's.

He reached for hers before long, pulled it close to his mouth, and kissed the back of her knuckles. Teddy glared at his brother. Nathan could see that his familiarity with Rosa was incensing Teddy, it was the only reason he was being so forward. Before Teddy could temper the emotion surely clear in his expression, Nathan gave him a knowing smile.

"Will you need me for anything?" his brother asked.

"I've got it handled, Nathan," Teddy said before Rosa could speak up.

"Perfect. Send word once you've located him. Or write if you need me for anything."

"Do you leave at first light?" Rosa asked, obviously sensing the building tension in the room.

"I do. I'll ride to Maidstone instead of taking a carriage, which should save me some time."

The remainder of their meal conversation turned to Nathan's trip to Maidstone.

Nathan placed his napkin on the table and stood. He placed his palm against the side of Rosa's face. "You'll find Daniel and I will do everything in my power to make amends with Anna."

Rosa took his hand in hers, lifting it away from her face as she squeezed it. "For both our sakes, I hope so."

Teddy felt his ire rising with every familiar touch. It wasn't like him to be jealous toward his brother; he knew Nathan was devoted to Anna, knew it with every fiber of his being. Still, he wanted to push his brother away from Rosa. He held still in his chair, watching their exchange, wishing Rosa had reached for him instead of Nathan, since he was the one who would help her.

Nathan leaned in close to Rosa and brushed his lips over her cheek. "Teddy will take care of you far better than I can."

Nathan watched Teddy as he spoke. Teddy refused to react, not sure what his brother's intentions were. Nor was he sure why jealousy had slapped him so hard in the face when he'd never been the jealous type before.

Teddy slid out his chair and stood. "Rosa, let me take you into the parlor. We can have some tea before we retire."

She turned toward the sound of his voice, her face tilted up, and her lips parted in a tempting manner. He did not act on that temptation, not with his brother standing so close, so aware of Teddy's reaction to Rosa. Pulling out her chair, he took her hand in his, intent on escorting her to the parlor.

"I'll leave you two to the night," Nathan said. Teddy didn't miss the undertone of speculation in his brother's comment.

"Good night, Nathan," Rosa said.

Once his brother left, Teddy turned all his attention to Rosa. "Do you prefer tea or wine?"

"Tea is perfect for this weather."

Teddy called over to the footman and asked to have tea brought to the parlor.

ROSA REACHED FOR THE TEAPOT as the maid set down the service one the table. Teddy had it in hand before she did and her hands fumbled clumsily against his.

"Let me," he said.

She took her seat again. "I'm perfectly capable of serving tea."

"You're my guest, so I must insist on serving you." He poured out two cups. "Sugar, lemon?"

She shook her head. "Black, please."

He touched her hand before placing the saucer and teacup into her hold. "Thank you."

"You are more than welcome. Now, what can you tell me of your brother's habits?"

She blew over the steam rising from her cup before taking a delicate sip of the hot liquid. "Other than the fact that Daniel has a penchant for gambling?"

"That's a starting point, yes, but I'll need to know any information that might aid me in locating him."

"The one great disadvantage of not being a part of his life is that I can only watch from afar, or so the expression goes. I always know how he fares and what trouble he's found as that finds my ears long before any good he does. I never involve myself directly in his life."

"Does he disapprove of the way you've lived your life?"

Probably the worst question Teddy could have asked, but he didn't backpedal. She thought maybe he wanted to know how she felt about her chosen path. There hadn't been many other options for her after being tossed out of her father's house. Young, alone, and frightened out of her wits, she'd agreed to take her first patron knowing that if she didn't, her life could head in a far worse direction.

"I don't imagine he knows."

Teddy refrained from asking anything more on the topic.

Setting her half-empty teacup on the table, Rosa stood, feeling as though she'd overstayed her welcome. "I think we should call it an evening."

Teddy grasped her hand to stall her and keep her from leaving. The feel of his fingers around hers bombarded her with feelings she didn't know how to address. It was something akin to desire.

"Don't leave on my account. I've been known to stick my foot in my mouth a time or two."

She ducked her head, hiding the sudden smile at his honesty. "No, I understand that you need to know more about me if you're going to find my brother. One of the reasons I came to Nathan was that he already knows about my past. That, and he has previous experience in finding Daniel."

Teddy still hadn't released her hand, and his warmth radiated through her. "Sit with me awhile longer and only tell me what you're comfortable revealing. I won't ask any other questions tonight, especially if they are painful for you. I can promise you that much."

Torn as to exactly what she should do, she knew there was no choice but to stay. She had to give him any information that might be useful in finding her brother. Slipping her hand out from between his, she perched herself on the edge of the settee with a long exhalation. She might as well get her tale out of the way.

"My father made it quite clear that my youthful folly had destroyed his reputation. I gave him no choice but to disown me." She took a deep breath knowing the details she provided would give Teddy a better understanding of how her brother had grown up, and how it would have shaped his character.

"If there is one thing I've learned over time, Rosa, it is that the heart can heal with distance and time. Forgiveness can still be granted, no matter how grave you think your actions might have been."

"That is a circumstance I will never be privy to. You see, I was once in love and tried to elope with the local earl's son. The weather—" She paused. It always brought her great pain to recall that night, and it broke her heart all over again. "It was raining hard the day we left. By the second day, we knew our fathers would be close to catching up with us and took to the road even after being warned by other travelers that the roads weren't ideal for a carriage.

"We rushed, you see. We rushed because of all the weather delays in getting to our destination. We wanted to be married before our fathers could stop us. They didn't agree with our union." She heard the clink of china being placed on the marble tabletop. After a rustle of movement on her left, Teddy sat next to her, the settee dipping and their bodies pressed together from shoulder to elbow. "Lightning struck close to the cart, spooking the horses. The carriage couldn't navigate properly through the muddy conditions."

She couldn't bear to detail the seconds before she and Michael knew they were headed for certain disaster. She'd held tight to Michael's hand as the carriage cab flipped off the road, the horses screaming, injured. She closed her eyes and took a deep breath. The memory made her too numb to cry.

"That was the accident that took my sight. And the life of my fiancé. So you see, forgiveness is not possible. The earl made sure of that before he even buried his son."

Teddy brushed his fingers over the back of her hand, over and over in a soothing fashion. "I didn't mean to invoke such memories. Please. Forgive me."

"My brother has not seen me since the day my father banished me from my house. He was still a boy. Even as he grew older I never reentered his life, fearing what he thought of me. I can only imagine the villain I was painted to be. It was when my brother was sixteen that his problems started. And I knew I could not let him learn from his mistakes like I had. Not once I understood the trouble he got himself in."

"You've been digging him out of trouble that long." Disbelief was strong in his voice. "Why didn't your father step in at that point?"

"I broke something in him when I left. He became reclusive. And I know he can't financially help Daniel, even if he wants to help my brother." Most of Rosa's musical engagements had paved the way for a more comfortable life for her family. She hated to think how her father supported the house without her income to help cover their expenses.

"You should never have had to take on the burden of your brother."

Rosa would not explain her need to atone for all she'd done wrong. "Yet it was within my means to do just that. I wonder sometimes ... Had I not been my brother's silent benefactor and had instead revealed myself to him, could I have persuaded him from the path he fell into so easily and willingly?"

Teddy wrapped his arm around her waist and he held her in his arms like a lover would. Thankful for the comforting touch, she did not move away from him, even knowing this intimacy was dangerous.

"His troubles are through no fault of yours, Rosa."

"Aren't they? I have tried to tell myself that over the years, but it feels like a lie."

"You know Nathan spent his younger days living through one soiree and house party after another, wasting the family fortune trying to erase the memories of our father and to destroy the dukedom he built."

Knowing Nathan as long as she had, she knew that it was Anna who had settled the duke's ways. Through Anna, Nathan had become a connoisseur of artists and had turned his focus away from the waste and complete debauchery he'd sunk into, finding something else to be passionate about. From some of the things he'd said over the years, she guessed that Nathan's childhood had been filled with more pain than any child should have to bear.

"What I'm trying to get at is that my brother had a choice to make, Rosa. He had to decide if his hatred for our father would eat up his life and allow himself to be destroyed by that, or choose to walk away from the path he'd taken. It was Nathan who eventually decided to be a better man than our father."

"I understand what you're alluding to, I do. And I'm sorry you couldn't experience a childhood with a father who doted upon you both." It went without saying that her father had once loved her and Daniel more than life itself, and she had single-handedly broken that love.

"Nathan had the brunt of our father's hard hand, since he was the only child, in my father's eyes, who would ever be duke. I was lucky to spend more of my time in my mother's company, even though my father accused her of making me soft. In truth he paid me little mind. His focus was on making Nathan worthy of the title he would inherit."

Rosa rested her head against Teddy's shoulder. She felt safe when she was in Teddy's arms. Was it that they had similar stories to share? She couldn't believe how freely she'd shared her past with him.

"Listen to us," she said. "How miserable our histories are."

With his hand cupping her cheek, he said, "Tell me the best way to find your brother, and I promise to do everything in my power to reunite you."

She wasn't sure how she felt about that, but she felt like she could almost take on the world if Teddy were at her side. And wasn't that a silly notion considering she barely knew this man.

"I don't know if he'll agree to meet with me." It was hard to admit that, but she felt she should point it out before Teddy got it in his head that this would be a happy ending between brother and sister. She'd been estranged from her family for too long to have such high hopes of reuniting.

"We'll worry about that once he's found."

Unable to help herself, she nuzzled into the palm of his hand. This man comforted her in a way she'd never allowed another to do. If she wasn't careful, Teddy would soon hold the power to be her undoing.

"He flits between gambling hells and whorehouses. His goal has always been to find the next quick, dirty hand of cards. He tends to have even odds, winning large sums of money and even property of other lords, then he'll throw all his winnings down on a bad bet. He's reckless, and that habit has progressively gotten worse over the past year. And I can't help but suspect some of his winnings are made underhandedly."

That reason alone was why he'd likely disappeared.

"When Johnson accosted you, he mentioned your brother borrowing a large sum of money."

"It's possible. He's done that in the past. Nathan has helped me settle a few debts that might have resulted in my brother's death had I not interfered."

"You don't think—"

Pulling out of his arms, she rubbed her fingers against his lips. "Don't even think it. You'll find him for me. I have to believe that."

"Where do you want me to start?"

"Nathan always spread word that my brother owed him money. While that has never directly turned my brother up, he's fished out information on his last whereabouts. My brother lives loudly and lavishly when he's in London, unless he owes someone money. Somebody will remember where they last saw him, or where he last played cards, and who he lost against."

"Then that is exactly what I'll do when I start with my clubs come morning. I know a few gentlemen who fit into the lifestyle you've described, Johnson included."

"Johnson won't help you." And Johnson was someone she wanted to keep Teddy away from. Though Johnson hadn't always been the way he was now, she wasn't sure there was a more vile man than the one he'd become.

"How can you be so sure?"

"Johnson can make things go very badly for my brother. I'm begging you not to ask for his assistance." She did not want to explain her complicated past with Johnson. A man she'd known in her old life, a man who had been her fiancé's best friend. How foolish was she to think she'd never have reason to run into him again? The duke had had a private function two years ago where they'd run into each other, and Johnson had pursued her with the tenacity of a dog after a bone since then. She'd brushed him off with a regularity that would dissuade most men, except, apparently, Johnson.

"If I come up empty-handed, I'll have no choice but to go to him."

"You must exhaust your other options first."

"You have my word that I'll seek every other avenue available to me."

She stood, knowing that it was time to head to bed. "Will you show me the way?"

"Of course." He took her arm, leading her out of the sitting room and toward the stairs.

"I'll head out fairly early in the morning, so I may not see you before you leave for your clubs."

"I'll let you know what I'm able to dig up when we see each other tomorrow night." They stopped outside one of the guest rooms. "Here you are," Teddy said releasing her.

Rosa missed his touch immediately. She would need to sort out these feelings she had for Teddy before they met again.

"Thank you for everything."

Gently clasping her hand, he raised it to press his lips against her fingers. The air left her lungs, and her heart picked up a notch in speed with the motion.

"Though I hate that we've met under these circumstances, I'm glad to help. And I look forward to spending tomorrow night with you."

Rosa reached behind her with her free hand, searching for the doorknob. When she couldn't find it, Teddy reached around her, his arm brushing lightly against her side as he did so, and opened the door for her.

His face was next to hers; she knew because she felt the heat of his breath against her skin like a lover's kiss.

"There's a bell pull to the left of the door. You can ring down for a maid for assistance. The bedroom is cozy: the bed is centered on the right wall, with two nightstands flanking it. There's a cushioned bench at the end of the bed and a slipper chair on the right of the window tucked beside the wardrobe." His voice was a seductive whisper in her ear even though he was giving her instructions on finding her way around.

She swallowed hard against the lump in her throat, barely able to get any words out. "Good night." Her voice was shaky and a little husky.

What would he do if she kissed him? She could invite him into her bedroom, but to what end? This wasn't her. She was always in control of her actions and she never acted brashly, even though she wanted nothing more than to be in the moment with Teddy.

Before she could regret how the night unfolded, she spun away from him and closed the door behind her. The deep breath she took in did nothing to assuage the state of her emotions.

She stood with her back to the door for a good ten minutes regaining her equilibrium and taking deep breaths to calm her racing heart.

She knew she was in a world of trouble if spending a mere few hours with him gave her this reaction.

Chapter Five

*How much has to be explored and discarde
before reaching the naked flesh of feeling.*
– Claude Debussy

LIGHT SHONE BRIEFLY BEHIND HIM, flashing its orange glow across the carpeted floor as an attendant led Rosa into his family's private opera box. He stood, dismissed the attendant with a nod, and took her arm to assist her the rest of the way. She wore that faint floral scent from last night that was fresh like a spring rain and as soft as the petals of flowers in bloom. God, the woman drove him mad with lust just by being in close proximity to him.

The box they occupied went dark as the curtain fell back in place. The wall fixtures set around the stage gave little light, as most had been lowered or snuffed completely while the orchestra set up for the opening act. They were effectively locked together in their own little realm of velvet and gilt. An effective illusion since the rest of the opera attendees need only look up and see them.

It was usually his brother who attended these events with his mistress at his side, though Rosa was not his mistress, and Teddy would not equate her to anything so base. Others would not be so kind in their assessment when they saw her at his side.

"Thank you for sending a carriage." He took her arm and led her to the chair closest to the one he occupied.

It wasn't too dark to see that her dress was crimson, the red as deep as the roses that once grew in his mother's garden. Her hair was coiled and held up with diamond-studded hairpins.

When she was settled in her seat, he slid his chair marginally closer to hers. She leaned forward to fix the bottom hem of her skirt where it twisted around her ankles. A single gem on the back strand of her necklace graced the upper line of her spine. He wanted to knock it off to the side, so it wasn't so perfect and glimmering against her skin, tempting him to reach for it and for her. He stopped himself before he made a tentative move to brush his fingers across the bead dangling over her spine. Instead he placed his elbow on the back of her chair and leaned in closer to her.

"How was your afternoon?" His voice came out deeper and needier than he wanted.

He wondered if she was aware of the effect she had on him. He'd spent a solid three hours in her company yesterday and he'd not been able to get her out of his head since then. There was no explanation he could think of that would draw him to her like this.

"Quiet and uneventful." Her intonation was soft and clear. "Have you found any new information regarding my brother?"

He felt like an ass for not sending a note to her maid or even having the decency to visit her before returning home to shave and dress before their planned evening together.

"I had no news today and no luck rooting out so much as a whisper about him. He's either incredibly secretive and trusts few people, or we do not mingle in the same circles. I'm hoping that some of Nathan's contacts will have answers to further aid me in my search."

"Other than the names of the few friends I gave you, I know no other acquaintances of his." He didn't miss the disappointment lacing her words.

"Does he have a mistress?"

"Not one that I'm aware of."

The way she said that seemed odd, like she was trying to hide something. He did not question her further in that regard, but tucked her reaction away for later consideration.

Seeing the distress he caused by not having hopeful news, he took her hand in his. "I promised I would find him, and I will. It'll just take longer than I originally anticipated."

"I know. The wait is difficult."

They sat close enough that he could make out her every feature. Her collarbone and shoulders were exposed in a bold scooped style at the front and back of the dress. Her skin was white as marble and so flawless that he wanted more than ever to touch her to see if it was as soft as silk. The corset she wore pushed her bosom high to catch the teardrop beads of her onyx necklace.

He had to pry his eyes from her and forcibly turn to watch the stage. He would not sit up here like a great buffoon gawking openly at a woman he was sure others would assume was a courtesan. She deserved more respect than that.

"The usher told me this was the last performance of *Rigoletto*."

"My secret is ruined," he teased.

"Not ruined, only made more exciting now that I know what we are here to listen to."

"So long as you don't forget about my oboist."

"I wouldn't dream of doing any such thing."

Teddy looked out from the box, watching the curtains move as the final pieces were added for the opening scene. Eyes from every direction were on them. He'd never liked the members that made up society, perhaps because he believed a man should do more with his time than play the games society was thick with. Sometimes it baffled him that he wanted to play his newest pieces for them. A necessary evil when one was a composer.

"Is this opera a favorite of yours?" she asked.

"Not a favorite, but I do enjoy some of the music." He was only here to listen to the oboist. The man was apparently well accomplished on his instrument. "Overall, though, I find the orchestration lacks depth, and disappoints during the crisis moments."

"The instrumentation is not designed to add to the story, but to support the singers. I think the lyrics for the most part would be lost amidst heavy orchestral interpretation. The balance works well for the operatic solos."

"I have always preferred orchestral works to operas. Perhaps because I am not in the business of writing operas."

It impressed him that she obviously knew music well enough to defend what she liked: a connoisseur in her own right.

"Do you find the premise for the opera romantic?" he asked, wondering what exactly she liked about it.

"Romantic?" She laughed quietly enough that it did not draw eyes their way. He wondered if she knew they were under social scrutiny.

"You say that as if you think otherwise."

"There is no real romance in *Rigoletto*. I have lived through my own hardships and even tragedy. What use do I have for others' sorrows, even in the form of an opera?"

Once again her blunt approach and honesty was refreshing. He wished he could make her forget the tragedy that had befallen her, erase the pain he'd seen in her expression last night as she'd revealed small bits about her past.

She gave a wistful sigh. "Besides, the tenor in this story is far too cruel to be considered romantic. He doesn't care that he's behind the demise of all his mistresses."

"I find it amusing that the characters in operas always bring about their own deaths," he said.

"The sadness is almost overwhelming and to think it's all due to the foolish naïveté of a young maid who knows naught of the evils of the world. I never thought her character deserved the tragedy that befell her."

"You're a romantic, Rosa."

She laughed again, this time louder and drawing the attention of those sitting nearest them. He gave those patrons a bored glare and didn't let up until they turned away first.

The curtains drew back, forestalling any further conversation. The first act opened with the palace setting and the Duke of Mantua marching out in front of the audience to sing of his conquests.

By the second act, Rosa grasped the edge of his jacket and tugged him closer so he would lean toward her ear. "Your oboist doesn't have enough of a part to be fairly judged."

"I was aware of that before we arrived." His lips were close enough to her ear that if he desired he could press a kiss there. He knew that the observers would think nothing untoward, assuming that they were whispering about the performance. As much as he wanted to take the next step, he held back.

"I need someone who has control over his instrument, not someone demanding to be heard."

She turned her head to the side so they were face-to-face. He couldn't stop himself from sliding his fingers over the little bone at her nape as he draped his arm over the back of her chair. She didn't lean away from him, which told him precisely what he needed to know: She was receptive to his touch.

Everything in his body stilled. Her skin was just as he imagined. Soft as silk. And he wanted to strip her bare, and feel every inch of her until he'd uncovered her most intimate secrets.

"You have me most intrigued with this piece you're working on."

What would she say if he told her he found her completely enthralling and fascinating, and the furthest things from his mind right now were the oboist and his concerto? Instead, he found himself asking, "Will you stay the night with me, Rosa?"

She sucked in a surprised breath. "We have already discussed the nature of our *friendship.*"

He cupped her nape with his hand, his fingers gliding along the pins holding up her elaborate curled hairstyle. "There are many types of friends."

"What is it you really want from me, de Burgh? More than my company, obviously, but do you really need my input on whatever it is you're working on?"

"We have an agreement I will honor, Rosa. We also agreed that you would address me by my given name."

Fingers reaching out, she found his chest and slipped her hand over the knot in his necktie. Her palm was warm. And her touch made him desperate to whisk her away from the prying eyes around them.

"Yes, but that was before you propositioned me, *Teddy.* I'm not so naïve as to fall for seeing your etchings, not even for the clear reason making a request of that nature ludicrous and impossible."

He couldn't help but chuckle. It was endearing that she could make a joke of her blindness. "That is something my brother is more likely to utter. Give me one night of your company."

Did she not feel the fire burning strong between them? Could she not taste the desire coating the air, drugging them into sensual intoxication? He knew he was not alone in feeling the attraction.

"And what will one night entail?" she asked.

"I want to hear you play again."

"Do you only seek a muse, de Burgh?"

"I enjoy your company."

Her breath hitched, the sound nearly imperceptible, but he caught it nonetheless.

"Have you heard enough of your oboist?"

"Yes." And before she could ask any more questions, Teddy rose from his seat and took her arm. Stepping away from the balcony edge, he pulled them toward the curtained area that was hidden from view. She did not pull away, not even when he placed his hand over the small of her back and pulled her flush against his body.

A low sigh escaped her mouth. He had never wanted a woman more than he did in this moment. He traced the seam of her mouth with his finger before he lowered his lips to hers. He hesitated for only a moment, wanting to give her plenty of opportunity to pull away. Give her the chance to prove she didn't feel the same way he felt.

Rising up on her toes, her mouth next to his ear, she whispered in a tone that was so seductive he barely held back from ravaging her mouth. "Are you sure one night will fulfill this yearning we have for each other?"

The scent of her perfume was an aphrodisiac in and of itself. The loose tendrils of her hair that had escaped her chignon teased at his nose. He wasn't sure of anything anymore, not where Rosa was concerned. He suspected, however, that one night would not be adequate.

"Just give me tonight. The rest we can figure out later."

WHAT HAD HAPPENED TO HER resolve to remain friends with de Burgh? He had given her a taste of her old life was what had happened, and she craved that as much as she craved the feel of his mouth pressed against her.

If she stayed the night with him, what would that mean for tomorrow? She'd not been intimate with a man since her fiancé's death, not that anyone knew that about her. Assumptions made asses out of most men and if they wanted to call her a harlot and courtesan, then so be it.

She'd only had three patrons since her fall from fame. The first was a painter she sat for day and night for four years, but that arrangement had ended when he'd moved to Paris with his lover. He had preferred the company of other men, but had used her in his paintings since her nudes sold for more than those of his male lovers.

The second had been short-lived, for she learned quickly that Lord Marsley had a penchant for locking away what he desired most. And she would not be hidden away from her friends by a madman who wanted to keep her in a cage like a songbird.

Then there had been Lord Hambleworth. Hambleworth had mourned deeply for his dead wife and so their arrangement had been without intimacies. When Hambleworth had passed away, he'd left Rosa with a sizeable income to keep her comfortable for the rest of her days.

Where exactly did Teddy fit in?

And why was she practically throwing herself into his arms at every opportunity, enticing him in ways she'd never dared to dream of with any other person?

He pressed her against the velvet-lined wall. "I'm going to steal a kiss."

"You'll make a spectacle of yourself," she teased, though her voice came out wistful and needful of his promise.

"No one can see us."

That was her only warning before he pressed one hand to the back of her head, angling her face toward his. The warmth of him enveloped her as he pulled her tighter against his body.

His lips found hers, the pressure soft yet firm. His teeth nipped, separating her lips. He didn't delve any deeper, but kissed his way along the column of her neck, his nose tickling a sensitive line along her collarbone.

Keeping a cool distance from men in the past had never been a problem, but Teddy was proving to be an addiction she could glut herself on. As much as she wanted to detach herself from her feelings and remain on friendly terms, that task was nigh impossible.

Opening herself up intimately to this man would eventually lead to heartache. Once her brother was found, Teddy would no longer be obligated to help her. He might not even require her assistance with his music.

Where would that leave her?

As his teeth found and pulled at the side of her ear above the onyx earrings, her traitorous body arched closer. It had been too long since she'd been touched like this, so long since she'd been desired in such a raw, carnal way in which she wanted to reciprocate each move, each touch.

As much as she wanted to revel in the heat surrounding her and igniting passions long vanquished by the realities of life, she knew they had to stop before they regretted their actions. Drawing in a deep breath, she forced herself to step to the side, her shoulders brushing against the curtained wall of the box.

It wasn't that she wanted to leave his arms—quite the opposite—but they needed to cool their heads and their bodies so they could leave with their appearances intact. With her fingers pressed over her fast-beating heart, she took another steadying breath.

He lifted her hand and kissed her gloved knuckles. "Trust me, Rosa." He pulled her away from the wall and toward the exit. There was a promise of so much more in the air as they left the opera house.

Chapter Six

*L*ove demands everything and that very
justly.
– Ludwig von Beethoven

ROSALIE CURSED HERSELF AS TEN kinds of fool for going
back to Teddy's town house. The carriage ride had been mostly
silent. Teddy hadn't made any further advances, confusing her
more than ever. What had she agreed to tonight? An affair? Or
simply to listen to parts of his newest composition? She wasn't
so naïve to think it was only the latter.

She rubbed her gloved hands together, trying to bring back
the warmth after sitting in a cold carriage for an hour. The butler
had whisked off somewhere with her overcoat and shawl. Teddy
had left her in the anteroom to inform the household staff of their
needs, telling her he'd return shortly.

Rosa brushed her hands over the round table in the middle of
the large anteroom. She'd been Nathan's friend for a long time,
but she hadn't visited his town house often enough to know her

way around well, and wouldn't attempt to find her way without her walking stick or on the arm of another.

She smoothed her hands over the cool marble surface of the table, wondering which direction she should take. The steady clip of shoes tapping on the hardwood floor approached her.

"I've instructed the staff to have something warm prepared for us, and to ensure my private chambers are heated sufficiently. They're lighting the braziers even now." Teddy took her hands between his, rubbing them briskly before taking her by the elbow to lead her down the corridor. "Why didn't you say you were so cold? I would have taken you straight to the drawing room."

She was glad to leave the chilly foyer, as he pulled her deeper into the house. "This is a natural state for me. I've never been keen on the winter months."

"We'll get you warmed in no time. There's already a fire lit in the sitting room. We can sit there for a spell while my chambers are prepared." He must have felt her hesitation, and clarified. "That is where I keep all my work."

"So long as you have a piano at hand, we can go upstairs now. That is, if you still want insight of a *musical* nature." She leaned in close to him in blatant invitation. What was she doing? Perhaps she needed him to spell out his intentions, because she didn't know what he planned for them or what he truly wanted from her. She had never been so flustered by anyone.

"The best piano in the house resides in my room."

"Better than the Broadwood?" She laughed a little at his outrageous statement. How often did you find more than one piano in a town house? Even while growing up in a larger country house there had only been one piano.

"That old Broadwood is for entertaining guests," he said as if that was answer enough.

Taking her hand, he placed it against the railing as he took her upstairs. When they neared the top, he paused, "Mind your last step. And yes, I do require your musical insight, though that isn't necessarily what I crave most at the moment."

"And what do you crave most?"

"I believe you already know the answer to that."

His hand tightened around her wrist with his admission, all the air in her lungs fled in anticipation and excitement. She wouldn't need the fire to warm her if he kept talking this way. Suddenly she wished he would kiss her again. She wanted his lips on hers with a desperation so unlike her. While he'd restrained himself from any further intimacies in the carriage ride over to his house, she wondered what it would take to shred his control.

"If I were to play a melody," he said, "could you play it back?"

His question pulled her thoughts away from his mouth against her skin and back to the present. "What an odd question. Why do you ask?"

"I keep recalling how beautifully you played last night without sheet music. I realized some hours after hearing you that you were warming your hands to Liszt's *Un sospiro,* which was published after your accident."

"So my secret is revealed." She smiled, pleased he had noticed. "Yes, I can play by ear."

There were few who possessed such a talent, few that she knew of anyway, and once again she worried that he would figure out her identity. Though she wondered if he would truly care that she had hidden that part of her past. He'd been the epitome of kindness since they met; was it possible for him to think less of her?

"So I have found my very own virtuoso," he said.

Unintentionally she stiffened next to him and hoped he hadn't noticed her momentary unease.

"I would like to see how far we can stretch your talents tonight. Are you willing to take me up on that challenge?" he asked.

"I'm no virtuoso," she said breathlessly, afraid for a moment that he would judge her for just how far she'd fallen. Once the door shut behind them, she swallowed against the lump of trepidation that made her mouth dry. "Please, play something of yours for me."

Taking her by the elbow, he led her farther into his bedchamber. A fire was indeed lit and the heat enveloped her almost immediately, ridding her of the chill that had settled in her bones during the carriage ride.

"I've brought in a bench so we can sit together at the piano."

"No need to fuss over me. I prefer to listen at a distance to start."

She dropped her arm and stepped away from his hold. He strode over to the piano, sliding the bench out across carpeted floor. The rustle of material told her he removed his jacket, giving his arms and shoulders free rein while he played.

"Are you sure you don't wish to sit?" he asked once more.

She was very sure.

She shook her head and crossed her arms over her middle as she waited for him to play. Aside from the four-handed piece they had played all too briefly, this was the first time she'd heard him play the piano alone.

He warmed up by playing a few chords, then started a simple tune. She wondered if this was one of his pieces. The upper melody followed two paces behind the lower register in a somber chord—A minor. He emphasized the solemnity of the piece by dropping an octave on the keyboard with the secondary melody.

She was tempted to pace the floor behind him, something she did often when she was thinking a musical problem through. Instead, she stepped closer to him, following the sound of the music.

Picking the piece apart in her head as the music unfolded, she listened to what he didn't play. She stood close enough to him that she could hear the damper being pressed down for the softer, pianissimo parts. Then, just as suddenly as his playing had started, all grew quiet. She paced a tight path, unable to remain idle.

Technically, the piece was simple; stylistically and to the untrained ear, it was nice to listen to; musically ... musically it did not move her. There was no thrill of excitement or emotional tingle of appreciation on listening to the piece. There was nothing to ground her in the song and keep her locked to it until it wrapped up. There was no hum in her blood that craved more.

She expected him to play something else, but he remained silent. The bench pushed out and he strode toward her, stopping outside the path she wore on the rug. She was aware of his body heat every time she walked past him. He waited, not rushing her thoughts, which she appreciated.

Brow furrowed, teeth biting into her bottom lip and her fingers drumming along her upper arm where they held tight, she tried to figure out what was wrong with the piece he'd played.

And then it came to her. He was testing her. Dropping her arms, she walked over to the piano, hoping she was headed in the right direction.

If he wanted to know whether or not she could repeat what she heard, he needn't test her; he only needed to ask her to show him that truth. There would be no difficulty in playing his piece back to him.

Setting her fingers on the chords he'd started on, she repeated the tune without embellishment or corrections to the missing notes she had identified upon first hearing it. And she didn't change the key it was played in, which strained the melody, making it grim.

As the piece concluded, she removed her hands from the keyboard and folded them together in her lap. The purely masculine scent of Teddy enveloped her as he leaned over her shoulder. Amber infused with sandalwood flooded her senses. Teddy played out a new melody, simple and one-handed.

He stopped and turned enough that his breath fanned out over her ear. "Now you," he whispered.

When she placed her hands over the keys, his were still there. She did not push him away, she allowed him to learn from her playing. She was a pianist, he a violinist; she was sure she had a few tricks she could teach him. As she played his melody, she switched into a complimentary chord of thirds, making the piece grander. Livelier.

As her finger slowed and finally came to a stop, she asked, "Is that what you had in mind?"

"You surprise me, and I know not why."

"People expect less from someone who cannot see."

She couldn't keep the bitterness from her voice. She had also expected less from herself after the accident, since it had taken her a full year before she could bring herself to sit at the piano again. It had taken her even longer to realize that the accident had only made her stronger as a pianist and as a person.

"I will never make the mistake of underestimating you. If you'll recall, Beethoven was deaf and his peers harder on him than other composers of his time."

"He was also a man of proven skill before the world was aware of his disadvantage as a pianist and composer."

"Others—fools—might think less of you for your blindness, Rosa, but I will never take you for granted. What I'm most awed by is that I've known few musicians who can claim such a tremendous talent like the one you've shared with me. How is it that you remain undiscovered?"

She could not tell him that she had once been revered and respected for her craft. And then she'd ruined herself in the eyes of polite society. Really, though, it was only a matter of time before he found out about her past. Would that be so terrible? It was a question she was asking herself with more frequency and she didn't know the answer.

He reached around her with his other hand, the heat of his breath moved away from the side of her face, and his chin brushed lightly over the top of her hair as he played a new tune in the lower register.

She leaned back, not quite enough that she touched him, though she yearned to be held in the cradle of his arms as he played around her on the bench.

TEDDY WAS TEMPTED TO LEAN right into her, take her into his arms, and hold her for the rest of the night. The desire to trace his fingers along her collarbone above the scoop of her vermil-lion-colored dress was almost too much to ignore. He kept his mind focused on the keys beneath his fingers and tried to shut off what the soft touch of her skin would feel like against his mouth as he kissed every inch of it.

It was safe to say he'd never met a woman like Rosa. She was the epitome of everything he'd ever wanted in a woman. She matched him in all things, starting with their shared love of music, which he liked to think allowed them to understand each other on a deeper level.

He stretched his hand an octave higher on the right, playing above the middle-C range. The change in tone forced his body into hers, letting the press of her shoulders rest along his chest.

Chin rubbing against her soft hair, he could smell the faintest scent of lilacs. He'd forever associate lilacs and springtime with Rosa. Being around her gave him a rush like cool spring water breaking through the ice after a long winter, waking him up from a slumber he didn't realize his life was in.

Closing his eyes, he started to play Beethoven's *Appassion-ata.* He wanted to absorb her into his body, to never forget this moment and the joy she gave him just by being here with him.

She patted the bench seat next to her. He had to stop playing for a moment as he settled in beside her and took the lower reg-ister. She took on the runs on her side of the piano. They both played with their own interpretations, creating an odd mishmash when their timing no longer matched and when Teddy forgot some of the notes. They laughed, bumping into each other's shoulders, then took the runs in proper unison for the remainder of the four-handed piece.

Though they played for nearly twenty minutes, it was over far too soon for Teddy. Rosa dropped her hands to her lap and pressed her shoulder against his once again. They were both breathing a little faster from the exertion the song required.

"I don't think I've ever had so much fun," he said.

"My head is liable to swell if you don't tell me how terrible on the pedal I was when I couldn't stop laughing. It's been so long since I played the *Appassionata* in its entirety."

"How about me missing half the lower register notes?" He brushed the back of his hands along the delicate line of her hands where they rested in her lap.

"You didn't do half as badly as you think," Rosa said.

"It was all good fun. The skill of ear you have to pick out and adjust to the tiniest nuance in a piece is astounding."

"It is the gift of a pianist. I'm sure you could do the same on the violin."

"Perhaps. I've memorized so many pieces and can play them with my eyes closed that I couldn't say for sure. What did you think of the first melody I played?"

He wanted to test her comprehension of the craft for theory. If she understood what his piece lacked and if it agreed with his assumptions—because he did know where and how it could be made better—then he knew he could ask for her assistance in adjusting the key themes of his latest work.

The Hanover Rooms opening was less than two months away, and too close for comfort when his concerto was nowhere near ready for public consumption.

She angled herself on the bench to face him. "First, you played it in the wrong key. If you played it in a relative major instead of A minor, the chords would stand out, and you could add the appropriate accidentals to accentuate the melodic theme. When you play it in A minor, you bury the better qualities of the melody, and create something akin to a requiem."

Pride for this woman filled his heart. It was a privilege to work with someone of her genius. "A very intuitive approach."

"Here," she said, lifting her hands over the keys once again. She played his piece in the key she had suggested. When she finished, she faced him again, her eyes never quite focusing, though he swore he could see the depth of her knowledge in her blue gaze. "Are you done testing my ability?"

He smiled and held back his laugh. Was he so obvious? "I was curious to know how great your skill was. I also noticed that you played music of your own making when we first met."

"Yes, it was my own," she confirmed. "Unfortunately, I have no one to help me write it down. No one with the skill required. No one I trust." He took note of the slight slump in her posture. Before he could ponder it further she straightened and gave him one of those playful smiles she was always tempting him with.

He knew then what he had to do. "I would be honored to write the music out for you." This way, they could still spend time together once her brother was found. She'd be tied to him for an indefinite amount of time.

"On top of your commission? I couldn't burden you with such a task."

"I assure you that it's no burden." Caressing her cheek with his knuckles, he added, "It would be a privilege. I'd also like to help you find publication for your work, if you desire it."

"Thank you," she said, pink tinting her cheeks.

Her hand rested over his knee as she leaned in closer to him. He thought maybe she intended to kiss his cheek, but he turned enough that their lips met instead. As she lingered, his hand cradled the back of her head. The soft, silken strands of her hair had him wanting to unpin it and run his hands through the dark tresses. He vowed to himself that he would do just that, and soon.

"Rosa," he muttered against her lips before running his tongue along the seam, seeking admittance. "I can't deny that I want you. I refuse to lie about how you make me feel."

She turned from their kiss, resting her cheek against his. Each of her inhalations was ragged and as needy as his. "You barely know me."

"Then let me see the Rosalie no one else knows."

"Desire passes with the first sign of fulfillment."

"That is an excuse for you to deny what's between us and nothing more."

"How can you be so sure?"

"I know what I feel and it's no passing fancy."

She pressed her lips lightly against his cheek, then stood from the bench. "The intensity is frightening."

It might frighten her, hell, it frightened him a little, too, but it was something worth exploring.

"We should get back to working on the composition," he suggested, knowing it would ease her nerves and keep her with him for a while longer.

It took everything in him to walk away from her when he wanted nothing more than to gather her in his arms. Picking up the stacks of music on his desk, his most recent attempt at writing, he fanned the papers out across the floor.

"I can hear you moving about. What are you searching for?" There was a husky quality to her voice he was sure hadn't been there a moment ago.

He could not look at her. If he did ... He might not be able to hold back another second from truly tasting of her lips. "I'm looking for the piano stanzas I jotted down a few days ago."

"You don't remember your own piece?"

"I don't because you have my mind scattered." The crinkle of paper filled the room. "Ha! I found it. Now, if you will please listen while I play for you."

He strode purposefully back toward the piano, took a seat at the bench, and played the melody that had been giving him trouble since the very beginning. Something felt off in the run, and though he knew the piece was missing something, that *something* remained elusive. When he stalled at the end of the theme, she said nothing, so he decided to play the rest of what he had.

She came up next to him, resting her hand over his shoulder.

"It's beautiful, Teddy."

As he played the melody over the middle-C octave, the back of his arm nudged her skirts. That gentle touch had her whole body relaxing into his, as if in invitation. He swallowed hard and maneuvered to a lower register, improvising a new section.

She settled herself on the bench next to him once again. The piece ended all too soon and the room grew silent except for the crackle of wood in the fireplace and the even ticking of rain as it hit the windows.

Unable to keep from touching her, Teddy brushed his knuckles over the side of her cheek and took her chin between his thumb and forefinger. Her mouth was slightly parted, her teeth nibbling at her lower lip.

"Will you kiss me again?" she asked, breathless.

"I hunger so deeply for you, Rosa." He traced the tips of his fingers along the line of her jaw. "I may not be able to stop with a kiss. What then?"

God, he wanted to taste all of her. But it was up to her how far they took this, how much she was willing to give him right now. He would accept nothing but all of her in the end. For now, they could take small steps in a direction she was comfortable with.

She laid her palm flat over his heart. "Why question your desires?"

If they did this, if he made the next move, it wouldn't be as simple as a kiss. And the truth of the matter was, whatever this attraction was, it was far from simple.

Instinct alone warned him that he needed to take this slowly, so in compromise with his conscience he promised himself that one taste would not be the end of the world. Releasing her chin, he brushed his hands through the soft coils of her hair, holding her gently by the nape as his mouth slanted over hers.

The second the exhalation of her breath brushed past his lips, he was done waiting.

The taste of peaches and black tea filled his senses as his tongue stole into her mouth to tangle with her tongue. He felt the moment she surrendered when she moaned softly and her body leaned into his hold. The rise and fall of her breasts with each breath was rapid, urgent. Arms around his neck, Rosa's fingers twisted and drew circles against his scalp. If a kiss could determine your compatibility with someone, then there was no question in his mind that they were made for each other.

One taste of her had been such a bad idea. He didn't think

he'd ever be able to pull away.

He felt the heavy pound of her heart where their bodies were crushed together. Sucking on her lower lip, he nipped at it before releasing it then soothed it with a gentler kiss. She matched every thrust of his tongue as their mouths tasted hungrily.

"Ask me to stop." His request was but a whisper against her lips.

She shook her head and pressed her mouth against his, giving him a sweet kiss.

"Ask me to stop, Rosa." He pressed his lips to her forehead, trying to rein in his need to claim her in an entirely different way than with a kiss.

"I can't. I—I don't want you to stop." She rained kisses along his chin and neck.

Wrapping his arms around her, Teddy held her tightly, locking them in an embrace. With her head tucked into the crook of his shoulder, she was in his complete control. He didn't move for some time, just held her as he warred with his better judgment to stop the madness that had ensnared them and let her go.

Even lost in the moment, Teddy knew that the danger in not pulling back was that Rosa would think him no better than any other man in her life. He had to refrain himself, take his time to get to know her.

He needed her trust, her friendship, and her love before he led them farther down their current path.

Brushing his lips over hers one final time, he let her go. Teddy hated the distance immediately.

Standing, he walked around to her side, took her hand, and assisted her over to the sofa. "Please stay a while. We can talk trade or about your brother. I want your company."

She shut her eyes and took a deep breath. "I think it's best for us to call it a night."

His jaw clenched. Despite that being the last thing he wanted to happen, he understood her hesitancy in remaining in his company if she wanted to fight their mutual attraction. "If that is what you desire, let me arrange for a carriage."

"Desire is a dangerous emotion."

"Not if it leads you in the right direction." He took her hand and led her back downstairs.

"Who is to say what's right between us?"

"Don't you feel how right this is?"

When she didn't answer him, he left to retrieve her cloak and his frock coat. Conceding to her wish to leave was growing more difficult with every step. He reminded himself again that she must think of him differently than she did of other men. The only way to achieve that was to be patient with her. Whatever was between them seemed to frighten her, where it only intrigued and spurred him into wanting her more.

After he hailed the cab, he opened the door for her, reluctant to say good night.

Temptation overwhelmed his better judgment and he gathered Rosa in his arms before he could think better of his actions. Taking a surreptitious glance around them, he checked that they were not being watched. Her breath hitched in her chest, her tongue darted out to moisten her lips, enticing him to take a bite.

When he did no more than hold her in his arms, she asked, "What are you about?"

Her voice had taken on that sultry, breathless quality that had his body aching for her.

"I want you to myself, and I'm sorry you feel the need to escape us."

As her arms snaked around his shoulders, the last of his patience wore right through. He was done waiting for a more appropriate time and place, and urged Rosa behind the open door of the carriage so the driver could not see them.

He lowered his mouth to the upper swell of her breasts, biting the flesh that teased him. He worked his way toward her collarbone, licking and nipping a path along her pale flesh. When she gasped and threaded her fingers through his hair, he knew she was his. Arms around his shoulders, she held him tight, encouraging him. Hands at the small of her back to pull her close, he dipped his tongue lower once again.

Could two people be more in tune to each other? Could two people meld any tighter with all their clothes on? He wanted to feel and taste all of her, every dip, every curve, every part of her flesh as he wrung passion from her body when he finally claimed her. Teeth grazing the curve of her breast, leaving it reddened, he tasted every part of her that he could without physically removing any article of cloth.

Voices broke through their private, stolen moment and he reluctantly released her, holding her in his arms, looking into her unseeing eyes. "Though I need to better contain my desire for you, I cannot apologize."

She took in a shaky breath.

"We need to get you home, or I'll do my damnedest to convince you to come back inside. I want you, Rosa. I have from the moment we met."

Closing her eyes, she pressed her palm against his cheek. "I fear the path we're on."

She was afraid of what lay between them, he could sense it in her words, in her body language as she started to pull away from him. Her honesty struck him so deeply that he wished he could brush her fears away with the wave of his hand. Instead of doing what he most wanted, he offered, "Let me accompany you home. I won't stay, I just want to see you safely off."

When she stepped away from him he felt his world shatter a little with the distance and wall she put up.

"Thank you, but I can manage on my own." She climbed into the carriage with her hand on the door so she could shut it behind her, separating them. He watched her leave, and stayed out in the street until he could no longer see the swing of the lamp on the side of the carriage.

FINALLY IN THE SAFETY OF her home, she shut the door behind her and pressed her back against the wood for a moment, thinking over the monumental evening with Teddy. Something far more than friendship had sprouted between them. Fingers reaching up, she traced her lips.

She could still feel the phantom touch of Teddy's lips atop hers: supple, strong, addictive ... everything a kiss should be. Even the taste of him lingered on her tongue, and the imprint of him warmed her skin as though he had seared her very flesh with each of his passionate caresses.

He had taken his time, tasting her tenderly, touching her like a man who couldn't get enough of the feel of her. The intimacy they shared had burnt a path right to her aching, hungry heart. She wanted him even now and felt the deep, craving ache in her body to have him. Why had she turned him away? Because she didn't trust herself around him.

And because she was falling in love with him. How could she not? The question was, did he return her sentiment?

As she made her way upstairs, she realized just how much she was at a loss in dealing with the feelings bombarding her. Teddy was merely helping her through a difficult time in searching for her brother. She read more into his actions than she ought. And while he said he needed her musical acuity, she knew that wasn't quite true; he just had to believe in what he was creating. There was no doubt in her mind that others would find his new work just as beautiful as she did. And she'd only had a tiny glimpse of the surface of it.

Where could this love affair lead in the end? She was a ladybird. A woman of ill repute and not worthy enough to stand next to a man of Teddy's status. There could never have or share more than their mutual love of music.

That was the key to making their relationship work; she needed to focus on his music and forget any sentimental feelings she harbored for Teddy.

As she made her way into her room, she trailed her hands along the polished wooden surface of the vanity in search of her hairbrush. When the bristles prickled her fingertips, she turned it about to grasp the handle and sat on the edge of her bed.

Perhaps the last few years alone made her yearn for the company and companionship of a man. It wasn't any man she wanted, though. Thaddeus de Burgh thoroughly consumed her thoughts.

She needed to shield her heart. She'd not be left broken and unable to pick up the pieces when he no longer required her services, when he no longer enjoyed the chase in pursuing her.

Why did he have to treat her as an equal?

What she did know was that in Teddy, she had found a friend who shared her passion and love in music. Everything they worked toward for his composition would make his debut at the Hanover Square Rooms the most talked-about event for years to come. And she would have a part in all that. But what would happen after that? Once her brother was found and Teddy's piece completed, what would be left for them? Would he write out her piano sonatas in the end? Or would he be done with her altogether?

Rosa sighed her frustration as she pulled at a stubborn knot at the end of her hair. She was being fanciful and foolish. And she knew that falling in love with Teddy would be a grave mistake.

Teddy was a man with the world before his feet. He would become someone amazing and respected, and he would never be able to do that with a woman of her reputation standing by his side. There would be no spot for her in his life once those around them realized just how brilliant a man he was. Because without a doubt, there would come a time when Teddy would be lauded again for his musical compositions.

He would have everything, and rightfully so, that she'd been denied. And while she felt no jealousy, only pride, that meant she had nothing to offer him once they concluded their time together. How could she ever expect to stand on equal ground with him when she couldn't even write her own music down to share with the world?

She shook her head as she set the brush down. For now, she

would live vicariously through Teddy.

And the rest ... the rest she would worry about when the time came to pass.

Chapter Seven

Never assume an inner or an outer pose,
never a disguise.
–Gustav Mahler

"DE BURGH." LORD HAGAN CLAPPED him on the back. "What brings you here so late in the evening?"

It was true that he rarely went out to his clubs at night, but he needed something to distract him, to keep him from going to Rosa and demanding she stop pushing him away.

"I'm in search of someone."

Hagan glanced at Teddy's half-empty tumbler, and the newsprint folded open on the table. Teddy hadn't wanted company when he'd arrived, but now ... After an hour, half a glass of whisky he didn't have the good sense to enjoy, and a mostly unread paper sitting in front of him, he could use a break from doing nothing. He motioned toward the chair across from him, inviting Hagan to join him.

"Anyone I might know?" Hagan asked, taking off his frock

coat to hang it over the back of the wooden chair.

Then it struck him that Hagan was a regular here day and night. Why not ask him about Rosa's brother? There was a good chance Hagan would know of him, he was much more a man about Town than Teddy had ever been.

"Daniel Montgomery."

Hagan made a derisive sound in the back of his throat as he pulled off his gloves and waved the club owner over to their table. "I didn't realize you'd fallen in with that lot."

"I'm looking for him for—" His companion? His lover— though Rosa wasn't yet his lover. He took another swig of the whisky. "A friend asked me to locate him."

"Ah. It makes sense then. Is your friend owed money?"

"Yes." A small lie would not hurt in this instance.

Hagan gave Teddy a thoughtful look, fingers splayed along the edge of the table. "Well, I doubt you'll find him here, or at any of your other clubs. Seems Johnson gave the boy heaps of money just prior to him up and disappearing into the night. There's some shady business going on there that you don't want any part of it."

Goddamn Johnson. Why did it keep coming back to that cad? Teddy's fingers curled tightly into a fist, his knuckles cracked. When he found that little prick, he'd wring his bloody neck.

And why in hell was Hagan warning him off?

"I see." Teddy scratched his chin pensively. "Though anything with Johnson is usually bad news."

When Hagan looked at him curiously, Teddy turned is focus to the paper he still held. He folded it and set it on the table. What would he tell Rosa? How would she react once she knew her brother was mixed up with Johnson?

"Honor bound as your brother's friend," Hagan said as he rose to his feet, "I should warn you that half the club is looking for Montgomery for various chits and favors owed. You'll not find Montgomery until he is good and ready to be found."

Teddy inclined his head. "And I am bound by honor to locate him."

Hagan gave him a slow, knowing smile. "A woman, eh?"

Teddy chose not to agree or disagree and instead shrugged.

Hagan clapped him on the shoulder once again before taking his leave. "Because it's you, and for a lady friend, you can try asking Montgomery's father. Though I hear he's taken ill and hasn't left his bed for a fortnight."

Teddy looked up at Hagan curiously. "And who precisely is his father?"

Good God, this search for information was hitting dead end after dead end. Now he'd have to tell Rosa that Johnson might be responsible for her brother's disappearance, but that her father ailed.

"My mistake. I thought you might know him. Lord Percy Montgomery of Sussex."

The corner of the paper Teddy clutched was suddenly crushed between his fingers. Not only was Rosa a baron's daughter, she was Lord Montgomery's daughter, a man known for his support of the arts, namely music.

He nodded a curt thanks to Hagan, hoping the shock he felt was not easily read on his face. Teddy needed to see Rosa—to ask and understand why she'd kept him in the dark as to her being *that* Montgomery's daughter. Miss Rosalie Montgomery. Despite knowing precisely who her father was, Rosa's name remained unfamiliar to him.

Shrugging into his overcoat, he left the club. Coming across a free hackney, he gave the man directions to Rosa's house.

He ascended the steps two at a time when he arrived, and gave a harsh pull at the knocker. A woman in a mobcap, rounded and matronly, answered his summons before he could pound the knocker a second time.

"The mistress of the house?" he asked.

Riotous curls swept around the woman's shoulders as she bobbed her head. "Come in, my lord. The house has bedded down for the night, but the mistress gave instruction to be summoned no matter the hour if you ever arrived for an audience."

The door opened enough to permit him entrance. Removing his gloves and feeling agitated for the first time in days, he paced the small foyer. Had Rosa lied to him purposely?

A footman who couldn't be a day over fourteen and still half asleep came and took his coat before leading him to a small sitting room just off the main foyer. The room housed only two sofas and a chair, a rounded table off to the side and an inviting mantel with a painting that depicted a woman at her piano.

"Teddy." Her voice was full of pain. He hadn't thought about the hour he'd come and how she might interpret that.

Her hair fell over one shoulder in a loose plait. Her night rail was covered with a soft lavender silk robe.

"Is something wrong? Has something happened?"

Some of his anger dissipated, knowing she'd come down the moment she'd been told of his arrival. He was sorry to have worried her.

He stepped forward and took her chilled hands in his. "I didn't mean to frighten you. I have not found your brother, but I had to come to you immediately."

As she exhaled, her shoulders relaxed marginally. He needed to hear the truth of what he learned tonight from her own mouth.

"Why didn't you tell me, Rosa?"

She slipped her hands out from under his and took a few steps back. When the backs of her knees hit the sofa, she sat heavily.

"What are you referring to?"

"I was advised to seek out your father if I wanted to locate your brother."

"My father?" she repeated. She turned her chin down, no longer able to face him, he thought. Her hands curled into the sleeves of her robe as a shimmer of tears glazed her eyes.

"I was advised that your father might have some insight as to how I should locate your brother. Funnily enough, I know precisely who your father is."

Rosa shook her head. "Daniel won't go to our father if he's in trouble."

"How well do you even know your brother to assume he wouldn't?"

She swiped the tears away from her eyes with the back of her hand. "Do not claim to know me or anything about my past. You know nothing about my family."

"Because you refuse to let me in," he said.

The hurt in her words was enough to have him reaching for her to gather her in his arms as he sat next to her. She struggled, but it was a brief fight before she gave up and pressed her face against his chest.

And just like that, the anger that had built from the moment he'd left his club vanished as though it never was. He brushed his hands over her back, wanting nothing more than to soothe her hurt, to erase everything that had gone wrong in her life, and stand in as her knight-errant as she'd claimed him to be.

She broke away from the embrace, and asked, "Will you still help me?"

"Why didn't you tell me, Rosa? Did you think it would change our first meeting? Change what I've started to feel for you?"

"Have you figured out who I am?"

"I feel like I do know you, but can't think from where. Your father was once a prominent figure and teacher, but stepped out of the spotlight before I went to train in Vienna. I know of your father, but I do not know him personally."

"We would have had the same teachers in Vienna, Teddy. Only a few years separate us."

She'd mentioned Vienna before, but hadn't elaborated just what she'd been there for. Teddy's first instructors had been Mendelssohn and Schumann in Leipzig. Johann Strauss senior had been his instructor when he moved to Vienna some eight or nine years ...

"What are you trying to tell me?"

"I played for royalty before my accident. I was someone." Her voice hitched, and she wrapped her arms around her middle. "Someone worth knowing."

"And you still are worth knowing." He rubbed his hand over the stubble peppering his jawline. "I would remember having met you."

"We never met formally. But I knew who you were, and you likely knew of me."

"Say what you mean to say already. I'll not play guessing games with you, Rosa."

"Amaryllis is my given name." She sat up straighter next to him, radiating pride for the first time since he'd come to her tonight. "Amaryllis Rosalie, after my grandmother."

Amaryllis Montgomery. That name had a certain ring of familiarity to it. A pianist. Vienna. Eight, maybe ten years ago, had he known that name?

When he didn't respond, she elaborated. "The Austrian princess named me a Royal and Imperial Virtuosa."

Dear lord. It struck him precisely who she was. He had no words; he didn't know what to say or how he should respond to this monumental revelation. The pieces of the puzzle started to fall in place and make sense.

"Rosa." Teddy placed his hands on her arms, wishing he could take away the pain she so evidently felt with her confession.

"It becomes clearer to you now, doesn't it?" She turned her head away from him.

"You should have told me. It is just another thing to bring us closer, not tear us apart."

"Are you so sure? You might have walked away from me had you known. Everyone else has."

He pulled her into his arms, wanting to give her comfort, knowing it pained her to have to reveal any of this to him. "Don't. Don't lower yourself."

"What choice do I have?"

"Tell me what happened between you and your father."

She shook her head. "I've already told you what I did to earn his contempt."

"I'll work doubly hard to find your brother, Rosa." Teddy ran his fingers over the thick plait of her hair, tugging at the end to draw her gently nearer.

She nodded against his chest. "Someone must have said something to you about my brother for you to come here so late."

"Nothing good, I'm afraid. It seems he owes half the men about Town something."

She pulled away from him, though not entirely out of his arms. "I can pay them off."

"Your brother will learn nothing of the trouble he has caused if you do that."

"You think to lecture me on my brother?"

"I only wish to protect you."

"You're far too late to do that."

He brushed loose strands of her hair away from her face. "I'm sorry we didn't know each other sooner. Had we, our lives might be very different right now. We will find Daniel, Rosa, and we'll work together to accomplish it."

"As we work on our music together?" Derision coated her comment. Did she still question his intentions?

"Yes. I can't change your past anymore than you can. What I can promise is that I would never judge you for what you think went wrong or what you did to survive."

Tilting her head back, he looked into her crystal blue eyes, and for the first time since having met her, he wished she could read the sincerity reflected in his own eyes.

"I wanted to ask if you'd consider staying at my house for a while. It'll be easier to work on my compositions and to write down your piano sonatas if we are constant companions."

She pulled away from him, forcing him to release her as she stood. He followed her, unable to let her escape too far. "Think about what you're saying. You can't move me into the ducal town house; it'll be social suicide."

"I am a second son. I have always had a strike against me."

"You can't possibly mean that. You aren't thinking clearly."

"Think about this for one second, Rosa. We've spent enough

time together to know we'll get on just fine. And I will not live my life in fear of offending anyone else's sensibilities."

"You are a titled man. You have no choice but to live by their rules."

"Is that what you believe?"

"It's what I know. With that title comes responsibility. You cannot invite your whore to live with you in a respectable house."

Advancing, he grasped her arms tightly enough to get her attention. "Never call yourself that in my presence. Never say that word to me again. You will never be a creature so vile and low as that."

She tilted her chin up and jutted out her jaw defiantly. "That is precisely how society has labeled me and they will never see me differently."

"Society, whom you deem so ever important, will talk about us anyway. And I don't give a damn what they're saying."

"Courting me isn't only a danger to your reputation. Have you so easily forgotten that your sister is of marriageable age?"

"I have not forgotten that she is tucked away at a boarding school in the south of France and is untouched by any scandal you think I'll cause by associating myself with you."

"You will simply counter everything I say. Don't listen to me if you don't want to, but know that society is far crueler to a woman for her transgressions or the transgressions committed by her family than they are to a man."

Teddy let her go with the same suddenness with which he'd captured her. On some levels, he knew she was right, but still, he wanted her. He didn't care what anyone thought of their union.

"This is the right decision for us."

"But for how long?" she asked calmly.

"For as long as you like."

She paced away from him, easily maneuvering around the furniture in her own home.

It occurred to him that he hadn't asked the most important question about her brother. "What's the real reason you never talked to your brother after being forced to leave home?"

She paused, then turned toward the direction of his voice. "My father forbade it when I was told to leave. He promised that should I disobey him, Daniel would be shunned and expelled from our family home as well."

Teddy stood in front of her and ran his hand down the side of her face. She pressed her face into his palm, taking the comfort he offered for a moment before she stepped away and continued her pacing.

"I'm confused by us," she said. "Are we friends or do we fall into bed and become lovers? I don't understand what you want from me."

"I've told you before that those are mere words and what we have isn't so simple as to be described one way or the other."

She sat heavily on the settee. "I promised long ago to never be any man's mistress."

"I'm not asking you to be my mistress." He sat next to her, taking her hand. "There is something special and beautiful about us together."

"You will be met with scorn if you continue down this path with me."

"I have felt reckless since the moment we met," he teased. Would he be able to wipe away the look of distrust that scrunched up her brow and caused her lips to purse? In time, there was no question about it.

"What now?"

"I will approach a few of Nathan's friends tomorrow. If Hagan, the man I spoke to tonight, had any information to share, others will as well. Now, can we sort out our arrangement?"

"I will agree to stay with you under two conditions."

"Name it."

"You cannot reveal my identity or what I've told you about my past to another soul."

"Done."

"That's not all."

All he cared about was the fact that she was agreeing to his mad plan. It took a force of will he was surprised he harbored to not take her in his arms and kiss her senseless. "Continue, then."

"Under no circumstances can you be seen in public with me. I'll not be responsible for you losing favor amongst your peers."

The little trickster. "I beg to differ with your opinion on that topic."

"This is not negotiable. And it is a condition of me staying with you and being your *companion.*"

"Has anyone ever told you that you're too smart for your own good?"

That earned him a smile. And he was happy to have eased the distress he'd caused on his arrival.

"Do you agree to all my terms?" she asked.

"Reluctantly, yes. This does not, however, mean that I will not try to persuade you to join me on a few trips about Town."

"You can try, but my answer will always remind you of our agreement."

"Why should you care at all? I would think that after all this time, you could not care less about the society that shunned you."

"Because I know how cruel the *ton* can be. I know your concerto will not be well received if you are not acting according to society's plan."

"There is one flaw with your assessment I feel I should point out."

"And what is that?"

"No matter the company my brother has kept"—it went without saying that he was referring to Anna in this instance—"or how recklessly he has acted over the years, no one would dare scorn him."

"The rules are different for him. He's the Duke of Vane."

Teddy chuckled at the assessment and contradictory standard.

"How long do you need to pack?" Now that she'd agreed to stay with him, he wanted her to come back with him immediately.

"You can send a carriage around in the morning. I will need

to make arrangements to close up the house for a short time, give my butler and cook some time off while I'm away."

Teddy stood and bowed over her hand. "As you wish, my lady. A carriage will arrive at seven tomorrow."

Before he could leave, she rose and clasped the sleeve of his coat, halting him. "Thank you for everything, Teddy."

"There's no need. I haven't done nearly enough yet. And I've forgotten something important about your brother."

"What?"

"Hagan mentioned Johnson having dealings with your brother."

She pinched her lips together and turned away from him. "You've done more than you can ever imagine. And we'll figure out Johnson's intentions soon enough."

Cupping the back of her head, he pulled her in close and brushed his lips across hers. The kiss was feather light and fleeting.

"You've made me a happy man today. With that, *you* have done more than you can ever imagine."

Then he left. Morning could not come soon enough. He'd set up his mother's room for her. It was the second nicest to his brother's master chamber and only two doors down the hall from his room.

There was no doubt in his mind that he and Rosa would eventually become lovers and spend more time in his room, but she would require a space to call her own.

He thought back on her words. About the threat of society scorning him. Did he really care what they thought? He cared how his work was accepted, but no, he didn't care what they thought of his personal and private decisions.

Chapter Eight

Can you change the fact that you are not
wholly mine, I not wholly thine.
– Ludwig von Beethoven

"I GAVE THE SERVANTS THE night off after they set up dinner in the breakfast room. It is far less formal than the dining hall."

Rosa took his arm, letting him lead the way through the house. After they wound their way down the staircase, they walked arm in arm down the long corridor; nearly to the back of the house, she was sure. All the while, the soft scent of his shaving powder and the starch on his shirt teased her close enough to him that the side of her breast brushed lightly against his arm with every step.

"I hope you don't mind the informality."

"Not in the least. You'll spoil me while I'm here."

And she still couldn't believe she'd agreed to this arrangement. Yes, it would make working together all the easier now that they could work together at any odd hour. And there would be less traveling between their houses, though admittedly, it was only a half-hour carriage ride. But those weren't the reasons she'd done it. She *wanted* to spend more time with him. She wanted to be closer to him. She wanted to better understand the feelings she had for him and this was the best way to do that.

"What is for dinner tonight?" she asked.

"Skewered lamb and carrots and greens in a raspberry drizzle. The divinest rosemary-flavored potatoes you'll have in all of London and a selection of cheeses and a fine *vin de Bourgogne* from Côte de Nuits."

"Do you plan on lowering my inhibitions tonight?" she asked, her tone clearly amused by the set up.

"Maybe. It is our first night together. We might as well enjoy it to the fullest before we work through the day tomorrow. As I see it, there is only one disadvantage to you staying here."

"And what is that?"

"Put simply, my dear, you'll have no escape from me now that I've lured you into the lion's den."

She couldn't help but laugh at his teasing tone. "I don't think I'll mind so much."

When he opened the door, warmth enveloped them and she could smell the coals burning in the grate. But more than that, she could smell the delicious scent of their dinner.

A chair slid across the carpet to her right, then Teddy directed her by her elbow to where she would sit. Removing her shawl, she folded it and placed it over the back of the chair.

She didn't miss his sharp intake of breath on seeing what she wore. She'd felt brazen and daring, knowing tonight would cement their relationship going forward. And she'd had seduction on her mind all day and wanted nothing more than to act on that desire.

The gown she wore was blush-cream in color, or so the seamstress had described it to her. The material was so fine that he would be able to make out the firm peaks of her nipples, since she wore no stays and the room still held a slight chill that the fire had yet to chase away. She'd forgone the hoops and frilly underclothes, too. The dress was a sheath of silk that hugged her hips before fanning out in layers of silk that gave it an elegance that trumped any formal evening dress she owned.

Before she could take her seat, Teddy had her in his arms. One of his hands rested over her lower back, the other found the curve of her bottom as he edged her closer to him. His mouth crushed against hers and stole the breath from her lungs. She didn't shy away from the kiss for one moment; she took everything he gave and still ... She wanted more. Her hands fisted around the sleeves of his evening jacket, his muscles flexing beneath her hold.

The firm assault of his lips was meted out over the curve of her neck, where he bit the flesh gently before laving the nips with the hot slide of his tongue.

As she twined her arms around his shoulders, he rasped out, "I didn't mean for this to happen quite like this."

His kiss eased, and he suckled at her flesh as he worked his way back up to her mouth. He pulled her bottom lip between his, his tongue caressing now instead of conquering as he coaxed her into a slow seduction of the senses. Arms tightening around her waist, he pulled her in until her back was arched over his arm.

"You had seduction in mind," he stated, his voice deeper than it had been before he'd started kissing her.

"Yes." There was no denying that truth when she was suddenly feeling weak-kneed in his arms.

"I lose all sense when I'm around you, Rosa."

She did too, but she wouldn't tell him so. A woman had to have some mystery about her. Her fingers threaded through the hair at the back of his head.

"You say that as if it's a good thing," she teased.

"I enjoy being lost in you. I want to be lost in you."

When he settled her back on her feet, the loss of his touch was like a wall going up, separating them. She stepped toward him, not knowing quite what she was doing, but needing him nonetheless. His hand caressed her cheek tenderly.

"If we don't sit and eat, I'm afraid I'll occupy your time in a much different way."

She took another step, feeling unsure of herself for the first time in years. She didn't know what she wanted from Teddy, but she did know they would be lovers before the night was through. She wanted him to kiss her again.

She reached her hand up tentatively, and swallowed against the nerves clogging her throat. She skimmed the smooth side of his jaw. "I want to be lost in your touch, too."

No sooner than the words were out Teddy was walking her backward. She had no idea where he was taking her, but she trusted him not to lead her astray. Hands around her back to hold her tightly against his body, he lifted her off her feet before carefully bringing them both down to the floor. The soft sheepskin rug beneath her back was warm and comfortable. She almost asked why it was in here but figured it was to keep your feet warm as you sat by the fire on a cold winter day. The heat from the fireplace sizzled along her arms chasing away the goose bumps.

TEDDY BRUSHED THE HAIR AWAY from her temples and gave her a sweet kiss on the mouth.

"You mesmerize me, Rosa."

Hand lowering, he drew teasing circles over her right shoulder, her collarbone, then lower over the upper swell of her breasts. Teddy kissed her chin, the tip of her nose and finally her mouth.

While he explored her mouth, his free hand inched up her skirts. He paused when his hands brushed against her bare legs and he realized she wore no stockings beneath. Bending her knee, he pushed her skirts high enough to reveal the slight curve of her hip and the milky white skin. The palm of his hand skimmed lightly over the short clipped hairs at her center.

"I never imagined ..." How did he finish that thought? He'd thought intimacy with a woman would be many things, but to be so overwhelmed and lost in the moment was something he hadn't imagined. Good lord; he might know the logistics of what came next, but he couldn't claim to be any sort of expert.

As his knuckles skimmed lightly over the crisp hairs at her center, her leg dropped open so she was fully bared to him. He swallowed hard. The folds of her sex were a rich pink, and as soft looking as her lips. He wanted to kiss her, delve his tongue in every fold and taste the nectar that coated her entrance.

As he trailed his hand upward along the inside of her thigh, she released a ragged breath. His exploration was slow as he brushed his knuckle over her core before retreating back to her thigh.

"You like to be touched like this, don't you?"

She nodded.

His hand lowered again, this time finding the wetness at her core as he pressed more firmly into her. Pelvis tilted up to him, Rosa arched ever so slightly as the moan she could no longer hold at bay rushed past her lips.

"Shall I continue?" he asked.

There was no denying the curious tone in his voice. He wasn't sure what he should do to please her. She didn't hesitate to give him direction; she reached for his hand, uncurling his fingers.

"Put your fingers inside me."

He pressed his forefinger deep inside her quim, not stopping until the palm rested snugly against her entrance.

He needed no coaching in what to do next. His finger slipped easily in and out, her sheath pulsating when he retreated as though she were trying to hold on to him. He was careful as he pushed in again, this time with two fingers. He watched as goose bumps rose along her arms. Her nipples peaked beneath the silk dress, begging for his mouth.

Leaning over her, he blew a hot stream of air over her bosom where it was exposed above the line of the dress. "You like that, too."

He kneaded her breast with his face. Rolling his cheek, jaw, and lips over the soft flesh. Her hand slid between their bodies and cupped the outside of his trousers where his erection strained. She loosened his trousers enough that she could slip her hand inside to touch him, and causing him to thrust into her hold.

His breath caught as her palm cupped the head of his cock before running her hand along the length of his shaft. She freed him from the confines of his trousers and pressed the head of his cock where his fingers were pushed deep inside her.

He pulled his hand free of her sheath and plunged forward with his cock. The impact of their sexes coming together forced another moan past her lips and a grunt past his.

In the next instant, he was on his knees between her thighs. The edge of his shirt skimmed her legs and stomach as he held still inside of her.

"Sweet Christ, Rosa," he murmured before pulling out and sheathing himself again.

Leaning over her, he grasped her head between his hands and kissed her hard on the mouth. She tucked her foot under the cheeks of his buttocks, urging the grind of his pelvis against hers.

Releasing her lips, Teddy held motionless above her. His breath was ragged and heavy, the sound labored as he held back from the inevitable. He was far from ready for this to end.

Caressing the side of his face, she whispered, "Teddy," and pulled herself off the floor enough that she could nibble on his earlobe.

She traced the lines of his back with her fingers. And he lost control.

This was heaven. This was bliss. Teddy rocked hard into her center. Sweet heaven, he'd never felt anything so perfect as her body wrapped around his.

Kissing a light path along her collarbone, he pulled marginally out of her before driving his cock up to the hilt. The sounds that slipped past her lips told him all he needed to know: She was enjoying every second of their lovemaking as much as he.

She held firmly to his forearms the faster he drove into her. His heart pounded so loudly in his ears that he was deaf to everything around him except her desire and the need to have them both lose themselves in this.

When she moaned "Teddy" again, he couldn't stop it from ending. He came with a roar of pure satisfaction, her sheath milking every last drop of semen from him. He lowered himself onto his elbows and kissed her lightly on the lips.

Damn it, he hadn't meant for it to end so quickly. And although he had been a virgin, he wasn't so foolish as to realize she hadn't experienced *la petite mort*.

He pressed his forehead to hers, still buried in her body and not losing his stiffness in the slightest. Damn it. What would she think of his bumbling attempts? She was far too polite to tell him his faults, but that didn't mean he didn't know exactly what he'd done wrong.

Then it hit him what else he'd done. "I didn't pull out."

He started to pull away from her, thinking he should wipe the evidence of what they'd done from her. She wrapped her thighs around his hips to keep him firmly seated inside her, and it didn't look like his cock was going to be very cooperative because he was still raging hard and he realized he needed her again.

"There's no need for caution," she said, brushing hair away from his forehead. "I would not have given myself to you if I thought there was any danger in our joining."

She rained a series of kisses along the side of his jaw.

"Is such a thing possible?" he asked, not quite understanding what she meant.

Her head fell back onto the rug and she placed her hands on either side of his face. "I was your first?"

He leaned down to capture her lips again, not sure if he should answer or not. But in the end, he decided to give her honesty. "Yes."

"Why didn't you tell me?"

"It's not important." What should he say? That he'd never desired a woman as he desired her? That he'd never wanted a woman as much as he craved her?

"It's important to me," she whispered.

Not wanting to elaborate on why he'd chosen her, he pulled

away from her and pushed up to his feet. He grasped her hand to pull her up as well. Her skirts fell smoothly around her ankles, though they were wrinkled where they hadn't been before. He hated to cover her up when he'd barely had the chance to explore her.

Her hand went to her stomach. "I am completely and utterly famished."

Had she sensed that he had no wish to discuss his virginity and was attempting to lighten the mood? Not that the mood had been shrouded in darkness. Though he certainly had a lot to think about. Teddy knew it wasn't only desire and infatuation for this woman that had led to them half-naked on the floor. And perhaps from the moment they first met and he'd realized just how amazing and marvelous a person Rosa was, Teddy had been falling in love with her. It all felt so quick, but it felt right. He'd never met a woman who matched him as thoroughly as she did.

"I look forward to appeasing all your appetites."

Teddy's hand brushed the length of her arm, lingering a moment longer than he needed to when he led her back to her seat. Retrieving the serving trays from the sideboard, he placed one in front of her and lifted the silver lid.

He lifted the decanter and poured out two generous servings of the Burgundy he'd told her about.

She closed her eyes as she swirled the glass under her nose and breathed deeply of the rich scent. "Like cherries covered in vanilla."

"And that's the taste that lingers, with an undercurrent of tobacco to smooth out the sweetness. Try it. Let me know if it's to your liking. The wine cellar is well stocked, and I can retrieve whatever you prefer if this one isn't quite right."

With her nose still over the rim of the glass, she took another deep inhalation. "It smells perfectly divine." She took the most delicate of sips. Teddy watched the motion of her throat as she swallowed the berry-colored liquid. Her sigh had his cock hardening further.

"It's delicious."

"Let me see if I agree," he said as his lips pressed against hers, his tongue sweeping out to taste the residue of wine on her lips. He wanted to linger, but they needed to eat before the long night ahead of them.

"We'll never finish our dinner if you keep doing that." Her voice was husky, relaxed. To his ears, it was the sound of a woman well pleasured.

"I can't seem to stop myself," he admitted. "You're like an addiction I want to indulge in all night long."

"Mm, I like the sound of that." Her grin was devilish and tempting him to do more wicked things.

He forced himself to take the seat across from her, but he watched her every move. "I suggest we eat before it's too cold to enjoy."

For a long while the only sound to be heard was the clink of silver against the plates as they ate the fare he'd had prepared. He looked at the sheepskin rug in front of the fireplace. Not quite what he'd expected, but just as good as what he still had planned.

"Will you spend the evening with me?" He bit into the last of his carrots.

They'd already agreed to spend the evening working on his music, but that wasn't what he was asking.

"Are you sure that's wise?"

"Completely. I want you with a ferocity with which I've never wanted anything else in my life."

She set her cutlery down and took a large sip of her wine. "You shouldn't say such things."

"Are you telling me you don't want the same thing? I know you do and I won't lie to you about how I feel."

"I never took you for a rogue with a wicked tongue."

"That title is reserved for my brother. I have only one woman on my mind and I'm bent on seducing her all evening long." He reached for her hand and drew circles around her wrist. "I want to make it very clear that I would never flaunt you as my brother did Anna like she was a prize won."

When she remained silent, he added, "I meant no insult, Rosa."

"I know. Anna has been long trapped by your brother's scheming. He had a collar so tightly wrapped about her throat that it was a wonder she ever broke away from him."

It was the truth. Nathan loved his mistress, but he also treated her in a way Teddy would never treat another person he cared for.

"Do I make you feel trapped, Rosa?"

"Yes." She ducked her head, but her hand turned so their fingers met and touched lightly.

He unclenched his jaw and forced in a deep, calming breath before he responded. "Then perhaps we should call it a night. I have an early day tomorrow at my club."

The last thing he wanted was to end their night, but if that was what she wished, then he would give her the space she craved.

"I think that would be the wisest course for us."

"We can start on my concerto when I'm back by midday."

She nodded. Why had she suddenly closed herself off to him? Had he done something wrong? Did she regret what had happened between them? Before long, they finished their meal. Teddy walked her up to her room, not sure how to make amends with her or if he should have to make amends for anything.

ONCE TUCKED IN HER ROOM alone, she wondered why she had run from Teddy. It had been her idea to give herself to him. And her idea to open up their relationship to more than their original agreement. Why was she running from him now when she'd run straight into his arms earlier? Was it his comment about Anna that had her all twisted up inside? His mention of Anna was a blunt reminder of who she was, what she'd done in her life, and, more importantly, what others thought of her.

She must never forget her place in society. Never rise above her station. She'd made the decision to become a courtesan, and that truth could not be changed.

She needed to get away from here, and away from Teddy. He was chipping away at the facade she'd hidden behind for so many years that she'd forgotten the woman she truly was before the accident. She didn't deserve a second chance at life, not when she'd survived the accident and Michael hadn't.

That she even considered her time and budding relationship with Teddy to be a second chance was part of the problem. It wasn't a second chance. It was so far from that. It was no different from the past arrangements she'd had with men.

Teddy was destroying the person she thought she was. He was tearing down the walls she'd put up to protect herself from further disappointments and letdowns. How could she face Teddy again, knowing this about herself?

She swiped the tears from her cheeks. Why couldn't she shut off the guilt? She gathered her composure, straightened herself, gathered up her walking stick, and found her way to her bed where her maid had set out her night clothes. Slipping out of her dress, she pulled on a more serviceable chemise. Picking up her walking stick again, she found her way to the slipper chair and put on her stockings.

What she must never forget was that there would come a time when Teddy would no longer need her, and it would destroy her if she allowed him to steal any more of her heart.

TEDDY LOOKED OVER TO THE piano with the sheet music strewn about the top. He'd been staring at nothing for a good half hour and it was getting him nowhere. He'd had to open his mouth and shove his foot in it. The very moment the words had left his mouth about the relationship between his brother and mistress, he knew he'd messed up the evening.

This was what happened when one courted scandal. Pull the tail of the devil and it lashed back at you.

He rubbed his hands through his hair, but mussing it up more wasn't getting him any closer to fixing what he'd done. What he wanted was to find Rosa and apologize. He needed her. Not just as his muse, but as a partner in what he was trying to accomplish with his music. As a friend he could speak plainly with. As a lover he could be himself with.

With her help, his concerto could be completed in a couple of weeks. After that, if he still worked with her, would she see that he wanted to help her with her own music, and spend time with her?

Pulling out his watch, he flipped open the casing. Not ten minutes had passed since the last time he'd checked, though it felt like an hour. He left his room and strode toward Rosa's. Thank God he'd sent the servants off for the night. He paused at her door, wondering if he should knock or simply enter. It wasn't too late to turn around and head back to his room. Perhaps the night apart would give them both time to think. No; he didn't want her to regret what they'd done.

He knocked softly before opening the door. Rosa lay stretched out on the sofa, propped on her side with her arm curled under her head and the other tucked around her middle. She had changed into something far less tempting than the dress she'd worn to dinner.

Shoulders shaking, she sniffled.

Approaching her slowly, he was surprised to see that she was crying. His steps faltered. On closer inspection, he noted that her eyes were swollen and red; her nose, too. She held a handkerchief balled up tight in her fist.

"Mary?" she said.

Mary was the maid she'd come to the house with even though he'd offered his own servants. Rosa had said Mary had been with her most of her life, so he had respected her wishes and invited Mary into his home.

He let out a frustrated breath of air as his eyes adjusted to the dim light of the fireplace. He knew he was the cause of her tears, and that made him feel like the biggest ass. "I'm afraid not."

Rosa sat up on the sofa. She turned her face so he couldn't see her, and wiped it with her sodden handkerchief. She gave a delicate sniffle and grasped the back of the sofa as she took a deep breath.

"My apologies," she said, still wiping away at the evidence of her state.

"I'm the only one who needs to apologize, Rosa. I never wanted to hurt you."

"Apology accepted. Now, if you don't mind, the hour is late."

Unable to leave her while she was upset, he stepped closer to her and placed his hands on her shoulders. Some of the tension left her body.

"Let me stay awhile, prove to you that I'm better than what you are thinking of me right now."

She shook her head in refusal.

"Let me comfort you. I can't bear that I'm the one who put you in this state." His finger trailed over her still damp cheek.

She curled her feet under her and waved her arm to the other end of the sofa in invitation. He took a seat next to her, dipping her body close to his. She turned her face toward the fire and away from him.

"Would you like me to light some candles?" she asked.

"No. I can see you in the firelight, that's all I need."

Unable to keep his distance, he pulled her into the circle of his arms.

When her sniffling lessened, she asked, "What are we doing?"

"Learning all there is to know about each other."

"What if we should lose sight of the tasks we've promised to fulfill?"

"We haven't yet. We won't."

"And everything else?"

"Why label it? What we have is beautiful and feels right"—he pressed his fist against her heart—"here is where it feels perfect for me."

She wiped the side of her face, not answering him, and he didn't press.

Standing, he leaned down and gathered her in his arms.

"Where are you taking me?"

"To your bed."

Setting her on her feet, he lowered his hands to the small of her back and felt for the tie in her half corset. When he grasped the strings, he loosened it enough that the contraption fell to the floor.

Next he gathered the chemise at her hips, bringing the lower half up around her hips before he drew the material over her head and dropped it onto the floor next to them. Her drawers he left on. He had to admit, he liked the feel of all those frills against him as he lifted her and set her on the high bed.

He rubbed the back of his hand over the top edge of those frills before scooting her up to the head of the bed, pulling his shirt off and tossing that to the floor, too.

The blankets were folded back so he slid her legs under the covers. He toed off his shoes and followed, curving his body around hers, wishing there wasn't a stitch of clothing separating them. If he removed what little they wore, he knew he'd never be able to keep his hands to himself.

It wasn't long before she reached behind her, stretching her fingers over his arousal. He grasped her hand and tucked it back around to her stomach, threading his fingers through hers. He would not allow her to distract him from his good intentions.

Chest pressed flush along the length of her back, he tangled his legs through hers. She'd figure out soon enough that he had no intention of bedding her. He needed to hold her to tell her how sorry he was for upsetting her.

"I didn't mean to make such a crass remark, Rosa."

"You didn't say anything wrong."

"The hell I didn't. It was thoughtless and reminders of the life you were forced to live will never pass my lips again."

He was only mildly distracted when she snuggled her derriere into his groin. "Thank you," she said.

He sighed. "Go to sleep, Rosa. It's been a long day, and we have an early start in the morning."

"You can't mean to *sleep* in here for the night."

"That is exactly what I intend to do. Is the thought of that distasteful?"

"I have never slept with a man." Her voice was hushed and held a note of marvel as though she didn't believe his good intentions.

He chuckled at that, his chest vibrating along her back. "Surely after all we've done, you jest."

"I do not mean in the sense of intercourse. I meant that I have never slept with a man next to me."

She tried to squirm out of his hold, but he only tightened his arms around her. He wasn't ready to let her escape; in fact, he refused to let her go.

"I don't care what you did and did not do in your past. I have every intention of staying the night." Sighing, he pulled both their hands up to rest between her breasts and placed a kiss on her bare shoulder. "Now, go to sleep or we'll never be able to get out of bed come morning."

Chapter Nine

A musician's nature can hardly be expressed in words.
– Gustav Mahler

ROSA TINKERED AWAY ON THE piano for a short time. Eventually she stopped, lost in her thoughts again. Teddy seemed to own all her thoughts.

At least she wouldn't have to face Teddy for a few hours. She wasn't sure what she should say to him after everything that had transpired between them since she'd been staying in his house. For three nights he'd come to her room only to hold her as they both fell asleep. She wasn't sure why he'd not tried to make love to her again, but she appreciated having him next to her at night. Actually, she was growing to crave his company.

"Why did you stop playing?"

"Hmm?" She turned toward Mary's questioning voice. "I wasn't, was I?" She frowned and turned back to the keys, placing her hands above them, not sure where she'd even stopped.

"I never thought I'd see the day." Mary's comment wasn't precisely an accusation, so she took no insult from it. Or at least she tried not to be insulted that she was so easily read.

"The day for what?"

"You've gone and fallen in love with de Burgh, haven't you?"

Rosa remained silent, mulling the words over in her head. Was it possible to fall in love with someone she barely knew?

"De Burgh will grow bored of my company as the weeks pass. I cannot mingle in the circles he does."

Mary's hand touched her shoulder.

"I think you like each other just fine enough not to be bored any time soon."

"I cannot be a part of his world, nor he mine."

"Don't be forgetting you were once a young woman of standing." Mary sat next to her on the bench, her arm wrapped around Rosa's shoulders.

She searched for her friend's hand and held it between hers. "I'll never mingle in his circles and I'll not dare reach above my station again. You know what that brought me when I was young."

It had brought her loneliness and heartbreak. Despair that had been so crippling she thought she'd never heal from the pain. She never wanted to feel the misery of losing the man she loved again.

Banishing the thoughts, she placed her hands over the keys once more and played a somber melody.

By the time lunch rolled around, Rosa was growing worried that she hadn't heard from Teddy. Just as quick as the worry gnawed at her, a letter arrived. When she clasped it in her hands, her maid asked, "Would you like me to read it?"

"Of course." Mary had been reading her correspondence for years; that Rosa should suddenly feel shy about sharing this letter was silly. She handed over the parchment. Anticipation filled her gut as her maid slid the envelope cutter and tore it along the edge.

Mary cleared her throat before reading, "Rosa, I apologize for not sending word sooner, I have had no luck where your brother is concerned. I have one lead that will keep me out till well past the dinner hour. The house is yours; the servants at your call. I will see you tonight. Teddy."

She let out a whoosh of air. Of course he wouldn't mention anything of a more personal nature in the letter, why she had thought he would ...

Could she still hope that her brother was lying low until he found the money to pay back whomever he owed this time? Hopefully Teddy found the answers they needed to solve the mystery of her brother's disappearance soon.

THE SOFT SOUND OF the piano filtered down the hall and made its way to her ears, the tune vaguely familiar the nearer she drew. Rosa had been readying herself to see Teddy for the past hour. She could resist the music no longer. One hand measured her distance from the wall, since she'd left her walking stick in her room. The other hand pulled up her skirts so she didn't trip.

On reaching his door, she turned the knob and paused when the recognizable tune washed over her. He remembered the song she'd played. Some notes were different ... off; he paused to fix his fingering, then resumed with corrections.

Why was he playing her piece? She walked toward the sound of the music.

When she was at his side, he stopped playing. "Excellent to see you. I was wondering when you'd arrive."

She heard the sound of the bench sliding across the rug. Teddy placed something small and hard in her hands. She tipped it to the side and cool liquid sloshed over onto her hand.

"Careful. I guess I should have thought better than to put that in your hands." He took the oddly shaped glass, and set it atop the piano with a heavy clunk. He flicked out his handkerchief and wiped the liquid from her hands.

"What were you doing?"

"Writing down your music. But I couldn't remember a few

of the passages, so you'll have to play them for me so I can jot them down."

Her hands trembled and her heart beat a little faster in her chest.

"You've gone stark white. Have I said something wrong?"

His hands gripped her unsteady ones. She opened her mouth to say something, but couldn't find the words she wanted to utter. Teddy's forefinger curled under her chin to lift her face. His lips were light upon hers and the last thing she expected in her shocked state.

He didn't rush the kiss. He took his time and explored her with a tenderness that melted her heart.

"You've rendered me speechless," she whispered when his lips left hers.

"I'm sure you've come for news of your brother. I fear I learned nothing while out today."

"I have set you on the path of finding a needle in a haystack. But I am beginning to fear for my brother's safety."

"Don't," he said. "I have only heard that he was on the run from people he owes money to. He'll have to come up for air sooner or later. Either to pay his debts or to face those he owes money to."

"I couldn't agree more on that. Johnson's part in all this doesn't sit well with me." And that had her worrying about what exactly Johnson was trying to prove. Surely he wouldn't hurt her brother to get back at her? No, she couldn't think that way. Johnson's issues lay solely at Rosa's feet. There would be no purpose in going after her brother to get back at her.

"I've known Johnson a long time, and while I don't trust him, I can't imagine him causing harm to your brother over a few quid."

"How can you be so sure?" Even she couldn't be sure of Johnson's character right now, not in the face of uncertainty.

"Have faith. We'll find him. Probably when he wants to be found, but we'll find him nonetheless."

He kissed her once again, the touch soft and alluring as though he wanted her to entertain happier thoughts. "Come." He took her hand and tugged her toward the bench to sit. She tucked her skirts under the keys and hitched up the back a little to sit more comfortably. Teddy sat next to her. "I do have friends looking for him as we speak, and they'll contact me as soon as they see or hear anything."

"Thank you," was all she could manage to say. Everything he was doing meant so much to her that she was beginning to think she was in a dream.

"Play your piece for me again, Rosa. I've jotted down as much as I could remember. But I'm afraid I'll do the beauty of this piece no justice without your help."

"You don't have time to focus on this. We can work on your music." He placed his finger over her lips, then rubbed it back and forth over the lower portion, pulling her lips apart before stepping around her.

"Play for me, Rosa. I want to do this for you. You've been immensely helpful with my concerto. I wish to return the favor you've bestowed upon me."

She nodded and settled herself at the piano. Her fingers played out a natural chord, so he knew which key she played in.

"I did have that down already. I guessed the time signature to be in twelve-eight. I couldn't figure out if you changed for a few stanzas to nine-eight or if you went back to the common time."

"Both." Her lips quirked up at the side, impressed that he'd noticed the odd switches in time. He really had been paying close attention. Though she supposed it wasn't too complex for someone of his skill to figure out the timing and key signatures.

Her fingers found the rhythm of the piece she'd played now for so many years. She didn't know where or how it was born. Come to think of it, she didn't know where most of her music came from, only that it was her own. And it often represented how she felt at the time. This piece had been about her loss and subsequent growth. Her search for life beyond the dark corridors of the half-existence she'd lived after Michael's death.

Letting up on the keys, she turned her head toward him. "Would you play the violin with me? Not today if you find the idea silly, but sometime soon? I've longed to hear your hand on the strings."

The scratch of the pen halted. "Why is that?"

She shook her head and switched to a light minuet.

"Are you sure we never met before?"

"We haven't, but I did hear you play once."

He set his pen down on top of the piano and got up from the bench. She missed the heat of his body at her side immediately. He didn't go far, though. His hands resting lightly on her shoulders so he didn't hamper her playing, he stood behind her. She changed to a gavotte, something faster, louder, her foot hitting the damper more frequently to douse the silence of the house around them.

He rubbed his hands down each of her arms. With too much ease and familiarity, he undid the buttons of her bodice. Cool air met her overheated flesh as he peeled the material away from the top swell of her breasts. She stopped playing and leaned back into him. His arousal pressed demandingly at her back.

Her hands fell away from the keys and into her lap as Teddy slid the bodice from her arms, stepping away only long enough to let the material fall to the floor.

"Don't stop playing. I want to hear what you're feeling right now," he said before pressing a kiss against her shoulder.

She turned, intent on leaving the bench when his hands landed on her shoulders and eased her back down onto the seat. "Play something for me alone, Rosa."

She pinched her lips together and placed her hands over the keys again. She played something of her own this time, something quick that had her shoulders and wrists bouncing to keep from slogging through the staccato notes and quick pace of the music. She chose this piece so he could not lay his hands on her till she decided she was good and ready for his attentions.

His knuckles grazed the bared skin between her shoulder blades, just above the corset and chemise. He touched her in the same way she explored the piano keys with the back of her right hand before she set out to play a piece.

He took his time, caressing his hands up the back of her neck and over the curve of her shoulders. He pushed the short sleeves of the lace-edged chemise lower, running his hand from the right to the left of her exposed upper back. Then he placed his lips to her shoulder again, first on her left, then closer to her neck. Featherlight touches like the softly beating wings of a butterfly; that was what his lips felt like against her oversensitized skin.

How she managed to continue playing, she couldn't guess, but the music changed to a more melodic, romantic piece as she leaned back into his embrace.

His hand smoothed over her collarbone and dipped beneath the edge of her chemise to skim his warm, deft fingers over the firm tip of her nipple, finally cupping her breast. Pushing the material beneath her breasts, he lifted the weight of her breast free of the corset. The feeling of cold air washing over her heated flesh was intensely erotic.

She stopped playing and turned her head to the side to press a kiss to his cheek. His lips met hers, then their tongues tangled and danced.

With a great deal of gentleness and control of his desires, he brushed his hand over the jutted point of her breast. She needed so much more, but didn't want to ruin this feeling building inside her. Not for all the world would she stop this moment.

Curling one hand around the back of his neck, she pressed their mouths harder together, wanting to taste more of him. His slow, steady pace remained constant, but he helped her stand and turned her to face him. Her one bared breast pressed against the rough cambric of his shirt.

Teddy let her go to slide the bench that stood between them away, before he pressed her back against the piano. Her skirts rang out their own tune against the keys—a mishmash of sounds as they fumbled with each other's clothes.

His fingers slid between her back and the top ledge of the Broadwood, working out the bows and ties of her corset. Before long, it was falling away from her. Next, he found the tapes that held the hoops under her skirts.

"Step forward so I can lift the hoops over your head."

She did as he asked. It was hard to be still while he took his time, his hands feeling her ankles and legs, squeezing her hips before he lifted the wires over her head. The rustle of material was replaced with the rasping of their breaths.

"Let me touch you, Teddy." Reaching out, she found empty air. Why did he evade her touch?

He was back before she could ask him that question, wrapping his arms around her and pressing her back against the piano once again. He'd taken off his shirt, and she took the time to explore the lithe muscles, kneading into the flesh of his upper back. His shoulders flexed beneath her touch.

Spreading her legs, he lifted her to sit atop the black and whites, the audible groan of the keys a reminder of where they were. The ledge where the music lined up pressed into her lower back, but she didn't care about the discomfort because she never wanted him to stop touching her.

When his larger frame aligned with hers, all that mattered was having him inside her body. Touching her. Caressing her. Making love to her. Why did she lose all sense when she was with him? Did that matter when this felt so right?

She lowered her hand, searching for the buttons on his trousers, and pushed them through the holes that fastened them in place. He stepped away from her only long enough to let them fall and then he was pressed against her again.

"Are you sure you want this?" he asked.

"More than anything," she answered before wrapping her arms around his shoulders and pulling him in for a deep kiss.

One of his hands guided his cock to the damp folds of her sheath and she moaned a little when he pressed forward.

"How does it feel for you?" he asked.

She bit her lip, unsure how to answer him.

He pressed marginally forward, teasing her as he entered her one slow inch at a time, not fully giving her what she desired. "Tell me, Rosa."

"Heavenly," she finally said, tightening her knees around his hips, wanting so desperately for him to take her with more force.

"Heavenly, how?"

"Like I'm coming apart from the inside out."

He bit her bottom lip and grasped her hips when she tried to thrust her pelvis forward. "Tell me more."

"I feel like I would die without you inside me. I need you so completely that I wish we were the only two people in the world we had to worry about. That we could get lost in each other and forget anything but us."

He slammed home so hard that a deep, satisfied moan slipped past her lips. But he still didn't give her what she wanted; instead he held still inside her, leaned over, and sucked the tip of her breast into his mouth. With her sheath spasming around him so close to release when all he'd done was touch her, her head fell back and she surrendered to him.

He released her breast with a loud pop and then his lips were meshed against hers and he kissed her so thoroughly she was panting beneath him. Holding her still, he finally pulled out only to slam back inside her. Her sex convulsed around the hard intrusion of his cock that filled her so completely. She wanted him again and again. The keys clanked and groaned beneath them, but she didn't care what kind of ruckus they made, she only knew that she wanted more.

He pulled away from her mouth so violently that she almost protested until he changed his footing so he could piston into her at a pace that left them both breathless.

Hands gripping her hips firmly to keep her where he wanted her, he said, "The things you do to me, Rosa."

She couldn't agree more, but couldn't catch her breath long

enough to say so. Not that she would have been heard over the piano's protests. Sweat dotted along her temples and ran a cool path over her cheeks. His pace, while still demanding, slowed marginally and he stood close enough that her breasts brushed against the material of his shirt with every thrust.

"Am I safe to stay inside you?"

She nodded.

"Then come with me, Rosa."

His mouth lowered to hers and his lips were gentler this time, sucking and laving instead of conquering. It had been so long since she'd enjoyed the feel of a man. She let go and gave herself to him fully.

The torrent of feelings and release flooded through her so thoroughly that Teddy had to swallow her moans and cries of ecstasy. Not that the rest of the household wouldn't have guessed the nature of their visit with the piano still ringing and banging out a mash of sounds beneath their gyrating bodies.

Teddy followed with his own release, pumping into her so hard that her body convulsed around his, lengthening her own orgasm. Once their breathing leveled out, he held her face between his hands, his thumbs touching the corners of her mouth. "We should move to the bed."

She could only nod her agreement. She felt so sated and pliant and unable to move an inch as the feeling of her release ebbed and she slowly came back into her body.

Grasping her rear, he lifted her from the piano and walked toward his bed. Climbing across the plush mattress on his knees, still holding her close to his body with his cock still firm and deep inside her.

He laid her down, his torso pressed along hers. "What do you like, Rosa?"

"I like this just fine. But I would prefer it if we removed our clothes."

The tips of her fingers brushed along his jaw. He shook his head at her request. "I want to take this slow."

"It's a little late for that, don't you think?" There was an edge of laughter in her voice.

Pressing his lips to hers, he demonstrated what he meant by taking his time. His tongue traced a teasing path over the crease between her lips. Taking her bottom lip between his, he released it with deliberate slowness. "I didn't have the chance to explore you the last time we were together. I want to know all your secrets, sweet Rosa."

"At your will." Longing filled her voice, but she could not take it back now that he'd heard it. She sat up to remove her chemise, but his hand pressed her back down.

"Let me," he said.

His mouth nipped a seductive path over her hipbone, his tongue flicking out between the shower of small kisses he placed to her outer thigh, knee, and shin as he rolled her stockings down.

He pushed her chemise high enough to expose her stomach and the bottom curve of her breast. She wondered what his expression held on seeing her, and wished he would climb back up her body so she could feel the set of his features to better understand how he looked at her. Would there be a crease in his brow as he concentrated on pleasing her? Did he bite his lip in the throes of lovemaking? Did he close his eyes and savor the feel of her instead of watching her every move?

As he kissed a light path over her knee again, caressing and tickling the soft flesh behind with his fingers, she reached for his shoulders so she could anchor herself to the moment a little better. She wanted him to take his clothes off and slide into her body once again.

He kissed the inside of her palm before her hand landed on his shoulder. "Should I kiss you everywhere? Or would you like to tell me exactly what you like?"

"I like everything you are doing to me," she answered breathlessly.

His hand skimmed up her thigh, his palm cupped her mound, and he held it tight for a moment. The fluttering of heightened awareness that concentrated in her stomach suddenly had the walls of her sex spasming and clenching in need of so much more of his touch.

"And what of this? Do you like it when I touch you here like this?"

"Yes," she moaned. Her legs spread wider, needing him to touch her deeper. Harder.

His hot breath replaced the pressure from his hand. "May I?"

She wanted to scream yes, but once again couldn't voice her thoughts the moment he blew a hot stream of air against her damp center. She felt a rush of dew and heard his groan of approval as he swiped his tongue over that intimate part of her body.

Turning his head away from her hot center he nibbled at her inner thigh. "You don't mind me doing this, do you?"

She shook her head and managed to say, "Don't stop."

Willing herself to remain motionless and to just feel what he offered, she fisted her hands around the counterpane beneath them.

With his hand pushing out her thigh, he urged her to spread her legs even wider. "Open for me, darling. I just want to see what all this pretty flesh looks like."

Before she even had a chance to be embarrassed about his candid request, his mouth settled over her again, his tongue slicking hotly over her core. He rumbled his approval against her heated sex.

Arching off the bed, she threw her head back in a soundless plea for more. When his tongue found her clitoris, she cried out, giving voice to the depth of her desire to have this man do very wicked things to her.

He pulled away long enough to ask, "So that's where you wanted to be touched most."

"Yes." Her voice didn't sound like her own.

Releasing his hold on her thighs, he spread the lips of her sex once more and set about tasting the little nub of swollen flesh that he exposed to the cool air surrounding them. Sucking the bud of her sex into his mouth, he released it long enough to rotate his tongue and lave lower into her cream before sucking that little pleasure spot again.

Letting go of the counterpane beneath her, she threaded her fingers through his hair to take a handful in her grasp. She couldn't stop herself, she couldn't be gentle; she needed him to rub so much harder. In mimicry of their early intercourse, she rocked her sex against his lips and the gentle, intermittent nip of his teeth. Sliding his hands under her buttocks, he tilted her so he could bury his face deeper and ate at her like a man starved.

He sucked away the cream of her pleasure and continued to kiss and lick at her most sensitive parts. It wasn't long before she was crying out his name, begging him to never stop. The sensation became so much she squeezed his head between her thighs and rocked hard against his mouth.

Sweet heaven.

Her body throbbed and convulsed around his mouth as she lost herself completely to the moment. His thumb thrust inside her sheath, pushing in and out at an unhurried pace. His tongue still worked over that sweet spot and then she felt as though she were flying free as a wave of pleasure crashed into her and washed through her whole body. The pleasure tensed then softened her limbs the moment she hit her crisis. Even the hand she tangled in his hair flopped lazily to the bed as she surrendered fully to the ecstasy of his touch.

Her legs fell open and her body grew slack as Teddy kissed her thighs and her hipbone before sitting between her spread knees. Hiking up her chemise, he pulled the material over her head and tossed it away. Then he moved away leaving her hot and hungry for more of his touch.

The sound of his shoes hitting the floor before the edge of the bed dipped as he sat, presumably to remove his pants. She was too satiated to even assist him. When the jut of his smooth cock landed on her hip, her body reawakened.

"I wish to return the pleasure you have given me, Teddy."

He stilled with the suggestion. When he didn't respond, she reached down to clasp his cock, and rolled the pad of her thumb over the tip, rubbing in the pearl of semen it had emitted.

His body came down to rest next to hers, and his hair brushed the side of her face. His lips branded her shoulder and collarbone. "If you'll recall, I said I wanted to learn all your secrets. I might have to taste every inch of you before the night is through."

"I want nothing more than to taste you as you have tasted me." She grasped the base of his cock and stroked it, pulling the skin back from the head.

When she attempted to scoot lower down the bed, Teddy caught her under her arms and rolled on top of her. Her legs opened to him immediately, putting the thrust of his cock against the sensitive folds of her sex.

"I'm not done playing with you just yet. But I will take you up on that offer ... later."

She wiggled a little, trying to lodge the head of his manhood deeper inside her.

"I desire to have you again."

"I more than desire you, Rosa. You've made a right mess of me. I can't get you out of my head, and thoughts of you have become so constant that I can no longer function when you aren't near to me."

His words fired through her body, acting as an aphrodisiac to her senses.

TEDDY DECIDED THAT THIS WAS the very definition of ecstasy: the feel of Rosa naked and wanting beneath his heavier weight, the laughter in her voice as she teased him into taking more, and the sweet taste of her body as she found release with him.

He couldn't get enough of this woman. She was the embodiment of temptation.

His Rosa. His sweet Rosa. He'd have her every way he could imagine for the rest of the night. Really, he wanted to make up for the night he'd denied her pleasure. Never again would he do so, because watching her come undone in his arms brought him a gratification so deep it kept him hard and wanting her.

When her neck arched, he nipped at the exposed skin, flicking his tongue over the erratic pulse at her throat. He molded his palm over her stomach and higher over her breast. He wanted to suckle her there, pull the tips of her breasts deep into his mouth and he would but he needed her promise for tomorrow.

"I want you all to myself, Rosa. Will you stay in bed with me tomorrow?"

She was silent for a moment. As she tilted her head back, he watched her suck her bottom lip into her mouth, nibbling at the delicate edge with her teeth. He wanted to run his tongue along the seam of her mouth, feel the contrasting texture of her strong teeth and the soft yielding flesh of her lips.

"If you that's what you desire ..."

He kissed her lips gently. "I want you to want it, Rosa."

"A whole day with no one but ourselves sounds like a splendid idea." Her eyes narrowed, puckering up her brows. "So long as you feed me."

His lips tilted at the corners in a smile.

"That I can promise." Hands wrapped about her hips, he pushed her back down to the bed and thrust back into her welcoming body.

Chapter Ten

My spirit is always with you, the knot made fast. I will never undo it.
– Clara Schumann

ROSA OPENED HER MOUTH FOR the treat Teddy offered. She was sharing yet another idyllic morning with Teddy. She felt like she should be doing something more where her brother was concerned, but was at a loss as to exactly what she could do. No word had come in days. And it was partially her fault that Teddy had stayed home instead of searching for her brother. She'd been reluctant to let him go, knowing that she couldn't keep him forever. Knowing that once their lazy mornings ended, she would have to face reality and forget the fantasy she'd been living in for the past week.

Was it wrong to indulge this way? Was it wrong to want to pretend that everything was perfect when they were tucked away together where no one could intrude? Every time the guilt crept up on her mind she squashed it down, wanting just a little more time with Teddy. Wanting a little more of this perfect life they shared before it all came crashing down around her. But it was time to put some distance between them. While they'd worked feverishly on his compositions and discussing her music at great length, his concerto was nearly complete and could soon be rehearsed by the musicians he'd chosen for his orchestration.

Something soft brushed over her lips as he slid the tangy morsel over her tongue. She shoved the melancholic thoughts away, wanting to focus on Teddy fully.

"Bite down," he said.

Fresh sweetness washed over her taste buds as her teeth bit through a ripe strawberry. Chewing the tasty fruit, she swallowed and hoped he had plenty more to share because she'd not had strawberries since summertime. "Where did you find such a treat in the dead of winter?"

"I cannot divulge my secrets, or I fear there will be a strawberry shortage in the de Burgh household." His voice held a note of teasing.

"May I have another?" She'd already found his hand with her mouth. When she tried to take another bite of the fruit, he pulled it away and she only caught the end. She licked the juice that dribbled down her lip. "Don't tease me so."

"Now, now. You'll have to work for this strawberry; it just so happens to be the last one."

Her mouth dropped open in shock. "But I've only had one. Tell me you jest?"

"I was hungry on my way up. I couldn't help but sample the treats. The strawberries in particular."

Pouting out her bottom lip, she asked, "What shall I offer in exchange for the berry?"

He brushed the nibbled end of the fruit over her bottom lip. The smell reminded her of the summers when she and her brother would pick wild berries in their fields.

"What do you suppose it's worth?"

She wrinkled her nose and contemplated exactly what the

strawberry was worth. "Hmmm ... I can think of a number of things in exchange for the last strawberry."

Stretching out her arm, she walked the tips of her fingers up his naked leg with slow deliberation.

"You should share these ideas."

Having a good idea of where he sat in relation from her, she pounced on him, tackling him down to the bed. Her robe pulled where her knee caught it, making it near impossible to shift over him so she landed across his torso. Not that she minded the position. He rolled them both over, reversing their positions.

Untangled, but trapped in a much more pleasant way, she said, "We could start with a kiss." She placed her lips against his chest and trailed the tip of her tongue higher until she reached just under his chin. "Or if you like, I could kiss you in a different direction altogether." Her fingers slid downward, showing him exactly what she meant.

She waited. She wasn't giving him what he wanted until he gave up the berry. He shifted her leg, his thigh pressing tight against her mound and she felt the thrust of his manhood against her stomach.

He caught her hands and raised them above her head, trapping them.

"Tell me you didn't eat my strawberry."

"Uh-uh."

His nose rubbed against hers, and she could smell the tangy fruit a moment before his mouth lowered to hers. She bit half of the strawberry and ate it with a gusto that had nothing to do with sating her hunger for food. He'd obviously eaten the other half, for his lips brushed against hers.

"You're a wretched tease."

"You should be nice considering I shared the last strawberry with you." He rolled away and pulled her up to a sitting position. The robe fell open to expose her breasts and she left it, hoping it inflamed his desire to taste her as he had last night.

"I've never eaten in bed with anyone. It's decidedly the most delicious way to break one's fast," she said.

"I'm glad to introduce you to something new. Open your mouth for the next treat."

She shouldn't indulge in his kindnesses quite so much, for she was bound to be disappointed in herself when left to her own devices; men eventually bored of the women they desired once they had seduced and conquered them.

When she opened her mouth for him, she could smell the scrambled eggs before she tasted them. They were fluffy but had cooled while she and Teddy and consumed the sweeter part of breakfast.

Cinching the robe closed and tying the sash tight about her waist, she held out her hand, hoping he'd hand her the fork. "I'm quite capable of feeding myself."

What she really wanted was to stop playing these endearing games with him. They must finish his concerto, find her brother, and then she could go back to her usual routine. Her need for more of this—of him—must stop. It was dangerous to want to depend on someone else.

"Here," he said, placing the fork in her hand and guiding her other hand to the small plate the eggs were piled on.

"I know I promised to stay the day, but I must get back to my room to bathe and refresh myself. Then we can start working on your concerto this afternoon. You must be anxious to finish it."

"I have a bathing chamber on the other side of my dressing room. We can save time by sharing the water," he suggested.

Buttered toast was pressed to her lips. She took a bite, thinking on his offer.

"We could." Though that was a very bad idea and one she wouldn't indulge in. She slipped out of the bed, knowing it was for the best. "I'll be back in a few short hours."

"I was hoping to convince you to join me for a rehearsal later today."

"You know I can't." She'd already told him that she wouldn't be seen with him in public, it had been her condition in staying in his town house. "Once your rehearsals start, you'll no longer need my assistance," she felt compelled to point out, though not for his sake, but for hers.

"What of our agreement? I haven't written anything but the bones of one of your songs. I owe you much more than that."

"You needn't worry about my work. Your hands are full right now, Teddy. My only concern is my brother, not my music."

She heard his sigh of frustration and wished they were in a more formal setting where she felt less exposed.

Changing the subject, she said, "I heard you working on some variations of Bach's violin partitas earlier this morning. Will you be playing it or do you have a violinist in mind for the opening?"

"I didn't mean to wake you. It's just something I have been working on for a separate commission. And you changed the subject rather cleverly." He tapped her nose, then kissed it.

"I simply wanted to emphasize the fact that you have a lot to deal with right now. That you are finding time for my brother at all is a blessing to me."

"Speaking of topic changes, I had every intention of spending the day working on your solo pieces since everyone will be at church this morning. The longer I am in your company, the more I find you and what you've created inspiring."

He reached for her hand before she could fully escape. She wanted to bask in the pleasure of his touch, relent and fall back into his arms, but she knew the best thing for them both would be to set boundaries before it was too late.

A part of her knew that it was already too late. She was in love with this man. And walking away from him would hurt.

"The depth of your ability is astounding and I feel privileged that you let me explore the beauty of your work." His words swelled in her heart, making her hate the fact that she had to deny him anything, even her company.

"You're only saying that because you've found a patch of light in what you're working on. Luck had me finding you at this time in your career."

"Don't play yourself short, Rosa. You give me reason to strive to be something more. A better man and a better musician."

Those words struck a chord so deep in her that she knew if she didn't pull away now, she'd be forever lost to him. With a strength she was surprised she possessed, she slipped her hand away from his and stepped away from the bed.

"You shouldn't be so candid. It's only a matter of time before the world sees the mad genius that has always been hidden in their midst. If it's anyone's time to shine, it's yours. My time was buried with my past."

"And I think your judgment is biased since you seem to like me," he teased.

She gave him a smile and she searched the floor for her clothes with her feet stretching out along the rug. "Perhaps."

"You're a better musician than I, Rosa. Don't try and deny that. I've been listening closely this past week."

She was not better than he. They were very different. She would never play in the public eye again; he, on the other hand, would become a household name. Celebrated and appreciated for the beautiful music he created.

"My playing hit its plateau long ago, Teddy. Surely you see this as the truth. I will never be more than a muse."

"I can't say I agree with your self-deprecating opinions."

He was wrong. It didn't matter that she had a widely celebrated past or that she'd been a genius in the eyes of royalty. None of it mattered now that she was blind, now that she'd lowered herself to becoming a courtesan.

They were both silent as she found her chemise and pulled it over her head.

Teddy was in front of her, handing her the rest of her clothes. "I could arrange for you to be heard." His offer was sincere, questioning. He wanted her to say yes, but she wouldn't.

"They would only see my disability. It wouldn't be about the music." She turned away, feeling tears threaten the last thread of her composure. She'd lived her fantasy for nearly a week; it was time to walk away before it was too late. "You will be the rage in London when you open up the Hanover Square Rooms. You'll be lauded widely and requests will come in from everywhere between Frankfurt and Vienna for you to play for them. The concerto that you've written is beyond what words can describe."

"I can only hope it's well received. Everyone will have high expectations after having written nothing for so long. I've not shared this latest one with anyone but you. I haven't even shared it with the musicians I've been putting together these past few weeks."

She sat on the edge of the bed and put on her stockings, once done she handed him the rest of her clothes, she'd need help doing up her bodice, she turned and gave him her back.

"The musicians will be ecstatic to have the opportunity to play this piece. I believe in your work and in your gift for music, Teddy."

"You are the only inspiration I need to move forward." Once he was finished tying her bodice, her turned her around. "You're a distraction that I couldn't do without."

She frowned at that. "You might think that now, but once our lives are back to some sense of normal, you'll hardly notice the change. Everything you've accomplished you've done on your own."

"Don't underplay your role in all this," he said.

"I didn't intend to. I just think you are losing sight of what is important in your life. I'll be but a passing memory."

"You're right, I can't think straight where you're concerned. Not when I'm with you, not when I'm away from you. While you might think you fill the role of mistress and companion, you're much more than that to me."

She ran the tips of her fingers down the side of his face, feeling the smooth line of his cheek and jaw. "I don't know how to even respond to that," was all she could manage. She didn't want to disappoint him, but they would inevitably part ways and she knew that would tear her up on the inside.

So she gave him a flippant response instead of being truthful to what she felt. "You know how to flatter a woman."

Fingers threading through hers, he pulled her hand away from his face. "I speak truthfully and from the heart."

She heard the frustration tightening his voice.

"I never said your words were false, but you have to realize that I have my own life I have to get back to. There comes a time when everyone has to move on and our time is closer to wrapping up than either of us wants to believe."

"You make it sound like we'd be no good for each other. I'm inviting you to stay. I don't know for how long, but I do want you here. I'd be happy if you stayed until winter finished." She shook her head, striving for fortitude, which escaped her with his sincere request. He pressed his finger to her lips before she could respond. "Don't answer now. I'm asking that you consider it."

Sensing he'd brook no argument, she nodded her agreement.

All Rosa knew was that she could not afford to lose her heart to this man. Staying here would destroy any resolve she had to deny him and losing herself in the process was a price she couldn't pay.

SHE WASN'T GOING TO STAY. She hadn't come back after making excuses to leave for a couple of hours, either. So the question was: What was she so afraid of?

Not having an answer to that question, he'd given her a little time away from him since she craved it so thoroughly. Instead of pursuing her like he wanted to do, he'd spent the better part of the afternoon scribbling down the finishing touches of one of her piano pieces. Did she have a title for it? He scrolled her name above the stave on the right of the page. Miss Rosalie Montgomery.

Carrying the music over to the desk, he dusted a handful of sand over the drying ink. One down; how many more could he convince her to share? Leaning closer to the music lit by soft candlelight, he blew the sand away from her name. It truly was a work of art, and only lacked a title. Grabbing the pen up again, he dipped it into the ink and scrolled *Sonata in C-sharp Minor* along the top. Now it looked much better.

Pulling his pocket watch from his vest, he flipped the cover open. Dinner would be in an hour. He should search out his lady friend in the meantime. See if she'd take a walk with him or maybe join him for an aperitif so he could play her piece for her now that he'd finished transcribing it.

Teddy made his way to her room and rapped lightly on the door. Her maid answered. "My lord," she said with a curtsy, then opened the door enough for him to enter. "His lordship is here to speak with you, Miss Rosalie."

Teddy took a quick look around the room. There was no mistaking Rosa's intent; she was packing her bags. "Have I done something to offend you?"

"No. Nothing of the sort."

Rosa picked up where the maid left off and folded articles of clothing and placed them in a neat stack on her bed.

"Why are you leaving?"

"I've overstayed my welcome. With your concerto nearly completed, you don't need me anymore. You'll start regular rehearsals this week and everything will fall into place once that starts."

"That's a bald-faced lie, and you know it."

She turned away from him, and sat on the edge of the bed, shoulders slumped forward, hands clutched around a shawl she'd been folding. "I can't stay. We are both becoming too distracted."

He walked farther into the room, fighting his first instinct to go to her and hold her. He knew doing that would only push her further away from him right now. "Tell me what you need."

"Time, Teddy. I need time. We've lost track of what we were doing."

"I can't agree with that. We're exactly where we should be, but if you need some time alone, I can give you a few days."

"I can't stay in this house with you."

No, of course she couldn't. Hell, he didn't even know what he wanted out of their union. Yes, he did. He wanted ... more. But what did *more* encompass? Rosa was used to living her life alone and outside of the rest of the world, and while he appreciated the need for privacy, being a very private man himself, he didn't want to be without her.

He sat next to her on the bed so they were shoulder to shoulder.

"A few days I can live with, Rosa. But we need to figure out *us* after that."

"I won't be the cause of your ruin."

"Is that how you will always see our joining? I'd say I'm flattered by your concern, but I'm feeling quite the opposite right now."

With his hand at her waist, her urged her to her feet and had her stand in front of him. He guided her until she stood between the vee of his thighs, both her hands captured by one of his. He kissed them before releasing them, then settled his hands firmly around her hips. "I never expected to feel the way I do about you. We've found something special in each other, and whatever it is, it feels right."

She pressed her palm to his cheek. "Your heart is pure and true, Teddy. I've known that from the moment we met. And I also know that you're going to make some lucky lady very happy one day."

He frowned at the assumption. She couldn't be more wrong. The only lucky lady he could think of was in his arms. "We are made for each other, Rosa. You're the only woman for me."

With a resigned sigh, she stepped away from him. "I need to continue packing if I'm to be home before night falls."

Whatever wall she thought to put up between them would be torn down in a few days, that was the only reason he was agreeing to her leaving. If he could take away her concerns about what people might think of them and about her brother, would that change her mind and keep her here longer? There was only one way to find out, and it involved finding her brother so she could put that worry to rest.

He stood and pulled her into his arms for a kiss before they parted. While she might be telling him she needed time by herself, that was the last thing her body was suggesting when she sank into the embrace. Her lips were soft, and easily coaxed into opening for him, but he kept it brief. He pulled away hesitantly.

Insisting that they could handle a few days apart, he kissed her cheek and left her.

Vane Estate
November 12, 1855

Thaddeus,

I regretfully write that I have found Daniel; or rather, he has found me. I've enclosed a letter for Rosa that only says I hope she'll join us in Maidstone, and that her brother will be staying on for a while. The truth of the matter is, Daniel seems to have gotten mixed up with the wrong lot, and was left beaten, bloody, and half starved at my servants' entrance. I don't know what circumstance brought him to my door, but I'm glad I was here to call on the doctor.

I stood vigil over his bed through the night, but he has surprised even the doctor with his resilience. I don't know if it's better to tell Rosa how badly off he is, or if it's better to tell her to come to the estate and hope he heals more before she reaches us. I will see you both soon.

Godspeed, Nathan

Chapter Eleven

*Mournful and yet grand is the destiny of
the artist.*
— Franz Liszt

ROSA WASN'T SURE HOW SHE felt about spending the next
few days with Teddy close by. While they'd only spent one day
apart, the letter from Nathan had come as a welcome surprise.
But she didn't fail to notice the tension surrounding Teddy since
he'd told her about Daniel. He was hiding something from her.
But what? Had her brother found more trouble than he could handle this time? She supposed she would find out soon enough.

"I know this isn't the best time to discuss this," Teddy said,
"but we have nothing but open roads for another three hours.
Have you put any thought into staying on with me?"

In truth, that was all she had thought about since leaving
his residence. And still, she had no answers where he was concerned. "We have both met our ends of the deal, now that Daniel
is found."

"I don't care about the bloody deal, Rosa. I missed you after only a few hours. Don't tell me the feeling wasn't mutual."

She continued tracing her finger over the cold glass of the window wondering what the scenery looked like. She wanted Teddy's arms around her so badly.

"We hardly know each other."

"So what's to stop us from getting to know each other better?" His tone was derisive.

She heard his frustrated sigh and hoped he was done discussing the matter. "We'll be in Maidstone for a few days, so we have nothing but time to talk then." When she could easily put distance between them. In the carriage that was impossible.

They didn't talk for the remainder of the ride, which meant Rosa was left to her thoughts.

So many conflicting feelings and thoughts tumbled around in her mind. This would be the first time Daniel would have seen her in nearly a decade. She wasn't sure how their first meeting would go, if he would hate her, or be happy to see her after her long absence from his life.

When her thoughts weren't wrapped around meeting her brother she thought of Teddy. Once he played at the Hanover Square Rooms he would be called on to write more music, to play more concert halls, to travel Europe to display his talents to everyone of importance.

That was the life he was destined for and she couldn't be happier for him. But her? She would never be able to face the people from her old life. She'd be shunned and turned away and that would only break her heart all over again. Leaving him was breaking her heart, but there was no other choice for them.

Finally, the carriage pulled to a stop. As the door opened, Rosa heard Nathan's familiar voice.

"How are you, darling?" Nathan took her hand and helped her down the steps. When she was on solid ground he embraced her in a hug, which was not something he usually did.

"What's all this about?" she asked as he set her back down

on her feet.

"I know I should have explained everything better in my note to you, but I didn't want you to be concerned should your brother's condition improve, which it has. He's finally awake."

"He's awake? Nathan ..."

"I had no choice but to omit a few facts from the letters I sent you and Teddy."

Teddy's arm came up under her elbow, before Nathan could steal her.

"What aren't you telling me, Nathan?" she asked, worry gnawing deep and making her stomach flip.

"Your brother found some trouble. He doesn't remember a lot of the details of what happened, because he was beaten pretty badly before being brought here. But the doctor's prognosis is positive."

She suddenly felt as though she'd lose her breakfast and had to cover her mouth with her gloved hand and take a few steadying breaths.

When she had her riotous nerves under control, she asked, "Did you know, Teddy?"

Nathan cleared his throat. "I was intentionally vague about your brother's appearance at my house."

Which didn't answer her question, and made her think Nathan was protecting Teddy. "Who hurt my brother?"

"Unfortunately, I don't know. The best thing we can do right now is ensure your brother gets better. The doctor assures me that Daniel will remember everything that happened in time, time being key in this instance."

Without a word, Teddy helped remove her jacket upon their entry into the house and handed her back the shawl she'd worn overtop of jacket in the carriage.

"Why do I feel as if you're preparing me for the absolute worst, Nathan?"

Nathan took her hands in his and turned toward her. "I'm not preparing you for the worst. He's on the mend, and that's what matters most right now. His speech is slightly slurred and you'll hear that it pains him to talk. I'm giving you fair warning only so you know what to expect."

Rosa took a calming breath. It was not calming; it was ragged, forced, and had water prickling at her eyes. What had happened to her brother that had Nathan afraid to give her the full truth?

Teddy placed a handkerchief in her palm. "These are not the best of circumstances for you to be reunited with your brother." His hand caressed the side of her face. "I wish I could have found him sooner. It pains me that I didn't."

"Neither of you are to blame. Without your help ..." She sniffled, hating to think what could have happened. "Daniel might have found himself in a more dire situation by the sounds of things."

He could be dead, her mind whispered. Her composure slipped again and her eyes welled over. She kicked the fear away. He was alive and at the duke's house, which meant he was safe.

She dabbed under her eyes and held her head high as she stuck her hand out toward Nathan. "Please. Take me to see my brother."

It was Teddy's hand that threaded through hers, and his strong presence helped to anchor her feelings, helped give her the strength for whatever she was about to face.

The first thing she was aware of when she entered the room was the crackled sound of labored breathing. Her steps faltered the closer she got to her brother. Having Teddy at her side was the only thing holding her up right now.

"Daniel?" she called out gently.

"He's asleep right now, but I've had a comfortable chair set up so you can keep vigil in here until he awakens," Nathan said. "He's been in and out of consciousness for the past few hours. It was obvious he hadn't been kept in an ideal place. I don't think he's eaten for at least a few days so he'll need some time to regain his strength."

"What's wrong with his breathing?"

"Two cracked ribs and some bruising around his chest. I'll spare you the details of what I believe happened, but the sound will lessen so long as he stays off his feet for at least a few days. The doctor thinks that happened a couple of weeks ago."

She nodded, feeling her heart break for a reason other than her predicament with Teddy. Her poor brother. What could he have gotten involved in that would result in this? "Will we able to find the person that did this to him?"

"I'm hoping that will come with his memory. Give him time, Rosa. Your brother has always been a fighter. He'll pull through this like he has everything else."

"I hope you're right." She reached forward, trying to find the edge of the bed, but Teddy was there, leading her to the chair Nathan had mentioned.

"I'll leave you two up here with Daniel," Nathan said. "I have some errands to attend to, and Daniel is in good hands with you both here at his side. The doctor will be back this evening to check in on his patient."

"Thank you," she said.

"You know that no thanks are necessary. I'll see you both later."

When the door opened and shut, she turned to Teddy. "I want to make it clear that my focus here is my brother. I can't thank either you or your brother enough for everything you've done for me so far, and I'll always be indebted to you for that."

"Nonsense. And we're far from done. I know this isn't the time or place to discuss our relationship, but we will have that discussion soon. I'll let you spend some time with your brother." He took her hand and placed it around her brother's hand. "His knuckles are a bit bruised, but I think you're okay to hold his hand if it gives you any comfort. I'll leave you here awhile and have tea brought up in an hour or so if that is to your liking."

"It is. Thank you."

When Teddy left, Rosa sat in the chair, still carefully holding on to her brother's hand.

"What have you gotten yourself into, Danny?" She knew he couldn't answer, but it helped to talk to him. They hadn't had a conversation since she'd left home and while she was worried and afraid for him, she was also nervous about what she would say to him when he finally woke.

THE TEA HAD COME AND gone hours ago and she needed to freshen up and get her things in order for her stay here. Daniel hadn't woken once since her arrival and she was afraid to miss a chance to speak with him.

A few minutes to herself would do her good, though, so she got up from her chair and picked up her walking stick and went in search of the door.

"Amy?"

She froze, her hand tightening so much around the handle of the door she thought she'd snap it off. Her back stiffened beneath the boning of her corset, and her shoulders bunched up a bit with the nickname, which was a shortened form of her given name. There were only two people in all the world who called her Amy, and one had died broken in her arms on a cold rainy night. Despite the memories it gave her, it felt good to hear the old nickname coming from her brother's lips.

With a deep, relieved breath, she turned around, her brother's name but a whisper from her lips. "Oh, Danny."

A sob caught her in throat as she rushed back toward the bed. He grasped her hands before she had to search for him and guided her around the side of his bed where she could sit on the edge of the mattress.

"It's been too long, sister."

She pulled one hand free of his and wiped the dew from her cheek with the handkerchief Teddy had given her. "I wish we could have met under better conditions."

"Now is as good a time as any." He squeezed her hand. "It's my own cowardly fault. You know Father said I couldn't see you. It was foolish of me to take the earl's word that he'd do us further damage should I contact you. He couldn't ruin our father more than he did."

The Earl of Warwick was Michael's father. The earl had also been the one to insist she be banished and tossed out into the street. And while her father had tried to persuade the man that it was the wrong path to take, the earl held more power than her father ever had.

She nodded. "I know."

"The earl died last month."

One of the first things Rosa had done to make peace with her past was forgive the grieving father for having her banished. While elements of that fateful night still haunted her to this day, she had refused to let her heart be ruled by hatred for how her life had turned out, and how the earl had had the biggest hand in her ruin.

"Does the earl have something to do with your injuries?"

"I can't remember much. I was at a den ..." Her brother stammered on his words, as though embarrassed by what he almost admitted to.

"You needn't fear I'll reprimand you for your actions. I'm sure you've heard the rumors of what became of my life."

"You did what you needed to do to survive. I love you no matter the outcome of our lives and would never judge you for the hard decisions you were forced to make, Amy."

She wished his words didn't cut so deep. After all this time, he was going to accept her with open arms? She'd missed him so much, and her father, too.

She dashed away more tears. "I go by Rosa now."

There was a pause. "Do you prefer that I call you Rosa?"

"Yes. I buried the past after Michael died. I had to, if I wanted to keep going on."

He rubbed his hand along her arm. "All right. Rosa it is."

"What of our father?" she asked.

"Father's not well. His mind is going and he hasn't been able to walk for a little over a year now."

She felt like her life was falling apart all over again. Life was cruel to give her back her father, only to give her a man broken over the years. But would he welcome her or treat her the way he had the night he'd tossed her to the curb and declared her a harlot?

"The earl made sure that Papa was all but destitute. Had I not found my own way, I might have ended up in squalor, too. I send him what money I can, not that it does him much good with all the medicines the doctors have prescribed."

When she could only sniffle in response, Daniel added, "Papa has been talking about giving you the **Érard** piano that the Austrian princess gifted to you."

"He should keep it." Her answer was instantaneous. That piano had reminded her of better times with her father at her side. She could not have one without the other.

"His hands are so swollen and sore with arthritis that he can't play anymore."

"Why didn't he come to me sooner if he wanted me to have it?"

Her brother sighed, the sound pained. "The earl was harsh on him. With you gone, the source of our money—your tours—dried up. Papa could find no other means of income. The earl made sure that no one would hire him on as a music tutor. I think the earl was mighty pleased to slowly destroy what was left of our father's spirit. Papa is but a shell of the man he once was, and has been since you left."

Her brother squeezed her hand with the pronouncement. His breathing was wheezy and ragged, and she wanted to hug him but was afraid to hurt him.

"Why are you telling me this now, Daniel?"

"I wanted to come to you after the earl died. I had every intention of coming to you in London. But I don't know what happened after the funeral in Sussex. I was at the earl's funeral, visited with Father for a few hours, then went to Missy's Den. That's where my memories of what happened just end."

"I don't understand how you ended up at the duke's estate, of all places."

"You're not the only one baffled." Daniel yawned.

"You're tired, and I've kept you talking too long."

"I don't mind, but I think I'll sleep a bit."

"I'll be here when you wake."

His hands went slack in hers and she knew he was already asleep. It must have pained him a great deal to talk at length with her. But she was thankful for the time they'd had.

She tucked the blankets back up around him and left him to sleep. She'd hurry with freshening up and getting a snack so she could stay with him through the night. She'd also arrange to have broth prepared for him, he'd be hungry eventually, and she'd help him while he was on the mend for as long as he needed her. They had so many things to catch up on.

For the first time since she'd realized her brother was missing, she felt her world coming together just a little.

ROSA HAD AVOIDED TEDDY FOR two days. And while Teddy respected the fact that she had a lot to catch up on with her brother back in her life, that didn't give her the right to completely ignore him. He'd been so lost in the final touches of his concerto that he hadn't looked up at the clock until nearly eleven on their second night there. It was far too late to see Rosa; she tended to be in bed before ten, as she liked early mornings with a cup of tea next to the piano. That didn't mean Daniel wouldn't be up, and it was high time he spoke with the man and introduced himself.

He rapped softly on the door, thinking perhaps it was too late, but he'd heard Rosa's brother talking to the chambermaid last night at a pretty late hour.

"Come in," Daniel called.

Daniel was sitting up in the bed when he entered, and he looked a lot better than he had on his and Rosa's arrival.

"It's good to see you looking better," Teddy noted.

"You're the younger de Burgh, aren't you?" When Teddy nodded, Daniel invited him to sit in the chair next to his bed. "Won't you join me for a spell? I've just woken from a long sleep and I'm wide awake, despite the hour."

Teddy took a seat in the chair and watched as Daniel pulled a deck of cards from under his pillow and took out various numbers before he shuffled the stack. "Hope you don't mind a game of piquet to pass the hour. I'm supposed to stay in bed for a few days, or so the doctor insists."

"It's been a while since I've played piquet, so you'll trump me in no time at all."

"Ah, it's not so hard. The question is: What do we wager?"

Teddy wanted to say he was surprised that a bet should be brought up at all, but from what Rosa had told him of Daniel, it made sense that he would wager even when he'd been close to his deathbed.

"I haven't a clue."

"What do you want if I lose?"

Teddy didn't want money, or any other assets. He would not put this man in more trouble than he could handle. "You'll answer a few questions about your sister."

"A dangerous game, that. But you probably know her better than I do."

"Almost nothing before her accident," Teddy admitted. And he wanted to know everything there was to know about her.

"Deal. And if I should win, why don't you tell me exactly what your relationship is with my sister, so I know if I need to hunt you down and teach you a lesson about how to properly treat a lady."

Teddy nearly grinned. If life was as easy as saying what he wanted and having it ... Rosa was many things to him, but it was her choice how they moved forward. Of course he wouldn't be able to give Daniel the answer he probably wanted to hear.

"Your sister is the better party to answer those questions," he tossed back at the man.

"Ah, but I'm asking you."

Daniel had a point. "We have a deal."

"I like a man of chance, de Burgh."

"I'm not one to take risks. Speaking of ..."

"I have no idea of how I got here. Rosa has been persistent in uncovering every detail from my last memory."

"Who was the last person you saw?"

"I saw a lot of people who were both friend and foe at the funeral."

"Rosa mentioned the Earl of Warwick's passing at lunch yesterday." That had been the only time he'd spent with her, and unfortunately, Nathan had been on hand and Teddy hadn't been able to talk to her.

"Is that all she said?"

"She explained the history she had with that man. The history your family has."

And that was how the night went on, vague discussions about Daniel and Rosa's childhood and Teddy skirting around the truth of his feelings, as he didn't want to put Rosa on the spot with her brother later on. Teddy won two games. Of how many, he couldn't say, but it was well past two in the morning before he made it to his own bed.

Chapter Twelve

I want but two things, your heart and your happiness.
– Clara Schumann

"ROSA," TEDDY CALLED AS HE made his way down the corridor.

She stopped, but seemed reluctant to turn around. He'd given her time alone with her brother over the past few days. But he was done waiting, especially since he knew she was intentionally avoiding him.

"Good afternoon, Teddy. I was just in the kitchen asking for a heartier meal to be prepared for Daniel. He's improving every hour, and it's time he got some real food in his stomach."

"Let me accompany you back upstairs. There was something I wanted to ask." It was minute, but he noticed the tension that raised her shoulders defensively. "You can't avoid me forever, even if you've done a good job of it since we arrived."

Her brows drew together. "I have been busy with Daniel."

"More busy, I think, than you need to be." He exhaled heavily.

He had no right to be treating her this way when she was going through a difficult time. "I'm sorry, I've missed you and it's driving me mad that I haven't had a chance to get you alone."

"I haven't spared a thought for even myself since we came here."

And didn't that make him feel like a jackass.

He caressed her arms, feeling so much calmer now that he had touched her again. "Did Daniel tell you that I sat with him last night? We played a few hands of cards."

"He mentioned it. Did he tell you anything that might give us a clue as to what happened to him while he was gone?"

"Nothing. His memory seems to be gone since his departure from Sussex."

He watched her chew contemplatively at her lower lip. "Something doesn't add up here. I wish I could help him figure this out."

"The doctor said his head took quite a blow, and in time his memory will come back." He gathered her in his arms, wanting nothing more than to comfort her.

"I want to believe the doctor," she said, "but time might not be on our side for this. You saw the shape he was in on our arrival."

"I can't tell you how glad I am that you couldn't be witness to that." Teddy rubbed his hand down her back, needing to touch her and make up for their time apart.

"That's not the point. The point is, someone went to great lengths to hurt him. What if they come back to finish what they started?" She turned her cheek to rest it over his heart. Teddy was just thankful that she took comfort in his embrace. "It scares me that Daniel can't remember. I even asked about Johnson, but nothing is ringing a bell for him."

"We'll figure this out." His arms tightened around her. "I miss you, Rosa, even when I catch a glimpse of you every day, I miss you. I long for the time when we were in London."

She lifted her head from his chest and started to pull away as though she just realized what she'd allowed. "It'll be a fond memory for the rest of my days, Teddy."

"There's nothing to stop us from creating more memories together."

His arms loosened, though he wasn't ready to let her go yet. He pressed a light kiss to her forehead and leaned down so he could reach her lips.

He kissed her finger instead. "I've explained my stance where we are concerned."

"Yes, you silly woman." He let her go because he couldn't keep her against her will. He had to believe that she would eventually come back to him. "It's absurd and endearing that you fear for my reputation."

"It's not something I take lightly."

He gathered her hands in his and kissed her knuckles. "And I understand that. But please, stop avoiding me."

She sighed heavily. "You need to head back to London."

"You won't be able to get rid of me so easily."

He turned them around and headed up the stairs toward her brother's room. Time was going to be the only way to persuade Rosa that he wasn't going anywhere. He'd have to discuss Daniel's predicament with Nathan and see if there was something they could do to help the siblings sort out the mess of their lives. Once Daniel was in a better position, Teddy would feel less guilt in pursuing Rosa. And pursue her he would.

"HIS GRACE'S INTENTIONS ARE GOOD. You can't fault him in thinking he knows what's best for you. It's in his nature to look out for those he loves," Mary said. "Now stop moving about so I can pin this braid."

Rosa clutched the edge of the vanity and clamped her mouth shut. She couldn't believe they were doing something so reckless. Or that she'd agreed to go along with the plan.

The duke had invited Johnson over to see if it triggered any of Daniel's memories. What would happen if Johnson had been involved with her brother's disappearance? What would happen if Daniel suddenly remembered everything and they were in a room full of guests?

That wasn't the worst part of all this. She knew why Daniel had asked so many questions about her relationship with the de Burghs and more specifically Teddy. And this couldn't be a more inappropriate time for Nathan and Daniel to interfere and play matchmaker like a pair of old society ladies. And Johnson ... What if he should approach her like he had so many times in the past? How would Teddy and Daniel handle that?

What irritated her most about this was that Teddy was still in Maidstone. While neither of them had expected to stay on for nearly a week, Teddy should have headed back to London after the second or third day. In reality, he should be in London setting up his orchestra for rehearsal.

Something was shoved into the elaborate bun Mary had created—probably a feather or a flower—whatever it was, Rosa didn't ask, she was too irritated with the train of her thoughts. Mary used a comb to tuck in some of the strands, then her maid stepped back and made a sound that told Rosa she was admiring her handiwork. "You'll be courted by everyone present. Now, what shall you wear this evening?"

"Something to remind those fools that I'm not some miss in need of a shining, heroic knight. Let my dress leave no doubt as to what I am."

"And what of Lord de Burgh?"

"He has more important things to deal with right now than chasing down the likes of me." Not that that would stop him. How did she deter him once and for all?

Standing, she let Mary cinch her corset, then walked over to the armoire. When a knock came on her door, she turned her head in the direction of the sound.

"I'm sure it's the duke."

"Here, I have your robe," Mary said, her voice drawing closer the moment before the satin was slipped over her underclothes.

Rosa tied the sash, sat on the stool by her vanity, and pulled the curls that fell down the center of her back over one shoulder.

"Lord de Burgh, what brings you here?" Mary said.

"Your mistress." His voice was rushed, perturbed as though he'd taken the stairs two at a time. "You're needed in the dining hall, Mary."

Her maid harrumphed and left without another word.

No one should dismiss her maid but Rosa. While she was ready to face the duke, Rosa was not prepared to confront Teddy. Not while she was at a disadvantage.

She curled her fingers together in her lap and waited for Teddy to say what he came to say. Fingers squeezing tighter together, she swiveled her chair in the direction of his footfall. He took her hands and pulled her to her feet. Now she wished she'd opted to be dressed instead of donning only a robe. Far too few clothes separated them and a part of her had ached for his company since their arrival but she'd known that it would be a mistake to allow any more intimacy.

He touched the sides of her face and held her with a reverence that had her breath catching in her throat. What was it about this man that melted the ice she'd always used as a shield around her heart?

He pressed their bodies together from thigh to chest. His breath was a whisper of warm air caressing her lips. "I needed to see you before the guests arrived."

She grasped his sleeve, fingers feebly clutching at him so he couldn't escape her. Without thinking about her actions, she stood on the tips of her toes, closed her eyes, and brushed her lips over his.

He didn't pull away. Not that she expected him to. Why was it she could never get enough of him? He was the kindle to her flame, she the bowstring to his violin. They were worlds apart, yet shared the same spirit and love for life. Could he be right? Could they be meant for each other? Her inability to hold back from kissing him told her that might be the case. That or it was nerves about what would come of tonight's dinner soiree.

"Rosa," he said, his voice hoarse. "We should talk."

"Can we can talk about this after dinner?"

Rosa pressed her forehead against his chest. Whenever she was in his arms she felt like this was the only place she ever needed to be. If they never had to exist beyond this point, life would be simpler. But life wasn't simple. And with the will of a stubborn bull, she forced her feet back to the ground and pulled away from their impromptu embrace.

"Don't pull away from me, Rosa. Not now."

"You know this is a bad idea. We cannot continue in this fashion. You have a life outside of me, Teddy, and plans that cannot be interfered with if you are to be the great composer I know you will one day be. With me at your side, people won't take you seriously."

"I don't care what others think. Not where you're concerned. Surely, you know this."

"I care enough to say we can't do this, even though it hurts to admit it. There is nothing beyond us here and now. Mistress and master. Lovers and consorts. Whatever you wish to call it. That is all it is."

"You want me to just leave—to forget you? To sever our ties without a backward glance? I'm not asking for forever because I know you won't commit to that. I don't know how else to ask you to try a life with me, taking it one day at a time." He pulled her into the circle of his arms again, his hands resting over her lower back. "We're a good team, you and I. And in my heart I know we are meant to be. On some level I know you believe that, too."

"I have thought on it. You have a life ahead of you, far grander than you realize. I'll only hamper your future successes."

"You're wrong. And after tonight, I'll find a way to prove that to you."

"Do you want it brandished about that you spend your days with your mistress? That you include your mistress in the process of creating your music?"

"Many a man does it. So shall I."

She shook her head and tried to back away from him, but he held her arms more tightly. Because he wouldn't listen to reason, she spoke instead from the heart. "You think you want this now, Teddy. But history always repeats itself and it'll be a matter of time before you tire of me. Where would that leave me?"

"You aren't even giving me a fighting chance here. Why can't you let go of the reins just once and feel the wind on your face?"

"I've had enough experiences of that nature to last me a lifetime. I care not to experience it anymore—"

He silenced her with a kiss.

She should have pulled away. Did he think his conviction alone would sway her decision? Her thoughts didn't get much further than that when he pressed his mouth to hers again, and she was lost in their embrace.

Just once more, she told herself. She needed this. Wanted this with everything in her heart.

It was a sweet kiss. Tender. The meeting of warm lips, the gentle seeking of two tongues too shy to take the first forbidden taste. He tasted of mint and coffee, a rich, strong flavor imploring her to taste deeper.

Oh, it would not end so simply, either. No longer caring how much this would hurt them both, she pushed his evening tails from his shoulders and off him before stretching her hands over his chest, working the buttons free on his vest.

"You should not be wearing," she mumbled as he nibbled his way down her neck and back up, "so many clothes."

His larger hands wrapped around hers to still her motions. "Be still, Rosa. I will do this only if you will consider coming back to London with me, even if it's only for a short time."

She shook her head and pulled her hands from beneath his. "All I can offer you is now."

He let out a frustrated air. "I'll leave you to dress for dinner, then."

She reached out to pull him back to her, but he moved out of her reach and she came up empty-handed. "Is that how it's to be?

You want nothing from me if I can't promise you a future?"

"As much as I want this ... It doesn't make it any easier on me, Rosa. It's better this way."

"I'll not beg."

"No, you won't, but it's what I've been doing. What you seem to expect of me after every refusal you throw my way." Silence remained after his hurtful but true words. "I'll leave tomorrow since that's what you so desperately want. Promise me that you'll at least come to the opening performance. Without you, I wouldn't have been able to do it."

"I would be thrilled and honored to be at your grand opening."

The back of his hand caressed her cheek. "Shall I call your maid up to finish readying you?"

"Thank you."

"Don't thank me. This is not an arrangement I will agree to for long."

THIS WAS NOT THE TYPE of dinner party Teddy had anticipated. All the guests were either Cyprians or gentlemen who spent the better part of their time in debauchery than actually doing something useful. Nathan sat at the head of the table next to his former mistress, Anna, who had been coaxed into attending on the grounds that he didn't want Rosa to feel uncomfortable without a friend present.

When he'd asked Nathan if he and Anna had worked out their differences, his brother had shrugged and changed the topic. Teddy hadn't pressed, but surely her being here tonight must mean they'd resolved some of their issues.

Daniel sat next to Anna, his body hunched slightly in pain. Rosa's brother had insisted on being up and about now that the doctor had told him it was all right to be out of bed.

Teddy wasn't lucky enough to be seated beside Rosa, but he watched her every move from across the table. Why had he agreed to go back to London without her? While it felt necessary when he'd suggested it, it hurt to make that choice.

Benedict Johnson sat on the left of Rosa. He hadn't acted oddly on seeing Daniel as one of the guests, which made Teddy think the man had nothing to do with Daniel's disappearance. But again, Daniel's memory remained foggy.

Creve and his mistress sat two seats down from Rosa and Johnson. Creve was known to live for the next gamble, and it was likely he'd bet against Daniel at some point. Though they knew each other, nothing more than pleasantries were exchanged.

Beside Daniel were two women Teddy did not know, but they made it a point to laugh far too often, as though that sound alone could seduce a man.

The one beside him was maybe thirty, decked out in jewels from the pins and clips in her hair right down to the rings adorning every one of her fingers. At least she kept those hands to herself.

"I'm glad to have you all here tonight. And to think, even my brother was able to join us at the last minute."

"Couldn't resist the opportunity to attend a house party when London is clearing out for the holidays," Creve said.

"Not with the delectable company you like to keep." That swine Johnson was staring at Rosa as he said that. The man sat too close to her, their arms nearly touching as he slid his chair closer to hers. Teddy had not forgotten the man's desire to land Rosa as his mistress. And that simply would not happen. But all this was necessary if they were to try and learn anything about Daniel's disappearance.

"I regret that I won't be able to stay on for the whole party," Teddy said.

His brother shrugged. "All you'll miss is good food, wine, and friends to share the cold winter nights, if you catch my drift. What more could we ask for?"

More than one guffaw sounded as the table toasted to that. Teddy took a small sip of the champagne and put it down. He watched Rosa, noting that the glass was cleverly placed against her lips, but she swallowed none. She must be too nervous to let herself be impaired by anything. She flirted incessantly with Johnson, laughing at everyone's jokes. She did something to Teddy when she laughed, something the other two women at the table could never do.

Teddy scarcely recalled eating any of the four courses served. All he knew was that his patience grew thinner and thinner the more outrageously she flirted with Johnson. Daniel didn't seem to mind the display, either, which only enraged Teddy further. They seemed to have some past together, all three of them.

Once dinner concluded and they all stood, Teddy was at Rosa's side before Johnson could take her arm and lead her into the parlor. He couldn't watch her spend another moment with that man.

Rosa turned her head in his direction and raised one brow in question. But she acquiesced with a nod and threaded her arm through his.

"Shall we adjourn to a more comfortable setting?" he asked Rosa before he turned to Johnson. "You should take Miss Sarah's arm, as she's without a partner."

It was hard to miss the murderous glare Johnson shot him, but he led Rosa to the next room with a smile on his face.

"What do you think you are doing?" she hissed almost inaudibly.

"Taking you into the parlor."

"You know that's not what I meant. I wanted to talk to Johnson to see if I could learn anything of the rumors where my brother is concerned."

"If you learned nothing over dinner, what do you expect to learn now? I could call him out for the way he stared at you through dinner. It was insulting and demeaning."

Lips pursed together, she took in an irritated breath then puffed it out hard. "You'll do no such thing. You'd be arrested."

"Who's to arrest me when I've killed the man?"

She yanked her arm from his. He pulled it back and gripped her hand firmly enough that the next tug did nothing but bring them closer. "Now, now, Rosa. You wouldn't want to make a scene."

"You were a perfect gentleman earlier. What in the name of Hades happened?"

"I came to my senses when I saw exactly how you planned to get information from Johnson. Flirting with danger is a bad idea, especially with a man like him. He's unpredictable, and I don't trust him."

"I'm not new at this." She actually seemed insulted.

"You seem to think you have a choice in the matter. I've agreed to go back to London, but if I have to stay to protect you from your own folly, all so you can solve your brother's problems, I will stay." He walked her around to the bench in front of the Broadwood. "Now that we've arrived in the parlor, why don't you play us a tune?"

"You go too far, to assume I'd play for a crowd."

"Come now, it's an intimate crowd, surely a tune can be conjured from memory."

"Why are you treating me like I'm no more than your whore?" Her voice was low enough that no one else heard what she said to him.

"Funny. Considering the way you're flaunting yourself to Johnson. I'm not your consort by any means, I'm your past lover. I might as well play the part of someone jilted by the object of his affections. It's a plan I far prefer over yours."

"I see why the majority of my acquaintances call you a volatile cad."

It was his turn to chuckle. She had no idea what he was like to those around him. Perhaps it was time to show her the type of man he could be when he was surrounded by buffoons and people he disliked.

"Do tell us what joke we've missed out on, Thaddeus." The query came from his brother.

He turned away from Rosa and smiled at the crowd gathering around the piano. "I've asked Rosa to play for us, but she's too

142

shy. Imagine that, too shy to perform for such an intimate group."

"Do play for us, my dear," Nathan insisted.

Teddy's head jerked around to the endearment falling from his brother's lips, giving him a scowl swifter, perhaps even deadlier, than any rapier. It wasn't hard to play the jealous lover when he didn't want any of the men in here entertaining ideas of Rosa as their mistress.

"I couldn't," she demurred. "Dinner was such an extravagant affair, and the wine flowed so freely that I'm afraid I'd accomplish no more than making a fool of myself."

Teddy leaned in close to her, his lips but a hairbreadth from her ear. "You drank not a drop, I watched you through every course of that meal. Play for the crowd, *my dear.*"

Her lips pursed again. With a pretty curtsy, she reluctantly took her seat at the bench.

"Brava, darling, taking on a dare from Teddy." Creve and his loud mouth couldn't seem to stop there, either. "Perhaps she needs something to fill that pretty mouth of hers, de Burgh."

The woman on Creve's arm tittered at the suggestion. "And what of me, my lord?"

"I've got plenty of ideas for you, dove."

Teddy turned away as Creve pressed his hand under the woman's gown to grope at her breast. His mistress had enough sense to push him away with another obnoxious snigger. "You should save that for later."

A footman came around with fresh glasses of champagne. When Nathan handed Teddy a glass for Rosa, he handed it off to Johnson, who stood on her other side. "Go take a seat, Johnson. I'm sure I can manage the bench for her."

"Rosie, are you all right with this devil hovering over you?"

"I'm fine, Johnson, though I feel I must apologize for his brash rudeness."

Johnson seemed to take that for some grand joke if that ruckus he considered laughter was anything to go by. Finally, he moved away from her and took his seat next to the Cyprian who'd unsuccessfully tried to engage Teddy in conversation over supper.

"What will you play for us?"

"Hmm ... I'm not sure." Her finger tapped at her lip thoughtfully. "Maybe a funeral march to show my appreciation of your effervescent presence tonight."

He ignored the rib and sat next to her on the bench. He ran his hand over the expanse of skin between her shoulder blades. She stilled next to him as he lowered his nose in her curls and inhaled her scent of lilacs.

"Stop that this instant."

"What if I said I couldn't help myself?" It was said softly enough to be for her ears alone. Pulling back from the warmth of her smaller body, he felt the lithe path of her upper arm all the way to her exposed nape. He knew he shouldn't press for more, but couldn't help himself with Johnson watching his every move. Teddy would leave no doubt that the blighter didn't have a chance in hell with Rosa. He firmly caressed her nape, then covered the jewels of her choker possessively before dropping his hand away and smiling darkly at Johnson.

Tucking his hands behind his back so he didn't take any more public liberties, he decided he might as well ask for exactly what he wanted. "Lift your skirts so I can see your ankles working the pedals."

She turned her head enough that their noses were level, almost touching. "I think not." The enunciation of her words were clipped, angered. Could it be that he evoked some emotion in her when he demanded she do his bidding? What would happen if he continued down this path? There was one way to find out.

He lifted her skirts for her.

Hand whipping out, she squeezed his wrist to stop any further liberties. "What do you think you're doing?"

"Showing Johnson what he can never have."

She elbowed him hard in the ribs, making him grunt. The whole while he was aware that Johnson had taken a step closer to see what transpired between Teddy and Rosa. "Leave me be, de

Burgh. If your intention is to anger me, you've accomplished it."

He took a deep breath. "Play something, Rosa. The guests are waiting and looking far too interested in our interaction."

"It's your own doing." She whipped a bit violently around on the seat and set her fingers to something quick and angry. He smiled before he turned to his brother and the other guests.

"She plays so flawlessly. So full of life. Just listen to the pure passion of the notes her fingers sing as she hits the keys. Herr von Beethoven would approve of your rendition," Teddy said.

"You mock me, de Burgh. I'd like to see you do better." She turned her head to the side when she addressed him, as though she were looking directly at him. There would be hell to pay for his actions, but he didn't care so long as Johnson got the picture and left her alone.

"Never a better challenge have I heard," Creve commented. "Thaddeus, you must show us your best. I'd almost demand it if it weren't for the dark scowl shading your face with such a ghastly impression of distaste."

"Yes, show us your facility with the musical language," Daniel suggested. "I'd bet on the pretty one to be sure."

"A grand plan." The snidely intoned comment came from Johnson's direction. Teddy didn't spare him a glance.

Spreading one hand over his chest in contemplation and to straighten his vest, he replied, "And steal this darling's thunder, I think not. She is deserving of all the praise and accolades you can bestow upon her. I'll not match her in skill on the piano, perhaps another instrument, but this is her obviously her first instrument, which I cannot compete with. You would set me to a losing bet, Creve."

"I think you've turned coward." Johnson must have felt the need to prove himself to Rosa. Why else would he continue on with his taunting remarks?

Teddy sneered at the man. "You've no chance with her, even if this was the Underworld and you were Hades himself. Tuck in your tail or I'll call you out, then we'll see who the true coward is."

The tune Rosa had expertly played for not more than a handful of minutes stopped. It was as though Teddy's words had sucked any joy or merriment out of the room.

"Enough." Rosa came around the bench and walked forward, her hands reaching out for anyone in her path. Johnson was there to catch her. His temper flared quickly and it was a struggle for Teddy to tamp it down and hold his stance instead of charging forward like a bull in rage.

"Vane," Rosa said. "I'm sad to admit that it's been a long day. I'm feeling rather tired and my head aches something fierce from the repressive behavior of some of your guests."

Nathan stepped forward without missing a beat. "My dear, it was a pleasure to hear you play. I hope to hear you again and soon."

Teddy expected her to curtsy and retreat alone. Instead she kissed Nathan's cheeks in a decidedly French style—an all too familiar style—and called for her brother. "Please bring me to my room, Daniel."

Teddy regretted every one of his actions immediately, but what else could he have done when Johnson stared after her as though she were the only bit of dessert after a feast.

Rosa had wormed her way into his heart so thoroughly that he'd allowed jealousy to get the better of him, despite knowing what had to be done tonight. The problem, though he didn't really see it as a problem, was that she was *his*. And had he not been in a room full of people, too observant already of his insensitive behavior toward Rosa, he'd have called after her. He'd have apologized. He'd have done more than stare after the swish of her skirt as she left the parlor because she wanted nothing more than to escape him.

Chapter Thirteen

My thoughts go out to you, now and then joyfully then sadly, waiting to learn whether or not fate will hear us.
– Ludwig van Beethoven

HOW HAD TONIGHT GONE SO terribly wrong? It hadn't helped that Johnson acted his usual self, even with Daniel present. Tonight was not what she'd expected.

Rosa shut her bedroom door, closing off the rest of the world behind her. "Mary?"

When no answer came, she threw her cashmere shawl across the room, not caring where it landed. It did nothing to calm her fury.

And then there was the focus of her rage: Teddy. Teddy, who up until now was always the perfect gentleman with her. What had he thought to accomplish with his crude, unnecessary actions in front of the duke's guests?

Reaching up and unclasping her sapphire-jeweled choker, she flung that across the room, too. Kicking off her slippers as she plucked out pins from her hair, she stormed through her room, giving a smarting to her hip when she bumped into the bedframe. She pressed her hand to the throb that radiated from her hip and walked to the bed, throwing herself down on the soft down mattress. She closed her eyes and counted to ten.

When ten came and she still wanted to throw something, she counted to one hundred.

And then she wanted to cry. But she didn't. Instead, she sat up and released the ties at the back of her dress to pull it off. Untying the underskirts and hoops, she shimmied out of the extra material, letting it fall to the floor in a crumpled heap. She didn't bother to remove her stays and undergarments. She just wanted to crawl under her multitude of blankets and hide from the world. She just wanted to forget everything about her trip here, about the duke, her brother, her life. She just wanted to forget the evening. And most of all, she wanted to forget *Teddy*.

"ROSIE ... WAKE UP, SWEET VIXEN. You were a dreadful tease over dinner. I couldn't get here soon enough."

A hand slid over her stomach to cup her breast on top of the sheet that covered her. Rosa pushed the offending hand away as she threw off the remnants of what had been a sound sleep. "Get off of me, you oaf."

The intruder leaned over her, his breath smelling like he'd drunk a whole tankard of whisky. He probably had.

"You mean to tell me you didn't ready yourself for bed to await me? I made it very clear I'd come to you tonight if you kept teasing me like you were." His words were a little slurred. But there was no way he didn't know what he was about.

"And I told you we wouldn't suit. How many other ways do I need to say it!" Her shove against his chest was unsuccessful. "Get off!"

"Not till I've had my fill of you." He tugged at the sleeve of her chemise, ripping it clean off her shoulder and exposing her breasts to the chill night air. "Well, now, those are some pretty bubbies you've got."

She pressed harder with her fists at his chest, getting in a good punch before he gathered her hands and held them in a tight grip above her head. Leaning down, he sucked her nipple into his mouth with so much force she screamed and tried to buck him off her with stronger force.

"Stop, Johnson." She twisted enough that her elbow met the side of his head, then he was pressing her hands above her head again, trapping her. "You'll regret your actions come morning when your mind is clear of the whisky. Let me go." There was no mistaking the fear in her trembling voice, and she knew fear made a man like Johnson hotter for his victory.

"I told you. You'd make me try harder to get you if you kept refusing me."

"Be reasonable," she pleaded.

"I am reasonable. Now spread your legs. I want to see if that slit of yours is as pretty as I think it is."

She locked her ankles and squeezed her thighs together with as much might as she could. "You won't like it if I do it for you," he said, his breath hot against her face. "I want you to like this. You'll like it like you liked it with Michael, just spread your legs for me."

"No!" She bucked up against him, hoping to throw him off. She twisted and tried to roll; nothing seemed to remove his weight. "Get off or I'll scream."

"I don't think so," came his vile voice before he shoved a hank of material in her mouth. "Won't matter anyway; what's Vane going to do for a whore? You were asking for it, have been all evening. You invited me up here is what I'll say. And after your actions at dinner, do you honestly think they'll believe you?"

She did scream then, as loud as she could but to no avail when the sound was muffled with the dry cloth. Her screams turned into silent sobs.

When he released one of her hands, she reached to her right and tried to grab for something. Anything. A silver candlestick holder fell from her fingers and rang loudly as it hit the floor. She cried harder, tears seeping down her face as he grasped her free wrist so tight it forced her to drop the book she'd gotten her fingers around.

"Naughty minx. Now I'll have to tie your hands."

Yanking hard, she tried to tug her hands from his, but he held fast and cinched her hands so tightly with a strip of material that she thought the blood might stop flowing to her fingers. Next, he wrapped the material around the bedpost assuring them both she was helpless to defend herself.

"There. Now you won't be going anywhere. I'd take the stocking from your mouth but I don't trust you not to call out. We didn't have to do it this way," he said, licking the tears on her cheek and temple like the cur he was.

She jerked her head away from him, then thought better and smacked the side of her head against his jaw. It stunned her and her assailant. The pain quickly waned, but only long enough for him to cuff her across the face with his open palm. Her lip split painfully at the side, warm liquid dribbling down over her chin and jaw.

"Now look what you've gone and made me do, you're bleeding. Stop fighting me, Rosie. I'll be good to you, you'll see."

Sliding down the length of her body, he wrenched her thighs apart. She managed a good solid kick to his knee and tugged against the material binding her hands to the bed. He got his torso between her legs and pressed heavily against her.

Leaning over her, he bit the skin on her thigh through her pantalets. Jerking away from him had her opening her legs wider to the dog and he started to tear at the material. When he was unsuccessful, his hand cupped her mound through the linen. Then he was pressing his nose there, smelling at her like she was an animal in heat.

Her arms strained against the material holding her hands above her head, and her fingers were growing numb. Wriggling her foot, she tried to slide her leg out from under his, but she was stuck beneath his weight. Pins and needles stretched down her forearms above her head. She felt numb all around and gave up her fight. Perhaps if he thought she was cooperating he'd let up. And if she had enough strength left in her, maybe she could give him a solid kick.

"Remove yourself, Johnson." The boom of her rescuer's voice had a fresh torrent of tears running down the side of her face.

"Get out of here, de Burgh. This is none of your concern."

Johnson's grip on her open thighs tightened before he suddenly lurched off her. Rosa locked her thighs together, and pushed herself up toward the head of the bed so she wasn't lying there helplessly. Her arms were tied in such a position that she was forced to huddle in an uncomfortable ball, but she put herself in a better position to kick out at Johnson if he renewed his attack.

"Come on then, you fool, show me how much of a man you think you are." The threat came from Teddy.

Rosa flinched when she heard a sharp smack of flesh on flesh and a resounding crack. *Please let it not be Teddy,* her mind chanted.

"You broke my bloody nose, you weasel," cried Johnson and Rosa breathed a small sigh of relief.

"I'm going to break a lot more if you don't get the hell out of my house."

"She wants me here."

She shook her head furiously. She didn't want him, she only wanted to help her brother.

"You don't honestly expect me to believe she welcomed your advances?"

"Why the hell wouldn't she? You saw her over dinner. Jesus, de Burgh, you didn't have to break my damn nose." Johnson sniffled; it was a gurgling, bloody sound. "You'll pay for this."

"This is your last warning, Johnson. Leave." Teddy's voice was low and the threat very real.

"I don't need any warning from you."

She felt the weight of someone coming up on the bed before

another sound of fists meeting flesh filled the room. A chair top-pled over and she heard the sound of glass—probably her vanity mirror—crashing on the wood floor as the men made their way around the room.

TEDDY WAS GOING TO KILL Johnson. The bastard. What in hell did the man think he was doing, taking advantage of his woman? What in hell did he think he was doing forcing a wom-an to do anything? Johnson threw a chair between them, flicked the blood off his cheek and mouth with a swipe of his hand, and glanced around the room for a weapon. At least that was what Teddy thought he searched for. And he didn't trust Johnson long enough to take stock of Rosa, so he dropped his fists to his side and waited to see what the blackguard would do next.

"I've done nothing to warrant such rash behavior from you." Johnson pressed tenderly at his swollen cheek. "Bloody hell, de Burgh, you've buggered up my face good."

"If you don't leave I will see you with pistols at dawn. I'm sure my brother will second me."

"You can't call a challenge, the magistrate would come down on us."

"I can and I will. You have about one minute. And if I ever see your face again, the challenge will stand and satisfaction will not be met until you are mortally wounded. You will leave this house without so much as a backward glance, and you'll never return."

"This is the ducal home, de Burgh. Last I remember, *you* were not the duke."

Teddy took a deep breath. Johnson was too deep in his cups this evening to realize how deep the grave he dug truly was.

The door to the bedchamber smashed against the wall a sec-ond time.

"The duke is now voicing his opinion," Nathan said. "I never want to set eyes on your swinish face again. Leave my home before I call the challenge myself."

The fight finally left Johnson's shoulders, he relaxed and came out from behind the chair he'd used to stop Teddy's advances.

When Johnson left the room, Thaddeus relaxed his fists and went directly to Rosa.

"Do you need anything, Teddy?" his brother asked.

He didn't even look at his brother as he answered, "Privacy, please."

Nathan left without a word, shutting the door behind him.

"Rosa. Sweetheart, I should have come sooner." He spoke as calmly as he could when the sight of her bleeding, swollen lip, and bruised cheek rekindled his anger toward Johnson.

"I'm going to remove the cloth from your mouth now. Try not to be frightened when I touch you."

She was shaking beneath him as he pulled the cloth from her mouth and loosened the rope that bound her hands to the bed. Angry red welts and burn marks from the material marred her skin.

The moment the material fell, she flung herself at him, her arms going around his shoulders, her face burrowing into his neck. He caressed her back, hoping the action soothed her. When she pulled away, he carefully examined her face and lip. The cut wasn't too deep, but had bled quite a bit.

He reached into the pocket of his vest and pressed a fresh handkerchief into her hands. "For your lip. I don't want to hurt you."

"Thank you." How civil of her. She must be frightened out of her wits.

"I'm sorry I wasn't here sooner."

She nodded and scooted slowly over to the edge of the bed. "Could you—" She motioned with her hand, as though not sure what she wanted to ask for.

"I have your robe." He wrapped it around her shoulders, then gently wiped the tears that had been crushed against her cheeks. "Tell me where you're hurt."

"He bit my leg, but I think mostly it's my head and wrists that hurt."

"Let me bring you to the bathing chamber, Rosa. If you prefer your maid, I can rouse her from the servants' quarters."

"No. I don't want Mary to see me like this. I don't want you to either, but it's too late for that."

"I have a plunge bath in my chamber, do you mind if I carry you there?"

She nodded and gingerly touched her jaw where a bruise was blossoming in an ugly purple stain on the lower portion of her face. "I think I need something cold for my face. It's throbbing, and my head is pounding something fierce."

He slid one arm under her legs, another behind her back, and lifted her slight frame into his arms and held her tight against his chest. "Everyone went to bed an hour ago, so no one will see us. You can stay in my room tonight, I will take another guest room."

"I don't want to be alone."

"Then I won't leave your side."

He left her room without meeting anyone in the hallway and quickly made his way to his chamber. He didn't set her down until he reached his bathing room.

"You won't leave me, will you?" Her voice wavered.

Lighting all the candles he had, he could see just how much of a mark Johnson had left.

"Let me retrieve a towel. I just need to get some supplies to clean you up."

Pouring cold water into a bowl, he set a linen cloth in it, then took another cloth and held it under the spray of hot water in the plunge bath. Kneeling on the floor in front of her he lifted her hands. Her wrists were spotted with angry red dots and lines of purple. "You'll have bruising around your wrists. But they're not cut. Are they bothering you?"

She nodded.

"I'm sorry I wasn't there sooner. I had intended to come to you earlier, to apologize. I should have."

Slipping one hand free from his hold, she touched his face with her fingertips. "Johnson would have found a way to do this another time. I'm thankful you were there to save me tonight."

"I'll make sure he knows he's never to go near you again. Not without dire consequences for him."

"Teddy," she all but sighed, leaning her forehead against his. "Perhaps you *are* my knight in shining armor."

"No knight, my lady." He smiled under her fingertips, loving how she traced her fingers over the side of his cheek, then back down to his lips as though she liked how his smile felt. "But perhaps a little in love with you."

She jerked her fingers away and took in a shaky breath. At least she kept her forehead pressed to his. Lifting the folded cloth in his hands, he pressed it to her swollen lip. She flinched and hissed in a breath. "I'm sorry," he said.

"Don't be. It'll heal in time."

"On the outside, but what about the inside?" Wiping away the blood from her chin, he pulled the cloth away, refolding it to use a clean part.

"I'm made of pretty stern stuff."

"You were very nearly raped. As much as it pains me to remind you of that, I think I must. You shouldn't have to be made of *stern stuff*, to be all right after what you went through."

"I'm scared."

"I know. And I'll be here for you."

Picking up her hand, he placed it against the cloth he held to her lip. "Hold this while I run you a bath."

When he stood up and moved away from her side, her hand slid along the length of his arm and over his hand, their fingers twining briefly. She followed him and wrapped her arms around his shoulders, again, clasping him tight to her chest. He returned the embrace, careful not to squeeze her too hard as he held her close and placed his chin atop her head.

She said nothing, just held him. So he did the same, smoothing his hands down the length of her spine through the robe. As much as he wanted to stay here and hold her like this and give her all the comfort she needed, he needed to take stock of the rest of her injuries. "Let me run your bath. It's the least I can do. Do you want me to call in your maid to help you undress and bathe?"

Rosa's head shook. "Please stay with me."

"Rosa, are you sure?"

"Yes. I don't want to be alone, and I don't want to see anyone else." She lowered her arms. "If you don't mind."

"I'll stay." He walked over to the basin he'd filled with cold water, picked up another cloth, dipped and wrung it out, and put it in Rosa's hands. At the questioning tilt of her head, he said, "To stop the swelling. Press it to your face and hopefully it'll bring down the bump forming on your lip."

"Thank you." She sat down, holding the cold cloth to her face.

Putting the stopper in the tub, he ran the water to a warm enough temperature that it wouldn't chill too quickly.

"I never imagined you to be a pugilist."

"I'm not, but growing up with Nathan ... He made sure I could fight."

"Is that an endearing trait in an older brother?"

"Adolescent boys can be a rowdy lot. If you stand up for yourself, you usually aren't picked on."

"The logic of men. I fear I may never truly understand certain aspects of your inclination toward violence."

His head jerked up. "I'm not a violent man, Rosa. That I can promise wholeheartedly."

"I didn't mean it that way." Her eyes closed and she inhaled deeply. "I'm sorry."

"No apology needed, love."

Lowering the cloth she held to her face and putting it on the bench beside her, she shrugged out of her robe and struggled with the strings on the back of her corset. Her wrists must have hurt too much to work out the knots.

He walked over to her, letting the bath fill. "Here, let me."

Kneeling, he slid his hands from her waist to the double-looped strings. Pulling them free, he loosened the binding enough that he could unhook the busk at the front, since he wasn't sure she could.

She took in a deep breath as the last hook released and the contraption slid off her body. Folding the corset in half, he placed it on the bench beside her. With a glance over his shoulder he checked the level of the bath. It wasn't even half filled. Turning back to her, he asked, "Might I see your thigh, where he bit you? I just want to make sure the skin isn't broken. It'll hurt to bathe if it is."

Standing up, she lifted the torn chemise over her head and tossed it to the floor, then released the ties holding her pantalets so she could step out of them.

"I won't hurt you. Trust me."

"I do. I'm nervous for some odd reason."

She sat down, bringing his eyes level to her breasts. There were red splotches and speckles of blood marring the perfect whiteness of her skin. She must hurt everywhere, for she had put up a good fight. The sight made him want to break Johnson's nose again. Maybe break something more meaningful: his arms, legs, something that would take a hell of a lot longer to heal than his nose.

His nostrils flared, helping him take a deep, somewhat silent breath as he tempered the anger rising in him. Rosa reached out and cupped his jaw with her hand. "You can't change anything. There's no sense in being angry. You saved me from any real harm."

"You make it seem as though nothing happened."

"I'll not forget his actions anytime soon. I believe I will remember them long past the fading of any bruising he left behind."

He settled his hands on her bare knees.

"I don't fear you, Teddy." She opened her legs, revealing a circular bite mark on her inner thigh.

He hissed in a breath. "How much does it hurt?" At least the skin wasn't broken, but it wasn't going to be comfortable for her to move around for the next little while.

"My face and lip hurt more." She stood, leaving his eyes level with the vee of her body. He came quickly to his feet.

"Into the bath with you," he said.

She nodded and gave him her hand.

He took it without hesitation and helped her into the bathtub. "Let me guide your foot in, I don't want you tripping, it's a pretty deep plunge." He did just that, then she climbed in on her own and settled into the water. He let it run for another minute before turning the taps off. "Can I leave you a moment to retrieve some clothes for you? I'll lock the door on my way out. Johnson has been banished from the house and will be long gone by now."

"Yes." She closed her eyes as she leaned her head against the porcelain lip behind her.

Chapter Fourteen

The painter turns a poem into a painting;
the musician sets a picture to music.
– Robert Schumann

THE DOOR TO THE BATHING room clicked shut. Raising her hands to her face, she took stock of the damage to her body. Her face hurt the most; the lip had to be swollen to twice its size and throbbed as much as her aching head. The lip had split on the bottom, toward the middle. Her cheek was tender, but would heal more quickly. Her wrists were starting to hurt.

Never had a man treated her so vilely. She knew some had strange proclivities, but she had always had sound judgment when it came to someone's character when she'd chosen her patrons. While she'd always had an unpleasant feeling when around Johnson—which she thought stemmed from guilt, as he'd lost a dear friend when Michael died—she had never expected *this*. Now she knew what her intuition had tried to warn her of. It seemed that Johnson's hatred toward her had twisted him into a man she didn't recognize.

Thank God Teddy had arrived in time.

The worst damage done had been to her nerves. Would she have a breakdown later—once the healing started, once the shock wore off? She couldn't seem to stop the shake of her hands as she reached around the tub in search of soap. A small hand towel toppled over into the water, as did the soap set atop it. She fished out the lavender soap and wrung out the cloth to hang it over the edge again.

A soft knock came at the door.

"Teddy?"

"Yes. Do you want my help with anything?"

"I'm sure the damage looks worse than it really is."

A chill raced across her shoulders as he opened the door and shut it quickly behind him.

"Sorry about the draft." His voice was a ways off; he didn't come closer. She bet he stood with his back to the door waiting for an invitation to sit, or to help her. She didn't need help, but his uneasiness being in her company somehow made her feel out of sorts.

"Will you help me with my hair? The braid came loose, and I'm afraid my fingers don't seem to work so well at the moment."

He was at her side in seconds, his fingers combing the hair back from her forehead. "I cannot braid, but I will pull it out of the water and pin it up for you."

She nodded her consent. He dipped his hand behind her back and pulled her hair from the water, squeezing it out before letting it fall over the lip of the tub. After he gathered it in his hands, she felt the familiar slide of bristles through her hair. Finished brushing out the knots, he pulled up thick strands of her hair and pinned them carefully in place in a low chignon. His motions were relaxing, soothing.

Her eyes grew heavy with fatigue. The throbbing over her face and wrists ebbed the longer the warmth of the water infused her body.

"My brother sent for a doctor."

She pulled her knees up to her chest and wrapped her arms

around her shins. "I don't think I need one. I'm glad I can't say the same for Johnson."

"He'll have to find one in London. He does not have a residence in Maidstone, and he is not welcome to stay at any of the local inns. He'll never be welcome in mine or Nathan's company again." She did not miss the threatening undertone in his voice. Nor did she blame him for such a passionate reaction. And admittedly her heart beat a little faster every time he rose to her defense.

"I brought up some concoction from the kitchen. It will help heal the bruising. It smells rather unpleasant, but it will soothe any stiffness. I also retrieved some clothes for you."

"Thank you." With the water cooling, she knew she couldn't stay in the bath all night, so she stood. "Is there a towel or a bathing robe?"

"Here." The soft linen towel was draped over her back and wrapped around the front of her. "I have a fresh robe for when you're dry."

She nodded, her teeth chattering at bit. She fumbled with the cloth, her hands still shaking, and her wrists aching.

After Teddy pulled the stopper to let the tub drain, he reached for the towel and dried her with impersonal strokes, rubbing the material over her shivering form to collect the last of the water. When she was mostly dry, he helped her into a robe, then he swept her legs out from under her and lifted her in his arms. "I'm taking you into the bedroom. I built up a fire for you."

She wanted to kiss him, but her lip hurt too much, so she settled for resting her forehead against the side of his jaw. "Will you take me back to London tomorrow? I can't stay here. Not after tonight."

"I'd take you to the ends of the world if you asked." He settled her down on a plush velvet sofa. "Where do you want to go once in London?"

"I don't know."

She wanted to stay with Teddy, but found she couldn't ask, for she wasn't sure if that invitation was still open. It seemed too intrusive to ask. If he did offer, she knew she wouldn't refuse him. She felt safe in his company. What woman wouldn't want such devotion, such compassion from a man?

"Will you reconsider my offer, Rosa? Will you stay on with me in London, let us see how our relationship forms?"

Her breath caught in her throat. And she nodded quickly. "Yes. At least for a short while. Until I don't mind being alone."

He gave a noisy sigh. "There won't be a day, Rosa, when I don't ask you to reconsider staying on with me. At least until we've better explored what lies between us. I know things change from here on out, in light of this evening's events. Just know that you have my eternal patience as you take time to heal, both inside and out."

"Thank you, Teddy."

His hands clasped around her face gently, his thumbs massaging into the temples as he kissed her forehead. "We will leave at first light tomorrow. It's one in the morning now, so we need to get this stinky sludge on you and get you to bed. Would you like to put it on or shall I?"

"I don't want to make any more of a mess than necessary. Or miss any spots. Please put it on for me."

He stood, she presumed to retrieve the salve. "If you're uncomfortable for even a moment, I need you to tell me."

"I will."

"Now put your leg to the side so I can see the marking on your inner thigh."

She bent her knee, and pressed it to the sofa, opening her legs to his scrutiny. His breathing grew harsher, and she knew it wasn't any form of arousal on seeing her exposed. It was anger.

When he took the stopper out of the remedy, she scrunched up her nose at the burning scent. "It does have a terrible smell."

She flinched and hissed in a breath when the cold cream was slathered over her leg.

"Sorry, I should have warmed it in my hand first."

"It's all right. Just a bit of a shock. I think there is a healthy dose of camphor in there. Actually, it smells like the stuff you put on horses when they've strained a muscle."

"I believe it is." Next, he massaged the salve into her wrists; it was warm this time. "Unrelated to the topic at hand, but I wonder, would you object to going to the music hall for a rehearsal tomorrow? It will be a good distraction for you. And I have some work I need to do there."

"Yes ... I mean no, I wouldn't object. I'd like to go very much." Really, she wasn't sure she wanted to be alone. Hissing in another breath, she reassessed her injuries. They hurt very much; at least her thigh did where Teddy had massaged the bite mark.

"My hands are covered in this grease. If you reach your hand straight out, you'll feel the handkerchief in my vest pocket." She did and pressed it into his hands.

"It smells dreadful, but it'll heal you up nice and quick. My mother used to put it on my brother and me after we got into a fight."

"I thought you said you weren't a fighter?"

"I'm not, but brothers will be brothers."

She gave a half smile for his attempt at humor and promptly frowned when her lip pulled and a little stream of warmth trickled down her chin. Teddy was on his feet the next instant, retrieving something from somewhere. A cold cloth was in her hand and placed gently on her face.

"I'll try not to make you smile." He cleared his throat. "I had the housekeeper wake your maid to have your bags packed. I didn't know you'd accept my offer, but I figured you'd want to leave here at first light."

"You've done so much for me tonight, Teddy. I don't know how to thank you."

"You needn't thank me. I've done no more than any man in my position would have done."

She shook her head. How wrong he was. "You've done quite a deal more than that."

"No more than you deserved, Rosa."

But she didn't deserve him.

"Teddy?"

"What is it?" He took her hands in his.

"Will you stay with me for the night?"

"I believe that is why you are in my suite."

"No, I mean, will you just ..." She might as well just spit out the words. "Will you hold me in your arms tonight?"

"You needn't ask." He kissed her between her brows, then to the top of her head. He lingered, inhaling her scent. "Your clothes are just behind you, draped over the edge of the sofa. I'll help you dress for bed if you can't do the ties yourself."

Reaching behind her, she found the pantalets and chemise. No corset in the stack of soft linens. She could dress herself, but was reluctant to do so.

She wore his warm dressing robe; it smelled faintly of Teddy. The comforting scents of lavender, bayberry, and Teddy were already wrapped around her.

"Are they not to your liking?" he asked when he turned back to her and she hadn't moved. "I can retrieve something else."

"No, it's not that, the bedclothes are fine." She stood and placed them on the sofa. He said nothing, so she couldn't walk in his direction. She did not know her way about his room, and it proved more than an inconvenience right now.

She wanted to be in his arms, she wanted to have another memory of tonight to replace the last horrid one. Nerves had her hands twisting into the robe's plush sleeves, which hung well below her fingertips.

"Teddy, say something so I can follow your voice."

"You've a most peculiar expression on your face."

Her stomach was full of butterflies as she walked toward his voice. "What kind of expression?"

"As though you've got something planned, something perhaps you shouldn't do."

"What is it you think I shouldn't do?" She took another step, knowing she was getting closer to him.

"It's the same expression, or rather, determination you cloaked yourself with when you joined me for dinner the first night you stayed with me in London." He audibly swallowed. "Rosa, what are you doing?"

Untying the sash of the robe, she let it fall open. "Are you anxious to be rid of me now?"

She heard the hitch in his breath.

"Give me another memory. Give me something beautiful tonight, Teddy." She shrugged the robe off her shoulders. The silk lining allowed it to slide from her body like a lover's caress. The cool air made the tips of her breasts peak before the material even had a chance to pool at her feet.

When he said nothing, she wondered if she had been too bold. Lifting her chin, she took in steady breaths and waited for him to say or do something.

"You should reconsider your offer," he finally said, closer than he had been previously.

She reached out her hands to find the buttons of his shirt. Her fingers trembled but she found that if she took her time, she could push the buttons through the holes. There was no objection as the first one popped free. Or the second. Or the third.

"I don't want to hurt you, Rosa."

"You won't. I trust you." The last button came free beneath her fingers.

"I can deny you nothing, even when I think it's a bad idea."

Hands pressing against the heated flesh of his chest, she explored the contours of his body. "How is it you stay in such fine shape when you lock yourself in the music room most days?"

"I ride."

She raised a brow.

"Horses, I ride horses. And I find occasion to fence with Nathan."

Reaching higher, she pushed the shirt from his shoulders, her breasts feathering over his torso. She followed the material down his arms until the cambric fell to the floor.

He made no move to touch her, or to take off his trousers. She didn't mind doing this slowly.

"Won't you at least touch me?"

"I'm afraid to."

"I need your touch. I'm cold, Teddy. Warm me."

"Let me carry you to the bed."

Next thing she knew she was off her feet again and in his arms as he picked her up and laid her on the bed. She sat up to push the counterpane out of the way. A few moments later, the bed dipped as he sat on the edge. She crawled over to him, pressed her breasts to his back, and laid the unmarred side of her face against his shoulder. He felt so much warmer than she. Wrapping her arms around him, she placed both her hands over his heart. Once his shoes fell to the floor, his hands encircled hers.

"Are you sure you want to do this?" he asked.

"Yes."

"If you need me to stop, say so at any time and I will."

"I won't ask you to stop."

His hands dropped away, and she was forced to release him as he stood. "Have to remove my trousers." There was a teasing quality to his voice that lightened her heart.

Reaching out she explored the length of his back before he could turn to her. Then she trailed her hands lower to cover his buttocks at the same time his trousers were removed. The flesh flexed beneath her hands.

"What is it you're doing?" he asked, amused.

"Exploring."

She laid her head over the curve of his backside. She'd have kissed it, to see what it felt like under her lips, but that would have to wait for another day. Hand reaching round to his front, she cupped the sac beneath his rigid penis. The skin tightened under her caress, pulling the cods taut.

He turned around. She'd have taken that fine piece of flesh in her mouth, but had to settle for rubbing her face along it since she knew her lip would split open again. Rising to her knees, she squeezed his prick between her breasts.

"Tell me what you want," she said. She wanted to please him, to forget everything about tonight except for the here and now. When he didn't respond, she said, "Teddy ... I want something beautiful and meaningful. Something to take away all the wrongs of tonight."

One of his knees tipped the mattress beneath her. She scooted up to the head of the bed hoping he'd not need more coaxing now that she'd gotten him this far.

Pulling a pillow under her head, she lay on her side and patted the empty space beside her. Teddy didn't hesitate to settle in close to her. His sex brushed over her belly, his hand rubbing over her hip and waist with gentle strokes.

"I'm afraid to touch you anywhere, dreading that I'll hurt you more."

"I'm not so delicate as that. Touch me where you want, Teddy. I want your touch so badly."

Kissing her forehead—it seemed to be one of the few places he could touch her without jarring her damaged face—his hand slipped lower to cup her buttocks and bring her closer. She threw one leg over his hip and tilted her pelvis toward his, the jut of his cock pressed against her entrance.

"Are you sure?" he asked again.

"Yes," she whispered against his lips. Then his shaft was buried deep inside her.

Their lovemaking was slow, gentle, a sweet exploration of each other. And Teddy gave her another memory of that night. One she knew she'd cherish for the rest of her days.

THE FIRST AWARENESS SHE HAD was of Teddy's legs tangled with hers. One arm was wrapped around her middle and tucked under her breast. Not ready to get out of bed just yet, she carefully turned in the circle of his arms until she faced Teddy.

"Good morning," he said.

"I didn't mean to wake you."

"You didn't. I just didn't want to get out of bed yet. But now that you're up, I should pack my bags."

"What time is it?"

"Five."

Rosa yawned, forgetting her lip and feeling the cut stretch. She clamped her hand over her mouth and let out a curse.

"How are you feeling this morning?" he asked. She could almost hear the frown in his question.

"Sore." She stretched her arms above her head, her breasts crushing against his chest in the process. "But the good soreness is mixed with the bad."

Lightly fisting her hands, she rotated her wrists. They felt bruised and a little stiff, but she thought maybe they'd feel better in another day. Maybe not healed, but good enough to play the piano again.

Teddy's hand caressed her rear and drew her closer yet again. The familiar ache to have him inside her made her wet and needy. His hand slipped into the crease of her rear, reaching forward to slick through her juices. He groaned on feeling just how wet she was.

"The last thing I want to do is get out of bed," he said.

She pressed her hands against his chest, rolled on top of him, and straddled his hips. His cock was stiff and pressed against her core, demanding entrance. "Can't we stay a little longer?"

"I don't imagine the house will be up for another few hours."

He lifted her hips where he wanted them and sheathed himself with a hard thrust that had them both groaning with the impact of their bodies coming together. The walls of her vagina flexed tightly around his cock. As their bodies moved, one of his thumbs rotated around her clitoris, bringing her quickly to her peak. Her hands found purchase against his chest as she rode him hard. It wasn't long before her climax hit.

Teddy sat up, his cock as far in her as it could possibly be, and he let her ride out the pleasure with his fingers scissoring the tender bud at her apex. The hot jets of his seed pulsed inside her as she rotated almost frantically around his hand. She didn't stop her movements until the pleasure became too much and her body could take no more.

She fell limp in his arms, unable to move an inch as she waited for her breathing to level out. She tucked her head into the crook of his shoulder and held him tight. With his fingers drawing lazy circles along the length of her back, Teddy held her in his arms without a word.

"We should leave before the household wakes," she finally said, still not willing to get off Teddy, for he was still in a state of arousal and her body though replete was unwilling to move.

"I made arrangements about an hour ago to have your packed things brought down to the carriage."

She wanted to smile, but had to put her hand to the side of her face on feeling the tenderness. She frowned instead.

Teddy grasped her hand where she held the side of her face. "We have to get moving if we're ever going to make it out of this bed."

"I know." Though she would much prefer to stay in bed with Teddy all day, she knew it wasn't possible.

He lifted her easily off him and set her on the edge of the bed. "I'll get a cloth so we can clean you up."

Arms outstretched, she fell back on the bed. The water was running in the next room so she waited for Teddy to come back, since she didn't know where to find anything in his room. She didn't even know where to start in looking for her clothes. The taps were turned off in the bathing chamber.

"I wish we could stay in bed for the remainder of the day," Teddy said. His hand pressed intimately between her legs with a warm cloth, and he wiped away the evidence of their lovemaking.

A soft knock came at the door. Rosa pulled the blankets around her.

"That'll be your maid with a change of clothes."

She relaxed a little, but still held the blanket close to cover her naked state. She heard Teddy open the door and he spoke too softly for her to hear what was said. The door closed a minute later.

"I can assist in dressing you, though I'm afraid your maid was not too impressed with the suggestion. It'll be such a hardship," he said with a hint of wickedness.

"Thank you." She threw off the covers and stood following the sound of his voice .

Dressed and ready to face what the day would bring, Rosa made her way down to the foyer on Teddy's arm.

"Rosa," her brother sounded shocked.

She touched the side of her face self-consciously.

Teddy released her. "I'll give you a moment alone. Montgomery, if you could bring her out to the carriage when you're ready."

"Of course," Daniel said as he pulled Rosa into the circle of his arms.

"I'll be fine," she whispered in his ear, feeling a fresh deluge of tears, which she refused to let fall.

"I wish I had been the one to see Johnson out."

Rosa pulled away from her brother's arms. "It's done. I honestly believe he was so intoxicated last night that he'll barely remember his actions."

"You're far too forgiving."

"No. I just want to think better of him. He was a decent young man, and I know it was long ago, but I always expected him to turn out better."

"It doesn't excuse his behavior."

"I know."

She also knew that she needed to put her almost-rape behind her, because she would not let that awful memory shape the person she was. She would not live in fear.

To distract her brother, she reached up to memorize his face. She remembered him being as fair-skinned as she, though his hair was lighter, after their father. There wasn't an ounce of the baby fat she remembered had rounded his features. His cheeks were sharp, his jaw well-formed and strong. Slight beard growth wrapped around his chin and above his upper lip, which were shaped the same as hers.

Moving higher, she felt the length of his straight nose and laughed a little to herself that her big, bad gambler brother who preferred the seedier side of life had never been in a fight that had broken his nose.

His brows were trimmed and prominent on his face, and slight lines crowed out from his eyes, as though he found reason to laugh often.

When she lowered her hands, she said, "Thank you. I normally ask, but it's been so long since I could see your face ..."

Daniel's hands wrapped around her upper arms. "There're no thanks necessary, Amy. We are siblings and despite our long separation, there's no reason we can't pick up right where we left off."

She smiled at that, stopping only when the skin stretched over her lip. Having her brother in her life again lifted her heart in ways she couldn't describe.

Daniel helped her into her jacket before they headed outside. "I'll visit you soon. I'd go with you, but Teddy made it clear that he planned to ensure your safe return to London."

"And I believe the doctor would be upset with you should you hurt yourself further."

"Don't worry about me. The duke insisted I stay on at the good doctor's advice. I promise not to do anything that might make the duke regret his invitation."

"I didn't expect you would."

A blast of cold air slapped her in the face as they descended the front stairs. Rosa wrapped her hands around her brother's arm, trying to warm herself.

Before she climbed into the carriage she turned to give her brother another hug good-bye. "We still need to discuss your financial troubles."

"Ah, Rosa. That you think of me so fondly warms my heart. My finances have been in order for at least half a year. In fact, I can pinpoint the day to Warwick's failing health." With her look of puzzlement, he added, "He always made sure we had little. Father's apothecary bills will decrease significantly now that the earl can't dictate the prices."

She opened her mouth to reply, though she wasn't sure what she could say. How had she not known about this?

"Don't worry yourself over it." He caressed the side of her face. "Father and I survived this long, haven't we? We Montgomerys are a resilient bunch and we're not so easy to get rid of."

"I'll still fret. I can't have found you only to have anything else happen to you."

"You won't, now," he said, helping her into the carriage. "Safe travels, sister. We'll see each other again before you know it."

Chapter Fifteen

Remain my true, my only treasure, my all
as I am yours.
– Ludwig van Beethoven

WITH NERVOUS FINGERS, SHE TUCKED the veil under the collar of her ermine pelisse just to be sure the lace wouldn't lift anywhere. It was amazing that Teddy had obtained access to the Grand Opera House. The opportunity to explore the old music hall would not be wasted. He'd already promised her a tour when his rehearsal finished.

It seemed strange to be in here without the constant din of conversation, and the presence of other patrons, with their whispering and gossip, their glances around to see whom arrived with whom and if they left with the same person. It was eerily quiet. So quiet, she practically tiptoed down the hall, not wanting to hear the click of her boots through the empty corridor.

She clasped Teddy's arm. He was down to shirtsleeves and his vest. He must consider this place like a home if he felt comfortable enough to remove his outer layers.

"They won't see me in the box will they?"

"And if they do?"

"I don't want to cause you any problems."

"You are no problem to me. If they want to make up their own stories as to your identity, I care not. They will see you, but you are veiled so they won't guess who you are—maybe some lady out with a gentleman not her husband, since you hide behind lace. Now stop fussing like a shy chit. You are far from one, my dear, and I think you well know it."

"I'm not playing coy. I don't want to be the start of some grand scandal with you at the heart of it."

"What? By having a woman secreted away in the royal box? Even if they thought you my mistress, instead of a lady, it's no bother to me. Nor should it be to you. Whose ears will their tales reach? No one of consequence, that's who." He undid the frog closure at her throat to take her pelisse off.

"What are you doing?"

"I thought that was obvious. You'll swelter under all these layers. I'll drape your pelisse over the chair by the curtain."

"I'll freeze."

"Hardly; you're afraid someone will see you. You are veiled, darling. I can barely make out your features when I'm standing right in front of you. Besides, you have your muff to keep your hands warm." Which was true. She wore long sleeves; they belled over her hands to keep her bruised wrists well hidden, too.

"I know. I just feel strange, all covered up as I am. I'm sorry."

"Don't apologize. It's been a long morning. It was an even longer night. We'll be here two hours at the most. Not long, really, once we get down to the grit of the piece. Have faith in me that I'll keep you well amused. Hopefully amused enough to make you comfortable and glad to have agreed to give me the day. When this is over, we'll go back to the town house and sleep the rest of the day away."

"It's not that I'm tired. I'm just nervous after last night."

"No one will hurt you here." Teddy held her hands between his. His touch was comforting and put her a little more at ease.

"I know." She sat in the chair. "The concerto will keep my thoughts on better things. Now go to your musicians. A number of them have stopped playing since you settled me in up here. Though it could be they've stopped out of curiosity."

"I'll be but a shout away," he said as he leaned down and pressed his lips to her forehead through the veil. "Try not to laugh too hard at their efforts playing some of the more difficult passages. It was rough when I did the initial run-through. They've had the sheet music a little over one week and only two practice runs." His fingers lingered on the good side of her jaw.

"I'd never laugh. I know what it's like learning music you're unfamiliar with. Perhaps one day I will show you how I pick a composition apart. It can be a very long and painful process. Now go to your musicians, I'd like to hear what they can play of this magnificent piece."

"As you will it, my lady." She imagined him bowing before he ducked out of the box. She gave the smallest of smiles to keep her lip from hurting, settled deeper into the high-backed, velvet-covered chair, and listened.

The musicians below her box warmed their instruments. She could pick out each instrument amongst the clamor: two oboes, a few flutes, and at least four clarinets in the woodwind section. There were fewer violins and violas than she expected, maybe ten or twelve. The cellist plucked out some pizzicato notes, limbering up his fingers. A bassoon player ran through a series of low notes and warmed his reeds. A roll of deep notes on the timpani sounded strong and clear. She heard brass. A lot more brass than was typically part of the orchestra, especially with so few woodwinds and strings to balance them.

The conductor's baton tapped against the podium, bringing silence to the room.

"Where is my pianist?" Teddy asked, his tone firm, angry.

Murmurs rose from the musicians, but they did not have a

definitive answer.

"Fine, we'll start without Klaus. If anyone sees him, tell him he'd better have enough sense to send me a note for his latest absence. Let's warm up with something familiar. I am for some Strauss. High notes to tighten your embouchure and some steady, heavy articulation to get your fingers flexed. *Radetzky March*." Papers shuffled as they pulled out the appropriate sheet music.

He tapped the podium to give them the tempo. It was a very lively tune to start the day.

The snare drum started a roll into the march, and the cymbal clashed before they played as one. The high trilled notes of the winds and strings followed the brass. She wanted to clap when the appropriate time came, but did not. Another time perhaps. It was exhilarating to hear the life of the orchestra breathing and singing so joyously around her. When the piece came to an end, she wished she could stand up and offer her praise. Once again, she did not.

The sound of booted feet reverberated through the hall as someone noisily made their way across the stage.

"Ah, Klaus, you've decided to grace us with your presence after all." There was no mistaking Teddy's sarcasm.

"Sorry, maestro."

"We've already warmed. Why don't you give us something on the piano? I think we should have a listen to something worth our while for waiting."

Chairs moved and papers shuffled then a sudden quiet filled the theater. She could not blame the ensemble for their wariness; she'd never heard such a dangerous tone from Teddy. He sounded as commanding as his brother, but somehow harsher, although the stage belonged to him, and he knew that his musicians would obey.

She heard the piano bench slide briefly, then the cover was opened with a loud clank. "What is it you wish to hear?" The pianist did not sound thrilled to be playing solo, but he wasn't fool enough to object to an order from the conductor and composer.

"Something worthy of the old **Érard**, I'd think. How about some Liszt?"

"I've no music to go by for Liszt."

"Of course. Then give us something you do know."

"I haven't brought anything with me other than your composition and the sheet music you put together for practices." The bench slid across the floor again.

Did he stand away from the piano?

"What were you planning to warm up with? Scales?"

Teddy gave a bitter laugh that made her insides twist. He was an altogether different person when he was on stage with his orchestra. Now she understood perfectly well why people thought him volatile at the best of times. She was glad to have never experienced this side of his personality.

"I have no patience for your antics today, and you are repeatedly late for rehearsal. This is the last time, Mr. Hendlesmith. Leave. You are not invited back."

"De Burgh, be reasonable." Now, when even she knew it was too late, the pianist's tone of voice came across as contrite and he went so far as to slam the cover over the piano keys.

"This is me being reasonable. If you wish to work with anyone in London again, you'll leave without another word. Otherwise, I suggest you pack your bags and head to Vienna. I fear they will not be so welcoming of you when you cannot show up to rehearsals, let alone performances, on time."

"I've had it with your holier than thou attitude. You cannot ask me to leave because I'm done with your lectures and reprimands. You treat me as if I were a child, never able to please you regardless of what I do. Good luck finding another pianist. Few will work with you after your last less than spectacular orchestration, and you know it for truth."

"Good-bye, Mr. Hendlesmith." There was silence for some time between the musicians and Teddy. She heard the pianist leave, the front door to the opera house whooshing shut with a draft of cold in the man's wake. "Take ten minutes everyone."

Rosa could hear Teddy's.

She sat back in her chair, wondering what Teddy planned now. He had plenty of time to find another pianist. She could name a handful living in the London area who would be thrilled to work on this piece.

The soft tread of Teddy's shoes grew louder the closer he came to the box. Then she could smell his clean scent when the curtain was drawn back. "I'm sorry you had to witness that. I knew I shouldn't have hired Klaus. Our last project did not go well."

"You've nothing to be sorry for. He won't be successful in this business if he cannot learn to control his outbursts to the maestro. And tardiness will get him nowhere."

"I've a favor to ask."

She did not like the direction in which this conversation was headed. And the last thing she wanted was to refuse him any-thing, but she knew she would not be able to say no to him should he ask. Though she would try to.

"Do not ask it of me. It isn't that I refuse to play, but that I cannot play with an orchestra. I haven't played with anyone in more than eight years. Before my accident, I rarely played in an ensemble larger than four."

"Just today, Rosa."

They both knew it would be for more than a day.

"Teddy—"

"I wouldn't lie to you, Rosa. Just a couple of days until I can hold trials for new pianists."

She sighed and pulled her gloves off. Thank goodness for the long, belled sleeves of her dress. She couldn't believe she was going to do this. Oh, yes she could. She'd been eager to work with other musicians for far too long now. And spending all this time with Teddy made her want a piece of her old life back.

"My wrists are a tad sore, but I should be able to play for a while. Movement will be good for them."

He took her hand and assisted her to her feet.

"My musicians have had very little in the way of hearing the piano parts with Klaus' continued absences."

How sweet that he was still going to give her a speech for his reasoning. Couldn't he see she was willing to help? She wouldn't have agreed otherwise.

"You helped me with this piece, Rosa. I know you can play it well. They are not virtuosos. Just men trying to make a little money on the side with their musical talent. I do have another musician in mind for the opening night of this piece. But for now, you know that the piano supports this concerto and the players won't truly understand their roles until they hear the whole of it. I've no one else to turn to on short notice. I know you can play it from heart, better than I."

"They will not take kindly to a veiled woman in their midst." A necessary point. But it would be taken better than her blindness.

"They have no choice, love. I promise to start auditioning another pianist come morning. It shouldn't take more than a week to secure one."

She checked her veil again. Not that she thought any of them would know her. It was a matter of preserving her privacy and hiding the bruising and cuts on her face. What if they thought Teddy responsible for it?

"You can warm your fingers and the keys while they finish break."

Tomorrow, or the next day, there would be someone else to play the piece. While she should be honored to play for him today, she was worried she'd disappoint everyone present.

His fingers twined around hers as he guided her down the hall and toward the stairs. She heard a few voices, so not all of them had gone for fresh air. The voices grew quieter, one by one, the closer she got to the stage where they were set up. Teddy's presence at her side was reassuring; she'd never falter under his guidance. She stood taller, knowing they scrutinized her, assessed her from the veil to the clothes that were of the newest fashion, but not something a young miss would wear as it was too bold and cut too low for a lady.

"Stairs to the stage are right in front of you. Four of them, a lip on the top step."

He whispered so the others would not hear. Did he hope to salvage her dignity by pretending she could see where she walked?

They finally stopped. It seemed all was silent around them, as the other musicians no doubt wondered what their conductor was about.

Standing behind her, he grasped her hips. She felt the press of his hands even through all the layers she wore, as he guided her over to the bench.

Running the back of her hand over the keys, she counted how many octaves the piano had. Six. A fine piano indeed and much like the one her father apparently wanted to give back to her.

She spread out her skirts so they weren't bunched up in the middle and tested the weight needed for the damper. She turned her head so it appeared she glanced over her shoulder, knowing Teddy stood to her left. "You requested something worthy of a great Érard."

"I think it too easy a task for you." Teddy's chuckle seemed a contradiction to the direct, no-nonsense de Burgh he'd been but moments ago with the other pianist.

Turning back to the piano, she played chords in A-flat major. Keeping her tone soft, slow, and soothing, she decided on a beautiful piece of love and dreaming. Something to calm the harsh tone that had invaded the room before she'd descended from the private box.

Liszt's *Liebesträum* came out clear and clean through the piano. She embellished some of the runs, exaggerated the volumes between pianissimo and forte to further test the ability of the instrument she played on. Not a weak note to be had, not a clunker of a key. It must have been well tuned before the practices had started for Teddy's ensemble. When she made it to the end of the piece, she held the final chords with the damper and let the sound die away on its own, finally lifting her hand from the keys when the strings ceased to sing.

Other than someone clearing his throat, it was quiet around her.

Teddy leaned in close to her. "Brava, darling. Now to introduce you to the ensemble. There's not a man who wasn't ensnared in the web of beauty you created. And in less than five minutes of being at the piano."

Before she could ask him not to introduce her by name, he stood with a click of his heels and called everyone to the stage to get on with their practice. "Rosalie Montgomery will be standing in as our pianist until I secure another. As you heard, she's quite accomplished. She's helped me with the arrangement and knows it as well as I do."

She stood and gave a slight bow of her head. "I'm thrilled to have this opportunity to work with you." She sat back down, hoping her name didn't seem familiar to anyone. Maybe because they didn't yet know she was blind, they hadn't made the connection.

No one voiced an objection to her presence. Instead, members of the ensemble stood and gave their names. A shame she didn't know what instrument each one played.

"All right, let's start from the top." Then he was tapping his baton on the podium.

She was glad he didn't ask if she wanted a cue for her entrances. She'd figure it out herself and embellish any mistakes.

But, as he told the orchestra, she knew all the pieces and only fumbled over two passages when playing with the full orchestration. No one seemed to notice, and if Teddy had, he hadn't said anything. More importantly, she didn't know the last time she'd enjoyed playing so much as she did now.

SHE PLAYED BEAUTIFULLY. THERE HAD been many curious gazes as he'd brought her up on stage. But those men, most of whom he'd worked with before, would not see her as a woman of ill repute. He well knew she worried they'd think her no more than his mistress.

She was so much more and didn't even realize it.

From the moment her fingers had caressed the keys on the *Liebesträum,* she'd enthralled every man in the opera house with her harmonious spell. Then, the way she'd played his concerto had left him speechless. He saw the looks of wonder on the men around him. The curious glances they gave her during the solos, the awe when her fingers played not a note out of place as the rest of the players struggled with some of the passages they were still learning. And she did it all without sheet music to guide her. Right enough, she'd worked with him for a couple of weeks perfecting the final version of this piece.

But she still amazed him.

He turned his gaze to his veiled beauty as he handed off his gloves to the butler. "I just realized I should have asked, but I wasn't thinking when I gave instructions before we left earlier."

"Instructions for what?" She released the frog closure on her pelisse. He slid it off her shoulders before the footman could help her.

"I've gone and had your things sent to my room. If you'd like me to set you up in your old apartment, I'll arrange it at once."

"I prefer your arrangement."

He breathed a sigh of relief and waved off the footman after handing him the pelisse. He was finally alone with Rosa, though he doubted either of them had much more on their mind than a late afternoon nap.

"Good, because I might have put up a fuss," he teased.

"I don't want to be alone." He could hear the fear still present from last night. While he knew it might take her some time to heal, every day that she held that fear he wanted to search out Johnson and beat the bloody hell out of him all over again.

"You won't be for as long as I can help it." He touched the edge of the veil, wondering if he should remove it or let her.

"In fact, I'd like to go up now if that's all right. I know there are few servants here, but I'll not have them staring at the evidence of my assault." That was why she made no move to take off the black swath of gauze. "And I want this veil off. It's suffocating and itches."

"I've sent the footman off. We are quite alone."

"I heard the door shut behind him." She was already removing her veil and hat.

When she was done, she pressed her face against his chest, leaning into him—in exhaustion, no doubt. With his chin resting lightly atop her head, he noticed the familiar scent of lilacs was absent because she'd bathed with his soap last night. "Thank you for everything today, Teddy."

"Believe me when I say this: It was all *my* pleasure."

He slid his hands down her arms and around her waist to draw her in closer. He didn't want to let her go. But he knew eventually she would want to leave again. When her hands stretched shyly over his, he smiled. "I enjoyed having you at rehearsal. You finally got to hear what you've helped me create."

"You exaggerate." She dropped her hands away to cover a yawn, then walked out of his arms, and held her hand out to him. "I want to lie down for a while."

"I will arrange to have dinner brought up in a bit. Do you want to go ahead of me? Or do you want me to join you?"

He walked her over to the stairs. Once her hand found the banister, she turned back in his direction. "I'd like to head up now if you don't mind. I think I can find my way."

"I will see you soon."

She took the stairs slowly. Was she sluggish because she was tired, or because of the added aches from yesterday? Waiting for her to turn the corner, he went directly to the kitchen to give his order for dinner and asked for a tray of tea and snacks to be brought up as soon as it could be prepared.

He took the stairs shortly after, hoping to give her a little extra time to settle in. Maybe he should have put her in her own room. She might have felt more comfortable, despite what she'd told him about not wanting to be alone.

When he reached his sitting room, her veil was set upon the sofa, her sensible walking boots kicked under it. Following the trail of clothes to his bedroom—her gloves, shawl, even her corset were thrown over the bench at the end of his bed—he found her snuggled deep in the mountain of blankets and pillows.

She was sound asleep. He couldn't seem to stop watching her. The swelling on her lip had gone down significantly with the aid of the healing ointment he'd put on her yesterday and again this morning. The bruise on her face had darkened to a purplish-green and spread beneath her cheek. Hopefully it would be gone in a few days. She looked fragile and too delicate curled up in his bed.

A knock at the door brought him out of his reverie. He opened the door and was greeted by Rosa's maid.

"Stop frowning at me. Your mistress sleeps. Let me take the plate of biscuits and you can take the tea back downstairs; she didn't get enough sleep last night."

Rosa had been restless last night, but it had been for more reasons than Johnson's attack. And when they'd finally gone to bed, her dreams seemed fitful, as she had tossed for the remainder of the night. It had kept him awake, as well, and the need for sleep had finally caught up with him, not that he minded.

The maid's eyes searched his, then she spoke in almost a whisper. "She's had a hard life. You can't get involved and make her want more than what she's got if you are planning to leave her in the end. If that's the case, you should let her go now."

Not wanting to reveal the depth of his attachment to Rosa— not until Rosa admitted that she wanted more—it took him some minutes to respond. "Your mistress asked to come here after Johnson's attack."

"Same reasoning still goes." The maid stuck out her chin stubbornly.

What a bold woman this maid was. But he respected her dedication to Rosa.

"Your concern is misplaced." He rubbed his hand over his

face and set the plate on the console table inside his room. "We'll ring for tea when we're up."

With a curtsy, she turned and left, though she didn't look happy to have him end the conversation. Closing the door, he loosened his necktie and the cuffs at his sleeves, took his vest off, and headed for the bedroom. It was time to catch up on sleep.

Keeping on his smallclothes, he slipped into the bed behind Rosa, gathering her close, one arm wrapped about her middle, and the other tucked under the pillow where she rested her head. With a light kiss to her temple, he settled in to sleep.

The next awareness he had was of her heated breath fanning over his bare chest. He reached out for Rosa, but she evaded his capture, tsking at his attempt. He smiled and tucked his arms beneath his head and curled his fingers together so he wasn't tempted to reach for her again.

"Did you sleep well?" He yawned the words.

"Yes." Her tongue circled the flat disk of his nipple. He shivered at the pleasurable feeling it roused in him. "Very well. Is it dark outside?"

He focused on the window on the north side of the room. He'd forgotten to close the curtains before climbing into bed with her. "The last rays of the day have stretched their golden fingers along the sky. Night will fall soon."

"You should have been a poet I think."

He chuckled at that. "I prefer my music, love."

The endearment caused her hands to stop their exploration for a moment, then she tucked her fingers under the edge of his smalls and pulled them below his hips. He helped her by lifting up his pelvis and kicking them off when they were around his knees. She climbed atop him, her thighs on either side of his, her pantalets gone. His cock stood to attention, brushing the soft curls at the juncture of her thighs.

Her hand clasped the base of his cock, uncapped the head with a little pull to the skin and then she seated herself fully on him. He closed his eyes and took in a shaky breath. She didn't move once sheathed.

Pulling himself up to a sitting position, he wrapped his arms around her, his head rested against the curve of her breasts. The tie on her chemise had come loose at the middle, his every exhalation made the satin ribbons dance away from him, then come back to tickle his lips as he inhaled.

Bunching up the material of her chemise to the small of her back, he slipped his hands beneath, first cupping the glorious cheeks of her backside, then massaging the length of her warm back. He couldn't get enough and wanted to touch her everywhere. Her movements above him were slow and languorous even as she rode him, taking him in and out of her body at a pace that left them both breathless. He couldn't help but press up harder every time she thrust down.

Unable to control his ardor, he grasped her shoulders to hold her tight, to still the movement of their bodies. "I'm going to let off far too soon if you continue."

"I don't mind, Teddy."

"I do. Just hold still a moment. I don't want this to end before I've got you next to me flesh to flesh."

"Mm, that sounds like a fantastic idea." Her voice was sultry and husky, full of desire.

She released him so she could pull the chemise over her head in a measured, teasing display that revealed one inch of flushed skin at a time to his gaze. The sight heated his blood and made him want her even more. When she uncovered one breast, he placed his lips against the pearled tip. When the last bit of material was over her head, she tossed it to the floor. What an erotic image she made: her sitting astride him unashamed of being exposed to his hungry gaze.

She ran her fingers through his sleep-tousled hair and arched her back, inviting him to taste her firm nipples again.

He kept his touch light, not wanting to mark her skin in any way. Her pelvis rotated in small circles, and he knew she was trying to find release. Her sheath massaged his prick with her gyrating, needful movements. He took her nipple into his mouth again, loving the texture of the firm, soft flesh beneath his tongue.

Her hips moved more vigorously as she rocked her center against him. He freed her nipple, and lowered his hand so he could stimulate the bud of her sex.

She brushed her hands through his hair and firmly yanked his head back. He licked at the skin beneath her chin and kissed the end of it when she pulled his head farther back. Lowering her forehead to his, she said, "I wish more than anything that I could kiss you." Her movements stilled, and she lifted a little so he could wet his finger on her fluids and slick them between her folds and over her clitoris.

"I know, love. Your lip will heal soon enough and then you'll beg me to stop kissing you."

With his free hand, he brushed his knuckles tenderly over the bump on the right side of her lip. His finger touched the tip of her nose. "Let me kiss you here." He replaced his finger with a fleeting press of his lips. Skimmed his lips over her brow. "And here." Her temple. "And here." The lid of her closed eye. "Here." Her other eyelid. "And here."

Her sheath flexed around his cock. She went motionless above him, her body poised and unmoving as he rubbed his fingers over the swollen bud. Then she threw her head back, her loose hair tickled his thighs.

She'd come to her crisis so silently.

He took her nipple into his mouth, felt the rush of wetness from her sheath and found his end in the next moment.

They stayed locked together, neither willing to move or release the other as their breathing calmed in the aftermath of their lovemaking.

HIS LIPS WERE FIRM AT her collarbone, tongue caressing the delicate line. Something seemed different in their joining tonight. Whatever it was, she couldn't put her finger on it. Well, she didn't want to examine it too closely for it resembled something strikingly similar to an emotion she'd sworn never to feel for another man.

"God, Rosa. I wish you'd stay here with me forever."

He kissed the pulse at the side of her throat where it raced as fast as her anxious heart. Their bodies were slicked with sweat; the tingling between her thighs did not seem to decrease after her release. She wanted him again. His words made her stomach somersault, her breath catch, and her fingers thread deeper into his hair until she massaged his scalp.

Instead of responding, she nuzzled the side of her face against his.

"Say you want this as much as I do," he said.

She wanted it so badly. But couldn't say it. Couldn't bring herself to admit it. Not out loud. Not yet.

"Don't make this more difficult, Teddy." She brushed back the damp hair from his temple.

"God, woman, you drive me mad! What is it you're running from? What is it that scares you so much you refuse something so perfect, so goddamned beautiful between us? I know you feel for me. I know this wasn't just a quick coupling for you. There is so much more if we're willing to take a chance on it."

She tried to roll off him, to do whatever she needed to do to escape this conversation. It had been so perfect, until now. There was no escaping the reality of who and what she was. This was all they could have. But her plan didn't work, for he refused to let her go. He pushed both his hands through her hair and held her face close to his. The tip of his nose touched hers.

"Do not run from me. I'll chase you down till I've got the answers I've long sought."

"I can't do this, Teddy. I never meant for there to be anything between us but the original arrangement. I didn't plan to care for you, but you seem to be there, for support, as a partner, as some-one I can turn to whenever I need you. This was never meant to be. I cannot do this. I should not feel the way I do about you." She knew she sounded lost and unsure of herself.

"And what is it you feel?"

"Too much to put a name to it."

"That'll do for an answer." He kissed her nose. "For now." He released her, and she left the bed to find the water closet. She no longer needed his assistance to find her way around his room, she was intimately familiar with these surroundings. "What did I say about you running, Rosa?"

"I'm not. I just need a towel." She made her escape and wondered how long she could take relieving herself and cleaning up with a wet towel. He'd come find her if she lingered too long, so she submerged the towel in the cold water. When she was clean, she wrung the cloth out and brought it with her back to bed.

She stood outside the bed, thighs flush with the mattress, and held the towel toward him. "Here, I brought this for you."

He took it to clean himself. "There are biscuits in the sitting room, but we should have something a little hardier. Do you want supper brought up here, or would you prefer to dine downstairs?"

"Either or," she answered. "I'm not overly hungry though. The biscuits might be sufficient."

He was no longer in bed and she tried to follow his voice but was unsuccessful. "What are you doing? I don't know where you went."

He didn't respond.

"Teddy, that's not funny."

"I'm right here," he whispered in her ear, his naked body lining her back. The crest of his rod rose firm above her buttocks. He placed a scone against her lips. "Shall we properly attire ourselves? Seems tedious when I'm just going to try and take all your clothes off again."

She shivered at his words, her nipples budding under his light caress as she ate the cheese filled scone.

"You aren't acting like yourself."

"I know. I told you, I've gone quite mad because of you."

"We can wear nothing at all if you prefer."

"I do like that idea. Sounds much better than wearing dressing robes."

And just like that, it was as though the conversation they'd had moments ago never happened. Teddy made it easy to spend time in his company. He always wanted her at ease. Never demanding outright she acknowledge that she was indeed falling in love with him.

She was in trouble.

This kind of love was far beyond anything she'd ever known. More than she could ever imagine or could have expected. And it felt like the greatest betrayal to Michael. It made her see what she had been missing all these years. What she could have had, had life been kinder. She could not choose between the two men. They were similar, yet so different. Perhaps because at the time of his death, Michael was still growing into the fine man he would have become.

She supposed it was possible to love twice. Had her life taken a different path, had she not embraced being a kept woman, maybe she could embrace this with open arms. But her past would always stand in the way of any true happiness.

Even though she felt safe staying at Teddy's town house as opposed to her own house in Town, she knew she'd have to leave Teddy sooner rather than later. Until she made that move, however, she'd take whatever kindness, whatever tenderness and affection he showered upon her. It would break her heart to leave him, but it must be.

Chapter Sixteen

Oh God – so near! so far! Is not our love truly a heavenly structure, and also as firm as the vault of heaven?
–Ludwig van Beethoven

AS TEDDY PROMISED, HE HIRED another pianist within a week. He even let her offer suggestions when he made his final selection. She was sad to have to stop playing with his orchestra, but it was necessary. And now it was time to leave his side or she might want a more permanent attachment with him.

"You don't have to leave, Rosa."

"We've discussed this at great length." What she was silently saying was that she didn't want to discuss it yet again. "I have always been independent, and I can't tell you how much I appreciate that you're helping me find new lodgings."

It was her fear that Johnson would come to her house that decided her. Not that she'd told Teddy that. No, she'd only said that she required something outside of the city, a place where she could have a garden all her own.

It scared her on some level that Johnson hadn't been heard

from since that fateful night that brought her and Teddy back together, that strengthened their bond—the last thing Rosa had planned on happening. Her hands curled in her lap as the carriage slowed.

"I can only ask you to stay so many times. And I've asked enough that my ego is somewhat beaten down and bruised at present," he said as he opened the door and climbed out, then turned to assist her.

Why had she allowed him to accompany her to her solicitor's office? She reached up to brush the lock of hair that had fallen across her brow as she descended from the carriage. Teddy took one of her hands to help her down.

"You know it's not possible. Gossip has already stirred where you and I are concerned. We needn't give the *ton* any reason to paint your name black before your big performance."

Teddy snorted and tucked her in tighter against his body as they walked down the street.

She'd known even before she'd left him the first time that their separation was going to hurt beyond compare.

"When you establish your new lodgings, you'll wash your hands of me, won't you?"

His cruel way with words stemmed from his hurt, she knew, so she ignored his question. By the end of the week they'd be on their own paths once again.

It broke her heart thinking about the end of their attachment. But it had to be done if she were to move on with the rest of her life. He would be so much more without her hampering him. He'd be invited everywhere, asked to play in the grandest music halls across Europe. That could not happen with someone considered no better than a whore at his side.

"You're not answering me."

"Because you paint me as heartless. Think of what the gossips will say if I stay."

"You know my thoughts on the gossips."

"Yes, you're as stubborn as a cat being ordered about as

though it were an obedient dog. You refuse to see the truth of the matter."

"Let them gossip. And you with the animal analogies, you really must find a more majestic creature to compare me to. I'm not nearly as nitpicky as a feline," Teddy said.

"If you don't stop fanning your feathers, I'll have to start calling you a peacock. Any negative whispers about us could harm your opening night. You can't afford to be snubbed by the *ton*. You need their support and excitement for your reintroduction as a great composer. This will carve the path of your future."

"They'll like the concerto regardless of what I do to amuse myself in my private life."

"See, now I'll have to compare you to a cock, strutting and clucking as though you were the most majestic being in the henhouse."

He laughed, tracing an invisible pattern on the back of her glove. "I prefer the peacock, darling. Let me get the gate." He released her long enough to lift the latch on the gate. Then he led her down the narrow, cobbled path to the back of the house where clients were seen.

"And I prefer not to be a part of those whispers, Teddy. I have to live my own life once you've moved on. I don't need them reminding me at every turn of what I became."

Frustration laced his sigh and tightened his hand around her arm. She bet he tugged at his necktie with his free hand.

"I knew what you were when I offered to help you. Did that stop me from wanting you? Certainly not. And has it stopped me from still wanting you? That tiny fact, which cannot even begin to define the woman you are, would never stop me from pursuing you, the *ton* can stuff it."

She mulled that over, biting at her lower lip, which had finally healed. She was picking a fight with him. It would make the day easier and harder all at the same time. She should have come to see her solicitor alone.

Teddy opened the door for her and released her arm so she

could precede him. The faint whiff of cigars hung in the warm, dry air.

They were greeted amicably. "Miss Montgomery, a pleasure, as always. You are a little early but I'm sure Mr. Robertson will be with you shortly. He's just with another client."

She inclined her head. "Thank you, Mr. Brown."

"And you, sir...." Mr. Brown prompted.

"Viscount de Burgh," Teddy supplied to the secretary.

Teddy never used his title when he introduced himself, so why did he do so now?

"My lord, my apologies. If you'd like there is a hat hook just on the other side of the door."

Teddy left her side, presumably to hang his hat, then he was there to guide her to an arrangement of chairs. He did not sit with her, though. He took to pacing the floor in front of her.

"Sit with me, won't you, Teddy?" She tried to keep her voice to a whisper, but the small office area made it seem as if she spoke to everyone present. She said nothing more after that. Neither did Teddy, probably realizing this wasn't the place to talk about their private matters.

Were his thoughts as tumultuous as hers? He had tried persuading her the whole carriage ride over that this was the wrong decision. That she should stay at his residence instead of finalizing the lease on her own accommodations.

A fire burned in a grate nearby, keeping the room warmer than it needed to be. Finally, a door opened. She turned her head in that direction. She imagined Mr. Robertson walked his other client out. She did not stand, as she did not want to bring any notice to herself or Teddy.

"Miss Montgomery," her solicitor greeted her.

Teddy had her elbow, ready to take her into the office, but she turned to him and shook her head. "I'll be fine on my own."

When he didn't respond, she knew she'd angered him, but it couldn't be helped. If she wanted to be independent of him, then she needed to make these arrangements without his interference.

TEDDY WAS SURPRISED THAT SHE hadn't allowed him to go with her into the office. He turned to see Mr. Brown watching him, pen poised above the blotter. He promptly looked back down to the ledger he was working on. Mr. Brown didn't look old enough to be a man of business with his baby face and cherub-like blond curls surrounding his face.

Rosa was gone for a quarter hour before she came out of the small office. What an image she made in her white muslin dress with a thick red sash about her waist. What would she say if he suggested she fit in well with the young misses about town? Her hair was tucked neatly under her white hat. Her eyes were downcast, then she raised her head enough that he could see the sad expression in her eyes. She rarely allowed any expression to show in her eyes. What made her show any now?

"Accommodations have been settled and signed for at the Hertford address. I can take the place as soon as Friday. I think we should go back to your town home so I can pack my things and then I'll spend the remainder of the week packing up my house."

"If that's what you wish." It certainly wasn't what he wished. But he'd not argue that fact here. How in hell was he going to convince her that moving to a small town outside of London just didn't settle well with him?

"Let's be off then." She held out her arm, which he didn't hesitate to take.

"It's a beautiful day," he said absently. "Do you want to walk around Hyde Park? I had a basket for luncheon packed for us, and we can feed the ducks our leftover bread."

He thought she'd refuse. She didn't answer him till they were seated in the carriage.

"That would be lovely. A pleasurable end to our arrangement."

How was she holding herself together so well? Was she so anxious to be free of him?

He took her on his arm and walked the path along the Serpentine once they were in the park.

"You've grown to dislike my company," he finally said as they sat on a blanket near the edge of the water.

She turned to him, her hand holding her hat in place as the wind tried to take it in its grasp. "Why would you think any such thing?"

"Because you've been pushing me away. As if you want me to dislike you. As if you want me to be angered by your words."

"I don't want you angry with me. But I admit, I'm uneasy about where our relationship stands. I think time away from each other is long overdue."

"And you're intentionally going in circles on this issue."

She leaned back on her elbows and tilted her head up toward the sky a smile on her lips, as the sun warmed her skin. She was like Aphrodite, infinitely beautiful in everything she did, everything she said, except when she was denying him the one thing he wanted most: her. She was the air for his lungs, the sun brightening his day, the moon offering light through the long night.

He leaned over her and kissed her. He couldn't help himself. It was nothing too long or too daring. It seemed as if half of London was walking through the park today and half those eyes were matchmaking mamas with their daughters watching, measuring his every move.

Right now he wanted her alone and all to himself. What could he do that he hadn't already done to convince her to stay?

He cleared his throat; it was something to break the spell around them. "Hungry?" he asked.

"For so many things," she teased, but sat back up. He handed her a cheese and cucumber sandwich.

There were questioning glances from many of his acquaintances as they ate in companionable silence. Those disapproving looks told him he should not be taking his mistress about Town so publicly. Yes, Rosa was right in how the *ton* would view their relationship. But he still didn't care about their censuring glances. He stared more than one member of the *ton* in the eye as they walked back to their carriages.

Most clutched their daughters' arms and rushed them away with a huff of dissatisfaction. Still, he couldn't find it in him to care. He broke up some of the old bread in the bottom of the basket and set it in Rosa's hand. "Come on." He pulled her up to her feet, and walked her to the edge of the Serpentine. "There are more than a handful of hungry swans."

"How many?" she asked, as she tossed her handful of bread pieces in the water.

"Four and one fledgling still covered in grey down."

That brought a smile to her face and it was the perfect end to their impromptu picnic.

Tossing her last handful of bread to the swans, she rubbed her arms. "We should head back before night falls, it's cooling rather quickly."

Once they gathered up their things, she let him take her arm and lead her back to their waiting carriage. With every step he took he felt like he was losing Rosa. Losing what they had. And for the life of him, he didn't know how to hold on to it as she tore herself away from him bit by bit.

Had it not been obvious he was stalling in bringing her back to his home, he'd have had the carriage go around the block a few extra times. He watched her gather the items of her vanity into a small leather box. They'd long ago run out of things to talk about. So he asked her about her new lodgings. The place she was moving to was a two-storey cottage, with a modest garden and private grounds. She would be taking her three servants with her.

"It'll be quiet, but no different than the house I grew up in as a child."

"Is there another reason you won't stay with me, Rosa?"

"I've given you my reasons." She tossed her ivory combs into the bottom of her toiletries box. So he'd angered her by asking this question yet again. It was better to have her mad than indifferent.

"Your reasons are not good enough."

"You'll be a man strutting about town soon, strutting that glorious concerto, and you'll have so many more to come. I'll be in the way. You'll see in a few days how much less you have to worry about without me underfoot."

"I quite like having you around."

She gave a short laugh that said otherwise. "You are a darling, de Burgh. The best companion I've been privileged to have."

"Reducing me to the level of mere consort. What's bothering you? You aren't normally this short with me. And what of Johnson? He has yet to show his face, and I'll constantly worry he'll make another try for you."

"He'll not bother me. I believe you made it quite clear what would happen to him should he go against your wishes. Besides, I won't be completely alone. Daniel will be joining me."

"He won't stay on indefinitely."

"No, but now that he's back in my life, we'll see each other a lot more."

Finished packing her toiletries, she closed the lid of the box and moved over to the wardrobe to remove her dresses. Her maid should be doing this. He thought perhaps she did it as an excuse to avoid him.

He sat on the edge of her bed and crossed his feet at the ankles. "You're avoiding my original question."

"Teddy. I'm afraid our affair has come to an end. I know no good way to do this when one person wishes to dissolve an association and not the other."

He scrubbed his hand through his hair, frustrated by the whole situation. "Will I see you again?"

"I think it best we don't see each other."

"I thought we'd gotten on amicably enough these past weeks that you'd see what a great pair we are."

She let out a heavy sigh. "I will always cherish the time I had with you. But this end was inescapable."

He stood from the bed, and gathered her in his arms, giving her a tight hug.

"I'll continue to fight for us."

Pulling away, he put his hands on either side of her face and gazed into her hauntingly beautiful eyes. "The inevitable is us, Rosa. Not just you, or me. Us. I wish you'd admit that as the truth."

"I can't give you the things you need in the long run. It's better to break this off before either of us is hurt in the process."

"I'll already be hurt if you do this."

"If there's one thing I've learned, it's that time eventually heals you."

He said nothing for long minutes, just sat heavily on the sofa and put his head in his hands. "I see now that you don't hold me in the same esteem I hold you."

"Let us part as friends, Teddy." Her shoulders slumped and there was no mistaking the regret in her tone.

"There can be no friendship after this. Don't you see that you will destroy the very essence of our relationship by denying your feelings?"

"I can't offer you more."

He gave a bitter laugh as he stood. "Why do I doubt your words, then?"

He walked over to where she sat on the edge of her bed. She tilted her head up at his approach. Unshed tears clouded her eyes. "I'm sorry."

"You've ruined me for all others, Rosa." Taking her chin in his hand, he brushed is lips over hers. "Do you know that?"

She shook her head, dislodging his grip.

He didn't wait for a response; in fact, he doubted she would respond. This was, after all, what she wanted.

"Good-bye, Rosa."

Turning on his heel, he walked away from the one person who meant everything to him. He turned his back on the woman he loved because she was too stubborn to let go of the prejudices she was sure would separate them.

Perhaps he was the blind one, seeing only what he wanted to instead of the truth. Surely if she loved him, she'd fight to stay with him.

WHEN THE DOOR SHUT BEHIND Teddy, she let fall the tears that had been a long time coming. This was harder than anything she'd had to do in her life. Walking away from the love they shared seemed far worse than losing Michael to the carriage accident and the miscarriage that had resulted. Leaving Teddy felt absolute.

To sum up her life, this was worse than cutting all her hair off to sell it to the wigmaker for a month's worth of food. Worse than having to sell her companionship to avoid poverty and living in the filthy backstreets of London. She actually felt her heart breaking in her chest.

Walking away was the only way she couald prove she loved him.

Her life had been destroyed after the accident, after she'd officially been ruined and the world, namely the *ton*, had found out about it. Without her, the world held infinite possibilities for Teddy. Without her, he would gain all the respect and fame he deserved. None of that would be possible with her by his side.

Teddy's music meant the world to him. If he could not perform because he was rejected on her account, she'd never be able to live with herself.

Even though doing this hurt like hell, it was better for them both. She wouldn't have to be humiliated and scrutinized by society, and Teddy was free to become the great composer he was destined to be. His music would live on eternally, and she was content knowing she'd helped set him on that path of immortality.

Gathering the rest of her dresses, she stacked them in a pile on the bed. Mary would pack them for her. All that was left for her to do was walk out the door. So why was she having so much difficulty doing that?

Chapter Seventeen

*After one has played a vast quantity of
notes and more notes, it is simplicity that
emerges as the crowning reward of art.*
– Frederic Chopin

WINTER HAD FIRMLY SET IN, and she rubbed her hands together to stave off the chill that had settled in her bones on her
morning walk around her new property with Mary. The gardens
needed work, but Mary had committed to turning the soil with
her. The house was larger than she'd expected, with two parlors
and quaint kitchen with a sitting area to take meals and only three
bedrooms on the second level, which allowed her to learn her
way around quickly. She'd moved in a week ago, though it felt
longer for not having talked to Teddy at all in that time.

She missed him.

On her return to the house, her brother met her. She hadn't
expected him to call on her so soon. Opening the door to the
sitting parlor, she led her brother inside. It was hard to smile and
be happy when she'd been miserable since the day she'd left Teddy's house. Teddy hadn't even seen her off, but that was no one's

fault but her own.

She heard some rustling of material; perhaps Daniel stood on her entry. She walked toward him, arms outstretched. He grasped her hands and pulled her into the circle of his arms.

"You called more quickly than I imagined. Have you healed well? Does the doctor know you traveled all this way?"

"I told you I had every intention of coming as soon as I was up for the trip. And, yes, the doctor was very happy with my progress. I can almost take in a deep breath without feeling any lasting pain."

She invited him to sit with her on the sofa. "Tea is being prepared. You must be chilled from your trip. Did you come all the way from Maidstone?" Which would have taken a full day on horse.

"No. I stopped over in London. I had to meet with someone."

"Have you been gambling again?" she asked, feeling a frown weigh down her brows.

"I wasn't gambling before I disappeared," he said.

She stilled. "Does that mean you remember?"

"That's why I had to come see you. Johnson did have something to do with the state I was in, but it wasn't me he was trying to get to."

"I don't understand."

"It was you he was after. Did he never make his intent clear?" her brother asked.

Of course Johnson had, he had to everyone present at the duke's soiree, as well. And then it dawned on her that he hadn't paid mind to her brother once that night, but had attacked her in the middle of the night. His only intention had been to hurt her.

Her mouth opened to say something before she closed it again, thinking about when Johnson's manner had changed toward her. He had become more insistent that she be his mistress this past year, more insistent she spend time with him alone. All she'd done was avoid him as often as possible.

For the first time in years, she wanted to know exactly where

Johnson was. It wouldn't be difficult to find her if he put his mind to it.

"To hold a vendetta so long ..."

"I wouldn't put it past him, Amy."

She felt a chill skate through her whole body. "What if you aren't safe," she asked.

"I can look out for myself. I'm worried about you."

She took a deep breath, which did nothing to calm the fear she felt "I can hire extra hands until we know where Johnson is."

"I'm going back to London to search for him. The duke has availed me of any resource I require. I will find him." There was a promise in his words that Rosa trusted implicitly.

Her brother took her hand. "Do you hate what you became, Rosa?"

"What do you mean?" Was he referring to her life now? Or what she'd done to have the life she now had?

"I mean, do you think so little of yourself that you're willing to let go of something that seemed so right to everyone around you?"

"Did you see de Burgh when you were in London?"

"Briefly. He asked after you, wondering if I'd already been to see you."

And she missed him more than she could put into words.

When she offered him no comment, he said, "I'll leave that alone for now, since you've enough to worry about with Johnson unaccounted for. I came for another reason ... to discuss Father."

The tea arrived, so she had time to think about what she would do with her father now that she could meet with him, if he was willing to see her. Though she wasn't sure how she would face him after their lengthy time apart, and after all she'd done that he might find shameful.

"Do you remember how much Father loved our mother? After you left, he talked about her a lot. I think you reminded him of her." Daniel cleared his throat. "What he did to you hurt him."

"I want to believe that."

"The Earl of Warwick was once in love with our mother."

She poured out two cups of tea, passing one to her brother, then sitting back in the sofa with hers. "You believed that balderdash from our childhood?"

"I know it for the truth. How is it you never figured out why the earl hated what you and Michael had so much? Hated that Michael continually defied his own father to spend time with you?"

"I doubt the earl loved anyone aside from himself. He treated his wife with abysmal disdain until she finally died, which I think she did to be rid of him. He wasn't much kinder to Michael."

"Father told me the whole story after some coaxing and a bottle of whisky one late night." Her brother laughed a little at the memory.

She blew steam away from her face and sipped the hot black tea. "Then tell me the tale."

"The earl was stodgy, cruel, and just plain awful. He and Father grew up together, even went to school together. It's very much a Shakespearian tragedy. Both were in love with Mother. It seemed Mother loved Father more. Do you see where this goes?"

"I do. But that was long before Michael and I chose to elope. Long before any of us were born."

"Ah, yes, that brings me to the other secret you wouldn't have been privy to, since you traveled so extensively. And when you were home, I was often at school. Can you think what the earl would have found out about me, that could be damaging to the heir to Father's estate?"

"You don't mean to tell me the earl thought you were a—" She couldn't say it, because she wasn't sure if that was the truth, though she had long assumed her brother preferred men to women.

"Molly. Yes, sister. You can say it. I was caught by the earl taking young Matthew Stoneleigh." There was a pause. She assumed it was to give her time to digest this tidbit of news, which took longer than she expected because the saucer beneath her teacup rattled and she had to set it down on the table in front of them. "It's a hanging offense you know; the earl made sure I understood that well enough."

"Stoneleigh? You didn't. He's not—"

"No, he's not. I just managed to convince him that all young men tried that sort of thing. I hated myself for a long time after that. He's married and has four children, a fifth on the way last I heard."

"Yet the earl never told anyone, did he?"

"He did not. His only condition on not breathing a word was that I had to keep you away from Michael and advise him of when I saw you alone together. A lot of good that did."

"Why didn't you ever tell me?"

"I doubt you would have understood my position, let alone my preference in bed partners. I daresay you'd not have taken it kindly back then."

She frowned knowing he was right in that regard. "Time has changed my opinion on a lot of things."

"And then after the accident, the earl was very clear about what he'd do to destroy our family if Father didn't force you to leave. Warwick insisted you were the reason his son was dead. And, might I add, the earl wanted Father to humiliate you as he banished you from our family home. I was helpless to do anything to help when the earl reminded me often enough that I should hang for my vices."

"You could have come to me in secret." She folded her hands in her lap. Was it really fair to ask that of him, though? "After I was removed from the house, that is."

"I couldn't. Fear is a strange beast. I was afraid the earl would make good on his threats. I never imagined you'd seek paid companionship."

"I'll not deny that I chose this life in the end. Nor will I apologize for the patrons I've taken on over the years. But you should know it was my last choice."

"I'm not asking you to apologize or justify your actions. You did what was necessary, and that's a good enough reason for me."

They were both silent, sipping their tea.

Her brother's honesty touched her deeply and she wanted him to understand why she'd made the choices she'd made, even if he didn't require an explanation. "After I lost Michael, I felt hopeless. Like my heart had been torn from my chest. I had one love left after that."

"Your music," he said without hesitation.

"Yes. But no one would hire me after my fall from grace, you see. It's a terrible position to be put in, a woman of means, of breeding, to suddenly have it stripped from me the moment the world believed I was some Delilah who'd seduced Warwick's son and led him to his death."

"I'm sorry you had to live through the rejection."

"Don't be. I think the hardest part of coming out of that dark time in my life was forgiving myself, understanding that I really had done nothing wrong. By society's rules I might have gone too far, but when I thought of the love Michael and I shared, there was nothing more beautiful or pure than what we had." She took a deep breath, and admitted what had always weighed heavily in her heart. "My only regret was that Michael died and not me. It would have saved a lot of pain in the end."

"Rosa—" Daniel took the teacup and saucer from her hands and set it on the table. His grip was warm around her fingers, comforting and offered something she'd missed dreadfully since he'd been removed from her life.

"It's been so long since I've talked about this." She shook her head, and slid her hands away from his to wipe away the tears filling her eyes. "The world knew me as Amaryllis Rosalie Montgomery. I dropped my first name when I entered into the world as a courtesan. I think people forgot the great pianist I was and it's as though that person never existed. I prefer it that way. So I ask you to keep my name to yourself. I don't wish to relive those dark years of humiliation and degradation."

Sharing this with him felt right. It was the start of healing their relationship after so many years apart.

"I have something for you." She heard the rustle of his jacket, then the crinkle of paper. "Before Papa started to lose his memories, he wrote you a letter. I've been carrying it with me for nearly two years. He made me promise to get it to you. He didn't want you to hate him."

"A letter?" Her hands shook.

"Would you like me to read it to you?"

"No." She'd had enough outpouring of emotion over the last half hour. "I'll have Mary read it later, if you don't mind."

"Not at all. I just wasn't sure if you'd want to share family business with her."

"She has been my only family for many years. I trust her implicitly."

Daniel placed the envelope in her hands. She took it reluctantly holding the parchment, eager to open it and know what it said. It was still warm from her brother's pocket, the paper soft and worn from being carried for so long. Fingering the edge of the worn envelope, she contemplated her next move.

"Can I prepare a room for you?" she asked.

"I need to head back to London to start my search. I would, however, like to escort you to London to see de Burgh's opening night next week."

While she wanted to avoid Teddy, she knew she couldn't miss this performance. "I would be delighted to attend with you."

"I need to be on my way." Daniel stood and paused for a moment. "Maybe I can take you down to see Father at Christmas."

She nodded and let him assist her to her feet. "Thank you, I'd like that."

Her brother kissed her cheek and left.

She tucked the letter in her dress, next to her heart. Mary could read it to her later, over dinner.

ROSA BROUGHT THE SPOON TO her mouth and sipped the pea soup.

"You have that look on your face." Mary set her utensil down and it might have been Rosa's imagination, but she had the impression that Mary fidgeted nervously in her chair.

"What look is that?"

"You aren't happy about something."

She placed her spoon on the table. "I'm just contemplating something."

Mary said nothing in response.

"I'm sorry. It's been a long day. A little strange with Daniel's visit. I never thought he'd be in my life again, not in a capacity that might matter." She put her hand out on the table, palm up. Mary clasped it and gave it a reassuring squeeze.

"Will you see de Burgh again?" Mary asked, surprising Rosa with the question. Had her brother mentioned something to her maid? It didn't seem likely, but one never knew.

"I think it's for the best I don't. I haven't seen him since our last day at the duke's town house." She stirred her soup with a chunk of break, no longer hungry now that Teddy was in her thoughts. She missed him fiercely and felt as though she'd made the wrong decision. "Our parting was not amicable by any means. And there were things said that make any sort of reconciliation impossible."

"You're wrong in that regard. He adores you."

"He'll find another woman to adore. He's a decent man, with a distinguished title. With me gone, every mama with a marriageable daughter will be courting him after his concerto is heard."

Rosa put the bread in her mouth and chewed it so she wouldn't have to talk.

Mary slid her bowl to the side. "Why do you have to say things like that? *He adores you.* Make no mistake in that regard. It might be easy for you to say he should find another, but how would you really feel if he did just that?"

"It would be better for him in the long run, don't you think?" Or so she kept repeating to herself whenever she thought of him.

"I don't believe you. While I understand that you miss Michael and losing him was difficult, you can't continue to live in the past."

"I'm not." She stood away from the table, tired of this conversation and wanting nothing more than to escape it. Mary, apparently in lecture mode, followed her from the room.

"Oh, Mary. I know you're right." Her chest tightened as she walked up the stairs to her bedchamber. "But it's too late for me to have that kind of joy in my life."

"You're too young to be talking this way."

"Am I? You always said I was an old soul." She took a deep breath, trying to ease the anxiety that had hold of her. "I might hate that I left Teddy's side when he wanted nothing more than for me to stay, but I would never forgive myself if I ruined his life. I love him too much to do that to him."

"I understand your reasoning, I do. But I'm here to tell you that you're wrong. You made the wrong decision. You are worthy of a life with him. You always have been."

Rosa took a seat at her vanity and started to remove her hairpins. Mary picked up her brush and combed out sections so it could be plaited for the night.

"There is one promise I want from you," Mary said.

"I already know what you're going to ask. I can't make that promise."

Mary took another section of hair and ran the bristles through it. "At least consider seeing de Burgh again before you sign your life away to being a spinster."

"If it makes you feel better, I will be attending his opening night with my brother next week."

"It's good you've come to terms with your brother, though I don't like this business with Johnson." Rosa told her maid everything after her brother had left.

As she released the buttons on the front of her dress, she remembered the letter her brother had given her.

"Speaking of the past and making amends with family." She pulled out the letter tucked in her dress. "Daniel gave me this.

My father wrote it before his mind started to go."

"Shall I read it to you?"

She nodded, ready to hear what her father had written. It made her long for his warm embrace. How she missed him in her life.

My Dearest Amaryllis,

This is the last letter I will pen to you, my darling child. You were the light of my life and the spirit I needed when your mother died. You gave me laughter and joy when I wanted nothing more than to crawl into despair. Your mother would say I'm being selfish and foolish like a boy. I think perhaps, knowing love as I did, that that was my sole reasoning for wanting to follow your mother to the grave. Life is a hard lesson, one I learned too little of and often too late.

I wish more than anything that you hadn't lost your Michael at so tender an age. That you were deprived of that love breaks my heart every day.

You don't know it yet, but will soon learn that I've watched you through the years. You have made the best of the worst. You strived for more and succeeded when most would have failed and found a lesser path. No matter what you've done, I've always loved you. There is no sacrifice too great for the cause of love—at least for this old heart that still beats strong for one held by death's cold touch.

I should have been stronger for you, I know that now, I knew it the fateful day you were forced by my cruel hand to leave our home. The light of our lives ceased to shine after that day. But it cannot be changed. God chooses the best path for us, plans His course for us for good reason, and I trust there is a reason it's happened this way. May He give you the stars and moon for all that you've suffered.

Live, my darling daughter.

Live life to the fullest. I know I should have given you that, but I failed in my duty as your father. Daughter mine, if you can find love and beauty in everything as you did when you were a child, then I know I will die in peace. I will be a happy man for having raised such an amazing girl.

Love Always, Papa.

Rosa was sniffling by the end of the letter, with tears falling freely down her cheeks that she didn't even bother to wipe away. "All this time."

"Your father always loved you something fierce. You couldn't see him when he asked you to leave that last day, but he had tears in his eyes, much like you do now. And I could see how broken his heart was, having to humiliate you the way he did."

"I wonder if he'll remember me now that he's unwell. Daniel thinks we should visit him at Christmas."

"A father can't forget his daughter. You were the light of his life."

"I hope I still am." She pulled down the counterpane and slid into her bed. "It's been a long day. Let's get some rest so we can unpack the rest of the house tomorrow."

"A sound plan. Good night, Rosa."

"Good night. And, Mary"—she reached her hand out, and Mary grabbed it—"thank you for everything."

"You needn't give thanks."

Rosa didn't agree. When she closed her eyes, she tried to forget about Teddy and prayed sleep would take her. She lay awake most of the night feeling like she'd made a terrible mistake. *Knowing* she'd made a terrible mistake.

Chapter Eighteen

I am resolved to wander so long away from you until I can fly to your arms and say that I am really at home with you, and can send my soul enwrapped in you into the land of spirits.
–Ludwig van Beethoven

"HOW HAVE YOU BEEN, ROSA?" Teddy watched her nervously pluck at the loose thread on the edge of the yellow damask chair.

"I've been well. We've finally settled into the house enough that everything has found a place and I'm not constantly tripping over things."

His brother had told him exactly where he'd find her house. He needed no reminders that his brother had had more contact with her than he had since she'd left him more than a week ago. Time escaped him these days. He'd been in one rehearsal after another, wanting only to bury himself in his work, as it was the only thing stopping him from going to Rosa. That had only worked for this long.

He couldn't forget the reason he'd come. The news he had to share. The moment he'd heard of Johnson's fate, he had wanted to be the first one to tell her.

She nibbled on one of the pastries she'd had her maid put out. She was uneasy and, he thought, doing anything and everything to avoid talking to him. The bruises Johnson had left were completely faded, there wasn't even a mark left where her lip had split. She looked happy and healthy, too. Better than when he'd first met her, which he figured had something to do with her brother being back in her life. He was delighted for her; really, he was, though it irked him slightly that he was all but miserable since she'd left him, while apparently she fared well.

He gulped down half of the tepid tea and set the cup on the table when he realized his hands were shaking and the spoon rattled on the porcelain surface. Every bone in his body wanted to gather her in his arms, and it took everything he had to hold back that desire.

"I came the moment I heard about Johnson's fate."

Her hand stilled halfway to the tray of sweets and she sat up with an added tenseness in her posture.

"Nothing you need fear, but he's been run out of the country after some bad dealings with a handful of lords' wives. The Earl of Mayberry apparently dueled with him. Johnson was shot, and it's rumored his health has been failing rapidly since."

The look in her face was shocked. "Are the rumors true?"

He reached for her hand, refusing to keep his distance now that he'd distressed her. "I didn't mean to upset you. I thought it would put you at ease, knowing he couldn't harm you."

"While I will never forgive him for the way he treated me, I would never wish him ill. He had his reasons for hating me."

Teddy's head shot up. Was she seriously going to forgive the cad so easily? "He didn't have the right to treat you the way he did."

"No, but it was our past, you see."

"Your past?" She'd told him that Johnson had pursued her and that she had refused him every time. What past could they possibly have had?

"And before you think the worst of me, you should know that Johnson was once a friend of sorts."

He didn't know what to say except, "Why didn't you ever tell me?"

"He was part of the life I wanted so desperately to forget and he was Michael's dearest friend. I disliked him in my younger years, too. The only reason he pursued me so zealously was because he wanted to destroy what little I had made of my life after Michael died."

"You could have told me, Rosa. While none of this excuses his actions, it explains why he was so cruel to you."

"You didn't answer my question," she said.

"The rumor was from a reliable source. Johnson is in Spain now, and the doctors are trying to bleed the poison from his blood."

Rosa looked away from him in contemplation. It amazed him that she could be so compassionate after everything that had happened between her and Johnson.

He combed his fingers through his hair. "I'm sorry I brought this news to you. I thought it might let you sleep better at night."

"It does in a sense. But I'm still saddened that a good man was wasted because of his hatred toward me."

She had to stop thinking everything was her fault. Which brought him right back around to them. "We didn't part on the best of terms, did we, Rosa?"

"We didn't. But it can't be helped now."

"You confound me."

What she didn't know was that her brother had paid him a visit not two days ago and had asked what his intentions were toward his sister. Teddy hadn't known what to say since Rosa seemed to be the one refusing his companionship—his love.

"Why did you come all this way to tell me about Johnson instead of penning a note?"

Stunned by her directness, he knew the only answer was the full truth. "Because I wanted to see you. Because I miss your company and your laughter. I miss your smiling face when I wake up in the morning. Is that what you want to know? Do I need to keep repeating myself and hope you'll eventually believe how dear to me you truly are?"

He tousled his hair again and rose from the settee to pace the sitting room. "Was I wrong to think we'd at least stay true to the friendship we developed? I've stayed away in hopes you'd come to miss me half as much as I missed you."

Face changing to something expressionless, she rose and made her way to him, stopping just in front of him. She wore no gloves and there was a small golden band on her right hand; he wondered if it was the one Michael was going to give her for their marriage. He wanted to laugh at himself. She'd made that man into a martyr. What hope in hell did he have in competing with that?

Taking her hands in his, he pulled them up to kiss her knuckles. "Can you walk away so easily from us?"

"My feelings were always torn where you were concerned, Teddy. I knew the best thing for me to do was to leave, and I'm glad you respected that wish and stayed away. And the answer to your question is no, I can't walk so easily away from us. It's breaking me more and more every day."

He traced his finger down the side of her face. "You see? This is the old Rosa I know."

"I had hoped you wouldn't want to see me after our parting. No good comes from your association with me, Teddy."

"I could never stay away for too long. It made me nearly mad with longing to be at your side. I'm miserable without you." He tucked an errant curl behind her ear.

Her head was shaking at his confession. "I'm no good for you in the long run, Teddy."

"Let me be the judge of what's right for me."

"You know that if you associate yourself with me any more than you already have, it will hurt your career. It wouldn't matter if I stayed in the background as your mistress, there would always be whispers. Besides, I think you want more than a mistress."

"I won't settle for a mistress, you're right in that regard."

"If we were to continue on as if the world around us didn't matter, it would catch up with us both. The *ton* loathes gentlemen of your rank sinking so low as to have a career, and they still dictate whom society as a whole loves and hates. It will ultimately be they who decide if you'll be a success or a failure to be dragged through the mud. I don't want the latter for you. You deserve so much more. But that might be your fate if you consign yourself to me."

"You're overthinking this. Society will have their say and their comments in the rags. But in time none of it will matter."

"It will always matter. You are the son of a duke and hold your own title. I'm but a common doxy in their eyes. I cannot face their hatred again. It was hard enough when I was scorned for my indiscretions."

Not wanting to hear the same speech she'd given him so many times, he placed his hands at the dip in her waist to keep them both steady, close, and prepared himself for the question he had wanted to ask her for days. It had been part of the reason he'd wanted to give her the news of Johnson. Part of the reason he'd needed to see her so desperately.

"And what if I offered you marriage? What would you say then?"

HANDS REACHING UP, SHE GRASPED the sides of his jacket to keep from swaying. She was sure her heart stopped for a full half-minute. Marriage was the last thing she had expected. The last words she would ever think to hear from his tongue.

"Teddy, don't do this." Her argument was starting to lack conviction when he could hear just how broken she was as she tried to refuse him yet again.

"Do what? Beg you to return to me? I've exposed myself to you, and you've pricked at my pride with the sharpest rapier in your arsenal. I've given you my heart, and you've scorned the very idea of love with me. I've given you my soul, and you've banished it to the coldest of shadows."

His words cut her so deeply.

"It's better that we remain friends if we must go on in any capacity." She couldn't believe she was refusing him. She hated herself for it, too.

"It's not better. It's a shallow existence I live through daily. I live for nothing without you. I hope for nothing. I feel as though I am nothing. I'm half a man, eviscerated by some slip of a woman. I go about the day, hating everyone and everything around me because you've taken what good was left in me. Don't refuse me now, Rosa. You'll destroy me and you'll destroy a future for us with your misplaced honor."

And she felt half a woman without him, she wanted to scream at the top of her lungs.

Taking on such a prominent position in his life would bring him down as she'd brought herself down all those years ago. Even if their union were sanctioned in marriage, they'd be scorned. There would be those who remembered her fall.

"You have a gift as a composer. I will not ruin that for you," she said firmly.

"Do you think because you refuse happiness for yourself that you might as well make me miserable right along with you?" His voice grew darker with each passing moment.

"Never would I wish such a thing." She cupped his face in her hands. "I tried to steer you off this path when I left London."

"Be my wife. A man can only be gutted so many times before he has to abandon hope."

She threw her hands in the air, completely frustrated. "You are the heir to a dukedom and hold title of viscount, you cannot marry your mistress!"

"I can, and I will if you'll say yes." His hands framed her face, his thumbs caressing back and forth over her cheekbones.

"Do you realize what you will be doing to your family name? It will die with you, Teddy."

"Now you are being overly dramatic. What gave you the impression we wouldn't have children if we married?"

"I'm sorry to disappoint you. There really is no delicate way to say this so I'll just say it. Did you never wonder why I didn't worry that you might impregnate me? After the accident ... it doesn't matter." She shook her head. "I cannot have children."

"Perhaps we will have to try harder." There was humor in his tone.

Her lips trembled as she held back a good stock of tears. She had to bite her lower lip to keep it still. "It's not so easy as that."

"How can you be sure?" Skepticism laced his voice. She did not want him to think she was making excuses, but he deserved to know the truth. Well, perhaps she needed stronger reasoning to fend him off. She didn't want to love him. She didn't want to need him. She didn't want to destroy his life as she had Michael's.

"I told you about the accident that caused my blindness. It was a carriage accident. I was with child at the time." She sucked in a breath of air, surprised she'd remained calm as she'd told him that. She hadn't told anyone about the baby. The only people who'd known had been Papa and Mary. "I lost the babe and with it, the ability to have children." She closed her eyes, feeling the hot flow of tears washing over her cheeks.

He did not hesitate in replying. "It doesn't matter, Rosa. I love you just as you are."

She clasped her hands around his, then stood on her toes to feather a light kiss across his mouth. She'd forever remember this moment. The smell of sweet pastries and the underlying scent of coffee on his breath even though she'd served him tea. She'd remember the smooth skin of his jaw, the dip in his chin, the crook of his once broken nose. The way he held her gently whenever she was in his arms, as though he was afraid she'd break.

And she was breaking right now, from the inside out.

He'd be a good husband. Caring. Kind. Loving. He'd be a good father, she was sure, but she'd not be the one to gift him with children. It took everything in her to turn away from him and walk over to the grate that covered the fire.

"I can't," she muttered, hating herself so much for not just giving in to what her heart wanted most.

The rasp of material told her he was straightening his jacket.

"I see." His voice wavered as he spoke.

Did he hold back his emotions as she did? Most likely. This was not a decision she made lightly. She wished he'd never come here. Wished she'd never agreed to that harebrained idea of an arrangement. She wished she'd never opened her heart and allowed herself to love. It brought so much pain in the end.

"Teddy." She shook her head, not sure what to say in the silence that descended upon the room. "I would destroy your life as you know it."

His steps were soft on the carpet as he walked toward her. "You couldn't possibly. You've destroyed my prospects with any other woman save you. The thought of being with someone else repulses me. How is it you've done this to me?"

"I'm sorry." Those were the only words she could give him.

"I don't want your apologies. You can give me exactly what I want, yet you hold back. You've given me a hundred reasons why we could never be together, but I know you're merely afraid to live beyond your imaginings. You need to break through the hardness you've shelled yourself in. Whether or not it was done for a good cause, you are hiding yourself from me."

"I hide, as you put it, because it's necessary."

"You still don't see. It's not necessary, not with me. You can put up a front for others, but you needn't with me. I want every last part of you, be it good or bad. If we cannot have children, so be it. If society shuns us, I will still stand tall with you at my side. If I'm not willing to hide, why are you? I know you are made of sterner stuff. But right now, you're nothing but a coward."

"Do you know what the Earl of Warwick did after his son died? He wanted nothing more than to destroy my life as he said I had destroyed his. He made sure that everyone knew my part in his son's demise. I was forced from my home by Papa because the earl would have it no other way."

"I fail to see how this is your fault."

"He was a powerful man and had the means to ruin my father if I wasn't sent off. In fact, he ruined my father after I left, in spite."

"Then it is your father's own failing."

"It wasn't." She wrapped her arms around her middle. "Our primary source of income was my touring and his teaching. He taught no one after that day. The earl poisoned everyone's ears against my family."

He gave a little tug at the curl above her ear as he wrapped it around his finger. "I fail to see why this means you cannot marry."

"There are too many eyes and ears that know me, Teddy. I could never stand by your side without their scorn tearing at us both. They know me, and they know what I've done. They also know what I became."

She liked to think she was a strong woman. In reality she wasn't. There were very few things that mattered to her: Mary and her family, for obvious reasons, her music, and now Teddy. Her music had kept her sane over the long years of heartache and sadness, through all the months of despair and poverty. Teddy mattered because she couldn't help but love him.

Had she not lost her sight in the accident, she would have gone on to Vienna alone to carve her own path. After the accident, that had been impossible. It took her so many months to learn to play as she now did. By that point, she'd already been thoroughly ruined and all doors had shut to her. All doors except to the wealthiest lords' bedchambers, though she chose almost none of them.

She bit the inside of her cheeks, hoping the pain would help her say all she needed to say. "I desired to marry once in my life. I wanted to marry the man I loved with all my heart. And I would have gladly taken his place in the grave. I might as well have been buried with him for all the heartbreak I suffered after his death."

"I'll not begrudge you the love you had for him. But I know you feel something for me." His fingers trailed over the tense line of her shoulder. She forced herself to relax, to prove his words wrong.

"I refuse your offer for the last time."

Straightening behind her, his fingers fell away, and he remained silent for some minutes. They seemed frozen in time. The frantic thud of her heart ceased in her ears, to be replaced by the crackle of the fire. It was the last tangible thing she could grasp, with the surreal feelings washing over her. It was the only constant moving sound to tell her time did not stand still.

It was a familiar feeling. It had happened twice before. Once when she realized Michael was dead, then again when her body had rejected the baby that died in her womb. This was the sound her heart made as it broke inside her chest, and this time she didn't think the pieces could be mended. Not with all the time in the world.

"I'm going to walk out this door, Rosa. If you change your mind, you know where to find me. If not ..." The warmth of his hand spread across the back of her neck. As always, his touch was light, fleeting, but she would not call it back once he released her.

Warm lips replaced his hand. She pressed her clenched fists tight against the mantel to keep from leaning back into him. To keep from turning around, throwing her arms around his neck, and begging him to stay. Then his lips were gone and cold air washed over her flesh like the caress of a phantom lover.

She closed her eyes and counted the seconds until the door closed.

When she was sure he was gone, she crumpled to the floor and cried. Silently, for she wanted no one to hear her. And more importantly, she did not want the sound of her sobs to call Teddy back. She wanted no comfort, for she did not deserve it.

Chapter Nineteen

I am happy, but shall be perfectly so only when I can fling myself on your heart and say, Now I am yours forever.
— Clara Schumann

"ROSA," DANIEL WHISPERED IN HER ear as she ducked her head through the carriage door. "You absolutely glow this evening."

She stretched out her hand for her brother to take. When she cleared the last step, he tucked her arm in his. "Thank you, Daniel. I'm sure you are a handsome devil yourself. You don't worry people will know our connection when they see us together?"

She had been nervous about that very thing all evening. Among other things of course. Foremost in her thoughts had been the words she'd rehearsed over and over in her mind, to be said once she was with Teddy again. Another week had passed since she'd spent time with him ... a week since he had left her crumpled in a heap of satin on her parlor floor. Not that her state had progressed much over the week. She felt herself being dragged down into some pit of despair, and she refused to let it take her.

No matter how she argued, she knew he was right. She was a coward. And she knew what she had to do.

She was done with self-pity. If a man who professed to love her would stand strong at her side, how could she do any less for him? What kind of person would it make her to shun one of the most beautiful things life had given her?

"Do you think I care what anyone thinks, Rosa?"

She smiled and felt a little more at ease. "Is Nathan meeting us inside?"

"I assume he's already here waiting for us. Did I tell you we have the best seats in the house, and that we'll be seated in the front row?"

Her brother couldn't possibly know how much this concerto meant to her. "You've only told me three times, but yes, and I couldn't be happier to be here."

She wasn't sure Teddy's invitation to attend still stood after the way she had treated him, and was glad her brother had asked her to come at all. She was so ashamed of her actions and with the way she'd ended things with Teddy. Pulling the cashmere shawl higher around her shoulders, she listened as her brother counted out steps and maneuvered her through the other attendees.

"Smile, Rosa. People are watching us, wondering who the ravishing woman on my arm is."

She lifted her head regally. Mary had spent two hours curling her hair and weaving pearls through the high chignon she'd styled it into. Her dress was the finest one she owned, a slip of ivory satin that spoke of riches. Whispers started up around them, but she couldn't tell if they were directed at her.

Then she thought, why should she care if someone recognized her? If she was going to put the past behind her, she had to stop worrying about anything and everything that was out of her control.

"They say this room seats six hundred," her brother mused. Did he notice her thoughts wandering? "But I swear there are at least eight hundred in attendance."

"That many." Pride for Teddy's accomplishment filled her heart. "I wish I could see it with my own eyes."

"I wish you could, too, love," came a new voice.

Rosa smiled and ducked her head in greeting. "Good afternoon to you, too, Duke." She'd never dare address him by his first name in a public setting. There were too many ears for such forwardness.

"How was your trip to London?" he asked conversationally of them both.

"Uneventful," Daniel answered.

"I'm sure the performance will more than make up for it."

"I know it will," Rosa said.

"Now, don't tease us, Miss Montgomery," the duke said, taking her arm. "You have already had a chance to hear it and you're bound to make a few people jealous."

She smiled brightly. "But never in its entirety. This afternoon's performance will be my first time truly hearing it."

Time went in a whirlwind after that. They partook of refreshments before making their way into the room. Teddy hadn't come to see them yet, but she assumed he was making last-minute arrangements for the big opening. She felt herself growing more and more nervous the longer she was here.

Her seat was on the end of the first row aisle and her brother's seat was next to her but the familiar scent of amber and bayberry greeted her senses.

"You look the perfect angel, Rosa." He sat in the vacant chair to her left. "The pearl drops in your hair reflect of the ivory of your gown in such a way that they look like fresh dewdrops."

"Teddy," she whispered, and put her hand to her throat, at a loss for words as her heart thundered like the pounding hooves of wild horses in her chest.

"You're the very image of Venus stepping out of her clamshell."

She turned to him, hating so much that she couldn't see his expression and his body language to determine his mood. All she had to go by was the tone of his voice, which said he was in good humor. There were a million things she needed to say to him, but how could she do that in a room full of spectators?

She settled on, "I've missed you."

She heard the intake of his breath just as his hand wrapped around one of hers. "I wasn't sure that you would come."

She curled her hand around his, entwining their fingers. "Words can't express how I feel right now, but know that I'm so proud of what you've done. There is nothing in this world that could have stopped me from hearing this performance."

Teddy was silent for a couple of minutes. "I made some minor changes to the concerto, but I think you'll love it all the same. The way the sound rings off the walls and fills this place makes one want to weep."

His thumb moved back and forth over the side of her gloved hand.

"What you've created has a magic about it that captivates the listener. I have great faith in this music. Great faith in you." She turned her head down, not sure what else to say. She'd rehearsed her apology so many times that none of those words felt adequate right now.

"The ushers are dimming the gaslights around us, which means I have to get back to the stage. I'll find you at the intermission. We have so much to talk about, Rosa."

Before she could utter another word, he was gone. Her brother took his seat next to her. "Did you make up?"

"Daniel," she admonished, hoping to hush him. "They're about to start."

"The speaker is just making his way to the stage," Daniel said.

"Good evening, ladies and gentlemen. It is my great pleasure to be here with you on the opening night of my dear friend, Thaddeus de Burgh's newest compositions. If you'll open your programme, the first piece tonight is de Burgh's newest concerto, *Sempre Fuoco, con Rosa,* followed by a new sonata. After the intermission we'll have a selection from Haydn's Symphony No.

85, *La Reine*."

A gasp escaped her, she couldn't help it, and tears prickled at her eyes. He'd named his concerto after her. It translated roughly to "ever with spirit and fire." Was that how he saw her? No, she was reading too much into the title, which had everything to do with the tempo of the piece. As the piece opened with a *cantabile melodia,* the audience grew silent in captivation.

The piano solo started soft and beautiful before it built into something grander, louder, so full of life that she swore she could feel the story it was telling. He'd found a pianist who truly understood the emotion and passion needed to play the piece. When the piano solo ended, the strings and brass took over with a big bang. It was glorious, and she didn't care that a tear or two had escaped as each movement was more intense than the last.

The applause grew around her at the closing of the concerto and chairs squeaked across the floor as people stood for Teddy, she among them. As Teddy spoke, his voice strong and clear, it shushed the stragglers who still clapped. She had always been right; Teddy would be the man he was always meant to be with this piece, a great composer revered by all.

"This next piece is very special to me. And while I cannot take credit for its creation, the beauty of this piece is sure to move you all. You won't find it in your programme, as I wanted this piece to be a highlight this late afternoon and for it to be a surprise for someone in this very audience."

Whispers of speculation rose up all around her. She felt her face heat as she wondered if everyone stared at her. Rosa's throat grew dry, and she opened her mouth to say something, but what? He hadn't? Couldn't? Would he?

"Allow me to present a *Sonata for Piano in C-sharp Minor,* though you shouldn't let the simple title fool you, its complexity is not only beautiful but also awe-inspiring."

Her hands clutched the arms of the chair and the breath halted in her lungs at the same moment Teddy's baton clapped against the podium and the piano came to life.

Rosa closed her eyes as a fresh deluge of tears threatened to fall. To hear her own music on the stage again filled the splinters in her heart little by little. How had she ever walked away from Teddy? How could she deny the love she harbored and unsuccessfully tried to hide?

"What do you think?" her brother whispered in her ear, probably seeing how moved she was by the performance.

Did he know it was hers? Had he been in on the secret? Had Nathan? It wouldn't matter, she still would feel the way she felt.

"It's beyond words," she whispered afraid to be heard. She bowed her head, wanting to hide her tears as so many different emotions bombarded her.

As the music drew to an end, her heart felt like it was soaring so high she wanted nothing more than to run into Teddy's arms. Voices grew in volume all around the room. She waited quietly in her seat, hoping Teddy would come to her, but knowing he wouldn't be able to do so right away. So many people would want to congratulate him on his success. Talk to him about the genius of his composition to ask him who had written the sonata.

"Would you like another refreshment?" her brother asked.

She shook her head dabbing the tears away under her eyes with a handkerchief. "You go ahead. I'm going to sit through this intermission." And wait for Teddy to come to her, for surely he would want to see her.

"I can stay with you if you prefer." Her brother's tone indicated he was worried.

"No, I just need a moment." She tucked her handkerchief in her hand and gave him a winning smile. "Thank you for offering."

Her brother squeezed her shoulder before leaving for refreshments.

She waited what felt like forever in her seat, not sure what she should do. There were still a lot of people in the room, but it had cleared out by at least half. She stood, not sure where she wanted to go, almost wishing she hadn't asked her brother to leave her here alone when she hadn't brought her walking stick to navigate with.

Before she could take her seat again, a hand gently wrapped around her elbow. "Rosa," Teddy said, spinning them away from the chairs and walking farther from all the chatter in the room. "I just needed a few minutes with you."

"Of course."

Neither of them said anything until Teddy shut a door behind them and she could tell they were alone. He pulled her into his arms and just held her. She breathed deeply of his scent, wrapped her arms around his middle, and pressed her ear to his heart. She'd missed him so much and it had been her own fault they hadn't been together these past few weeks.

"I wanted to tell you my plans for your sonata, but wasn't sure you would come today."

"I would have said no. But hearing it come to life on the stage made me realize how wrong that decision would have been. Thank you for giving me such a beautiful gift." Her lip trembled, she was unsure how to express just how much that had meant to her.

"It was a small token of my affection and respect for you. Your music is meant to be shared and appreciated by everyone, no less and no more than my own compositions." Teddy released her, and said, "Tell me you liked the concerto."

"It was perfect harmony to my ears." Oddly enough, it was their story she heard, in the sorrowful theme. "The main melody was beautiful and chased the ascending chords like the music was overlapping stories of love and loss." She laughed; her nervousness had her carried away. "Now you have me speaking in riddles. It was more beautiful than I could ever have imagined."

"Tell me more about the scene you envisioned?"

"I'm not sure. I suppose it could be any sort of story," she said. "It was serene, but romantic."

He brushed a curl from her temple and pressed close enough to her that they touched from hip to thigh. He leaned toward her, his lips near her ear, the soft tendrils of hair escaping her chignon tickling her nape as it brushed back and forth with his every exhalation.

Could he hear the hitch in her breath?

"You told me that every piece tells a story. I want you to tell me what you saw when you heard that concerto."

"The French horn, when it started, felt like it was the start of a young man's journey. There was a dissonance in the chords that lent to his confusion for which path he had to take. Maybe it was confusion about what he wanted?" She paused, her head angling to the side, exposing the delicate arch of her neck to him. She wanted him to reach out, run his fingers along the skin there. "No, it wasn't a man, but a woman, running toward something."

It was her, she knew.

"What if I said she was trying to escape from something?" he asked.

She shook her head. How could she be escaping when she stood here next to him? "And what of the oboe following the main theme by half a beat?" He slipped his finger into the edge of her right glove and pulled it below her elbow. Her breath caught as he circled his finger over the bone at the side of her wrist.

"Will he eventually catch her?" she asked.

"Let's call the oboe her lover. Always one step behind, never fast enough to catch her because she refuses to be caught. She slips through his grasp no matter how sure he is that he's finally got her." His fingers threaded through hers.

"Maybe she has reason to escape?"

He kissed her lightly on the mouth. Her lips remained parted, but he didn't kiss her again.

"Fear, maybe," he said. "But she has no reason to run, not from anyone but herself. I imagine she knows it, too."

His hand traced a heated path over her exposed arm.

Throat dry, she swallowed, hoping she'd find the courage to say what she'd been rehearsing since the day after he left and she'd realized just how monumental her mistake was in denying her love for him.

"I do know it."

"Rosa." He said her name barely above a whisper.

She raised her hands to his cheeks. "That piece was the most beautiful thing I have ever heard in my life."

"What we have is more beautiful."

"And it scares me, Teddy. I'm sorry for how we parted."

"Why did you really come today, Rosa?"

She shook her head, biting at her lower lip, unsure how to voice her fears and desires.

"Will you run from me again?"

"No," she said firmly. "Ted—"

His finger pressed to her lips, shushing her. She closed her mouth waiting for him to say what he wished. But he said nothing. His lips replaced his finger over her mouth. She did not hesitate to return the kiss, finding herself pressed against his front as they kissed each other with an urgency that told them how much they had missed each other.

His hands held tight on either side of her head as their lips parted. They both breathed heavily. Closing her eyes, she took in the nearness of him.

"I'm sorry, I didn't mean ..."

She shook her head. "Don't, please don't say you didn't mean to do that. I know you did. I'm glad you did. I've missed you, too."

"Missed is too bland a word to describe how I felt without you in my life. What made you change your mind?" Teddy asked sincerely.

"So many things. Things I've known but denied for too long now. You were right, I was afraid. I'll never be accepted amongst the *ton,* but I cannot let the vapid tongues of others dictate how I live my life."

He wrapped his hands around her back, bringing her more snugly along his body as his hand caressed the length of her upper spine.

Snaking her arms around his neck, she gave him a shy smile. "Will you even have me after all the horrible things I said?"

"That depends on what you have to say now."

"When Michael died ..." She threaded her fingers through the hair at the back of his head. "I never thought it possible to care for another person. It happened so long ago now that I sometimes forget what it was like to love him. I wondered if my grief was made greater by losing the child or being unable to help Michael as we lay in the overturned carriage."

"Oh, Rosa. You don't have to relive your sorrows for me. I want to start fresh, to see what life brings us."

"I'm scared of what will happen because it's not something I ever imagined possible. And I've been such a great fool."

"You were only trying to protect yourself from further hurt."

"Have I really protected myself? You named me a coward, and rightfully so, Teddy."

"How can that be when you are standing here with me?" He kissed her forehead, then her lips.

She pressed her cheek to his chest and listened to the steady cadence of his heart. "Had I not been a coward, I would have come to you before now. And you were right about something."

"What was that?"

"That I feel something more, something worthwhile when I'm with you. I love you. I think I've loved you from the moment we met."

His breath caught at her pronouncement. She fidgeted with the sleeve of his jacket and waited for his response. None came, but his hold around her back stayed strong. She felt tears fill her eyes and tried to keep a smile on her face.

She'd come this far and shared what was in her heart; there was no reason for her not to say all of what she'd been rehearsing in her head for the past week.

She raised her head and faced him. "Will you still have me? Will you marry me after all my silly stubbornness and unwilling-ness to believe in you, in us?"

She swore she felt her heart in her throat and could barely breathe as she waited for his answer. Tears slipped down her cheek.

"You little fool." His thumbs brushed away most of the wetness. "Why are you crying?"

"Because you haven't said anything."

"I'll never change my mind about you. Haven't you figured that out yet? And, yes, I still want to marry you, because I love you, Rosa. I always have and not for one minute could I stop loving you."

She laughed and more stupid tears fell down her cheeks. Tears of joy.

Soft linen was brushed over the wetness of her face. She took it from him long enough to wipe her nose, then threw her arms around his shoulders.

"What if I make a dreadful wife?"

"Not possible. Now come, we'll introduce you so the attendees can see who the brilliant writer of the sonata is. And we'll announce our engagement before the last symphony is played. I want everyone to know you are the only woman for me and that my music wouldn't have been possible without you at my side."

Epilogue

Ever thine. Ever mine. Ever ours.
– Ludwig van Beethoven

Two years later

ROSA PULLED THE ROCKING CHAIR up to the piano, settling herself into the cushioned seat to play a one-handed melody in the lower register. Today had been the first day she could get out of bed by herself. It amazed her that she could be so tired and worn down from having a baby.

Though the doctor forbade them from ever having a second child for the sake of her health, she was thankful she had given Teddy a son.

All the pain she felt now and the weakness from the labor was nothing compared to the joy that overfilled her heart when she first held her baby.

The floor creaked behind her, and she turned her head to the side. "Mary, is that you?"

"It's me, sweet," Teddy said.

Teddy was bound to be furious with her being down in the music room. There wasn't enough space for the old Érard her father had given back to her, so they kept her piano in the music room. It just so happened to be her favorite piano in the house to play.

"I thought you were out at a rehearsal today?"

"The weather is horrible. Carriage ended up stuck in mud at the end of the laneway, so I walked back and sent a rider with a message to the music hall."

Teddy had played music halls all over London after the night he'd played the concerto he'd named after and dedicated to her. A number of her works had also been published with her husband's help. He was still trying to convince her to take the stage herself, insisting no one could do her pieces justice because according to him, there were no better pianists than her.

While they'd moved around a lot in the last two years, they had stayed in this particular house in London for two months with the pending birth of their child. During that time, her husband hadn't once mentioned her playing for the public.

"Come sit with me." She held her free hand out to him.

"Of course." He slid over a stool to sit on and placed a kiss over her knuckles. "But what are you doing out of bed? The doctor said you needed at least another week to regain your strength."

"I felt well enough." Though she was tired and refused to admit that or he'd put her right back in bed. "I haven't played in nearly a month. I'll not while away another day in bed, Teddy. I need fresh air and music. I miss my music dreadfully." She demonstrated that by playing a soft ballad with her left hand.

Teddy brushed his hands through her loose waves before he kissed her temple.

"For a little while, but then I want you back in bed. Your father is visiting with Daniel in a few days and I don't want them thinking I don't take care of you."

She smiled, knowing she'd won this argument. "Take the

middle register. I don't want the high notes to bother the baby's ears."

"Isn't he a bit young to be learning the piano?" Teddy teased.

She smiled, turned in his direction, and kissed his jaw. "What if he's to be a musical genius?"

"I think there is enough musical talent in our family. But I'd like nothing better when he's older."

They played for half an hour, all soft pieces that were of a slower tempo, and only pieces she could play one-handed, since she refused to put their son down.

When she yawned loudly, Teddy said, "Let me take you back to our room, Rosa. You look like you've run a few laps around the estate and the circles under your eyes are darker than they should be."

He gave her no choice in the matter. Before she could answer him he was pulling out the rocking chair she'd painstakingly dragged to the piano, lifted her in his arms babe and all, and strode determinedly out of the music room.

"We'll move to another room in the house tonight. The one with my old Broadwood so you don't have far to go when you want to play. How does that sound?"

"Like a dream." Placing her head to his chest, she closed her eyes, inhaling the scent of her husband and her newborn baby. How heavenly. Their son lay tucked against her chest, still sound asleep.

"Why do I have to be so tired?"

"Because you gave me the most beautiful baby a man could ask for." He kissed her forehead.

"I don't like being confined to our bedchamber."

"Then I'll stay home another week and make sure you have someone with you to go around the grounds and to get around the house properly. Poor Mary's run off her feet looking after you and the baby." He was quiet a moment, as though making up his mind about something. "In fact, I'll not hear another argument on the matter. My mind is already made, I'll stay home. I can't lose you, Rosa. It would destroy me."

He set her down on her feet when they were back in their chambers.

"I'm fine. I just prefer to be up and about, or I'll never heal from the birth. You are needed for rehearsals and I don't want to keep you from that. I won't hurt myself. I was careful when I went downstairs earlier." She'd known Mary would put her right back in bed, and had waited for the right moment to escape her maid's ever watchful eyes. Not that she would offer up that tidbit of information to her husband.

"I know, but I'll always worry."

She sighed, knowing she had to cede this argument to him. If she were well enough to go around the house on her own, she wouldn't be this tired right now. "I promise to stay in bed until I'm fully healed if that makes you happy."

"It does. You know what would make me even happier?"

"What, pray tell, would make you happier," she said with a great yawn she couldn't be bothered to cover.

"A nap."

She chuckled at her husband. There was nothing better than them curling up together in the middle of the afternoon. "I think that is a wonderful idea. Will you put Michael in the bassinet?"

"It would be my pleasure," he said, lifting their son from her arms and into his.

She leaned forward and kissed her son's head. Once Teddy set Michael in the bassinet, he scooped her up in his arms and carried her over to the bed. She was placed on the same side where her baby slept, then Teddy's arms wrapped around her from behind, and tucked her in close against his front.

"I love you, Rosa."

"And I you, Teddy. Promise me you will take me back to the music room after our nap."

"I promise. Now let's rest since our son sleeps."

Rosa pulled his arms tighter around her middle and settled into the pillow. There was nothing better than being wrapped in the warmth of her husband.

This was exactly how they were always meant to be.

Thank You!

Thank you for reading *Tempted by You*! I hope you enjoyed it!

Would you like to know when my next book is available? You can sign up for my newsletter here
http://tiffanyclare.us4.list-manage2.com/
subscribe?u=f6ad24630b0efece8e16bfff1&id=38d370ac2b,

visit my website http://www.tiffanyclare.com,

follow me on Twitter
@tiffany_clare https://twitter.com/tiffany_clare,

or like my Facebook page https://www.facebook.com/pages/
Tiffany-Clare/102596663174362.

Reviews help other readers find books. I appreciate all reviews, whether positive or negative.

If you'd like to find out more about my books, please turn the page!

Coming Soon: Desire Me Now Trilogy

Desire Me Now Trilogy
Avon Impulse
2015

I'm so excited for the **Desire Me Now trilogy** my next dark, sexy historical romance series, that will be released through Avon Impulse. This three-book series is set in the Victorian era. These books are focused around Amelia, an educated young lady running from her past, who accepts a position as a personal secretary to Nick, a powerful businessman with secrets of his own.

The release schedule for each book is as follows:

Desire Me Now – May 2015
Desire Me More – August 2015
Desire Me Always – November 2015

If you would like to be kept notified of all the latest news with the **DESIRE ME trilogy**, please sign up for my newsletter http://tiffanyclare.us4.list-manage2.com/subscribe?u=f6ad24630b0e-fece8e16bfff1&id=38d370ac2b.

Acknowledgements

I wrote this book a number of years ago and tucked it away for another time. It was my homage to the art of music, something that was a huge part of my life for many years before I traded my clarinet for a pen. As a young woman The Romantics and Classics were such a huge inspiration that I knew I needed to include their words of love at the head of each chapter. All the Beethoven quotes are from the Immortal Beloved letters he wrote to the mysterious love of his life. Those letters were the biggest inspiration for writing this book.

As always, so many people helped me shape up this book so that I could share it with my readers. Elyssa Patrick, you are amazing. I would never have made it to the end without you constantly prodding me. Helen Breitweiser you didn't want to give up on this story when you had it in your hands because you saw its potential; I can't thank you enough for that. I couldn't end this without a shout out to my amazing copy editor Martha Trachtenberg, you are the best at what you do!

Thank you to my friends, Simone St. James and Maggie Robinson. You were part of making this book perfect. And my husband, Scott, who made the cover for me, and put up with me commenting over his shoulder for every tweak even though I know you know what you are doing.

About the Author

Deciding that life had far more to offer than a nine to five job, bickering children in the evening and housework of any kind (unless she's on a deadline when *everything* is magically spotless), Tiffany Clare opened up her laptop to write stories she could get lost in. Tiffany writes historical romances set in the Victorian era and is currently working on her Desire Me Now series for Avon Impulse, which release in 2015. She lives in Toronto with her ever-patient photographer husband, two kids and two dogs.

You can sign up for Tiffany's new release e-mail here
http://tiffanyclare.us4.list-manage2.com/
subscribe?u=f6ad24630b0efece8e16bfff1&id=38d370ac2b,

visit her website http://www.tiffanyclare.com,

follow her on Twitter
@tiffany_clare https://twitter.com/tiffany_clare,

or like her Facebook page https://www.facebook.com/pages/
Tiffany-Clare/102596663174362.

Other Books by Tiffany

Standalone Books

The Surrender of a Lady http://www.tiffanyclare.com/book-shelf/the-surrender-of-a-lady/
Tempted by You http://www.tiffanyclare.com/bookshelf/tempt-ed/

The Hallaway Sisters

The Seduction of His Wife http://www.tiffanyclare.com/book-shelf/the-seduction-of-his-wife/
The Secret Desires of a Governess http://www.tiffanyclare.com/bookshelf/the-secret-desires-of-a-governess/

The Dangerous Rogues

Kiss Me, Kate (a prequel novella) http://www.tiffanyclare.com/bookshelf/kiss-me-kate/
Wicked Nights with a Proper Lady http://www.tiffanyclare.com/bookshelf/wicked-nights-with-a-proper-lady/
Midnight Temptations with a Forbidden Lord http://www.tif-fanyclare.com/bookshelf/midnight-temptations/
The Scandalous Duke Takes a Bride http://www.tiffanyclare.com/bookshelf/scandalous-duke/

Coming 2015: Desire Me Series

Desire Me Now – May 2015
Desire Me More – August 2015
Desire Me Always – November 2015